COLD REBOOT

There was a moment's utter silence, coinciding with the second before the beat dropped on the dance floor.

Then Freya moved. A fist into the gut of the woman beside her, the baton unhooked and extended in one motion. She lashed it across the woman's face before she could recover and then slammed it with bone-jarring force into the arm of the next nearest onlooker as they went for a gun in a chest holster.

The man with the gun yelled as his arm went dead beneath Freya's baton strike. She cracked him over the head while throwing out an arm, catching another attacker she half-sensed, half-saw was lunging at her over the bench with her elbow. There was the crack of broken face bones. It had all taken about five seconds.

"Nobody move," Freya snarled, grabbing the shoulder of her hostage. She was in her element now, every sense heightened, life and death separated by the gentle squeeze of a finger. In the wildness of the moment a part of her realised she had missed this.

The rest of the room froze.

ALSO AVAILABLE

WATCH DOGS® LEGION

Day Zero by James Swallow & Josh Reynolds

Daybreak Legacy by Stewart Hotston

WATCH DOGS®

Stars & Stripes by Sean Grigsby & Stewart Hotston

ASSASSIN'S CREED®

The Ming Storm by Yan Leisheng

The Desert Threat by Yan Leisheng

The Magus Conspiracy by Kate Heartfield

The Golden City by Jaleigh Johnson

ASSASSIN'S CREED® VALHALLA

Geirmund's Saga by Matthew J Kirby

Sword of the White Horse by Elsa Sjunneson

TOM CLANCY'S THE DIVISION®

Recruited by Thomas Parrott

Compromised by Thomas Parrott

TOM CLANCY'S SPLINTER CELL®

Firewall by James Swallow

Dragonfire by James Swallow

BASED ON A UBISOFT ORIGINAL

WATCH DOGS®

LEGION

COLD REBOOT

Robbie MacNiven

First published by Aconyte Books in 2023

ISBN 978 1 83908 223 8

Ebook ISBN 978 1 83908 224 5

Cover art by Martín M. Barbudo

Distributed in North America by Simon & Schuster Inc, New York, USA
Printed in the United States of America
9 8 7 6 5 4 3 2 1

ACONYTE BOOKS

An imprint of Asmodee Entertainment Ltd

Mercury House, Shipstones Business Centre

North Gate, Nottingham NG7 7FN, UK

aconytebooks.com // twitter.com/aconytebooks

To Tobiáš Špringr, one badass little (big) brother-in-law. Hope you enjoy the book!

PART ONE

SETUP

1
Bad Morning

Thomas Bauer had a bullet in his gut.

He could feel it there. It was agony. It made him want to double over, to clutch at his stomach and scream.

Instead, he clenched his jaw and fumbled in his jacket pocket. His fingers were numb and shaking. He couldn't tell if it was because of the shock, or the pain, or the cold. It was so damn cold. An early January morning in Berlin. The only heat came from the fiery anguish in his lower torso, and the blood he could feel, wet and warm, running down his legs.

He managed to find his wallet and pull it free. His fingers were red, and left stains on the soft leather as he opened it. It was almost impossible to think, but he forced himself to. For Freya.

After what felt like a fumbling age, he managed to get a little, dog-eared Polaroid free from its leather sheath. He dared snatch a look at it, at the small, smiling girl, freckled and pigtailed, now partially smeared with her father's blood. Fingers trembling, he lifted it to his lips and kissed it. Then he ripped it in half, crushed it, and dropped it over the edge of the bridge. It vanished into the ice-skimmed waters below.

He heard footsteps on the wooden boards behind him, light and measured. He didn't turn around. Instead, he forced himself to keep looking down into the canal.

The Jungfern Bridge wasn't where he had expected to die. It didn't have the grandiosity of the Friedrichsbrücke, with the towering dome of the Bode Museum behind it, or the Oberbaumbrücke and its two towers. The Jungfernbrücke was a little canal crossing, twenty-five metres from end to end, overlooked by hundreds of windows in dull apartment buildings on either side, its wooden boards now marked by Thomas's blood.

The footsteps stopped beside him. He could hear a slight, wheezing rattle, unhealthy lungs struggling with the bitterness of the morning air.

"Get on with it," Thomas growled in German. He braced for the end, closed his eyes, but instead of a second gunshot he heard the flick of a lighter, and smelled the addictive stink of a cigarette.

He turned to face his killer, supporting himself on the bridge's railing.

An unremarkable man. A little under six foot, cropped, dark brown hair, slight stubble, over thirty years of age. Thomas had almost expected as much. This was the Gespenst, the Ghost, a being infamous in Berlin's criminal underworld. He could not do what he did if he looked like anything other than a dull, ordinary person. The only points of vague interest were his eyes – they were grey, watery, though not disconcertingly so. At first, they appeared resigned, bored almost, but that wasn't entirely true. The disinterest could not quite hide the gleam of excitement. The Ghost was enjoying this.

Wordlessly, he drew on his cigarette, then offered it to Thomas. Thomas shook his head.

"Bad for your health," he said. The Ghost grunted with something that might have been amusement, then turned to one side, leaning on the railings next to Thomas and looking along the length of the canal. His cigarette smoke coiled languidly in the freezing air.

"Does your employer want me to die this slowly?" Thomas demanded through gritted teeth, shivering now. He felt a spike of anger at the man's arrogance.

"No," the Gespenst said, not looking at Thomas. "But a second bullet would be wasteful. You have a minute left, perhaps two. My job is done."

There was a thump as Thomas's wallet fell from his nerveless fingers and landed on the bridge's planks. He was too weak to try to retrieve it. It didn't matter anyway. All the IDs were fake. The only genuine connection was little Freya, now ripped in two and drifting along the Kupfergraben towards the main body of the river Spree.

"Getting rid of the evidence, friend?" the Ghost asked, moving away from the railing and kneeling in front of Thomas. He picked up the wallet and thumbed through it, idly tossing cards out onto the bridge's planks. "You really think you can keep the rest of your family safe from me? My employer pays too well for them to remain hidden for long."

Thomas tried to answer but found he could not. He could taste blood, choking and metallic. He swallowed hard, but it kept coming. He realised he couldn't feel anything. The cold was gone, and so was the pain.

Sudden tiredness overwhelmed him. He found it impossible to stand. He slumped, slowly, against the edge of the bridge, struggling to draw breath. He looked up, and found himself gazing into the cold, watery eyes of a ghost.

"You won't find her," Thomas Bauer managed to tell him as he died. "But if you do, she'll be ready for you."

2
Summons

Freya had hit her hundredth bench press when the call she least wanted came through.

It arrived courtesy of Chalmers, the owner of the gym she worked at. He was a decent enough guy when it came to employees he considered valuable, and Freya was his best personal trainer. That meant he didn't mind her using the equipment for an hour after the place had closed early on a Monday. It was her favourite time of the week, when she was left to her own devices, Rammstein blasting out over the speakers and no one to pester her. An opportunity to get a proper sweat-and-burn going.

The hundredth rep completed, she was starting her rest period when the ear-achingly loud rendition of "Mein Herz Brennt" cut off. She stood up and turned fast, but it was only Chalmers, approaching her across the gym floor.

"Sometimes I wonder what you do when you're not here, Frey," the thickset Cockney said with a half-smile. "Because anyone who reacts that quickly to their music being turned off is a real piece of work."

"You know me," Freya replied, trying to shrug off her own abruptness. "Just a single mum trying to get by."

Chalmers paused, looking at her thoughtfully. He had been well built when Freya had first started working for him, about eight years ago, but was now locked into what she thought of as the body's doom spiral – no matter how hard he worked out, he couldn't quite keep himself as toned as he had once been, muscle steadily turning to fat and tension to slackness. At some point it was probably easier to give up. Freya was glad she had a decade or so to go before she started experiencing the same.

"You need help?" Chalmers asked, his expression becoming serious. "Money? Want me to speak to your landlord?"

"You offering me a raise?"

"Calm down," he scoffed.

"You said we'd talk about it this week."

"Yeah, well, week's only begun."

"What do you want?"

"Your Optik's blowing up," Chalmers said. "Rattling around inside your locker. Sounds like someone wants you in a hurry. Don't know why you don't just keep it on like most people."

Freya masked her annoyance. An Optik communicator's primary components were the tiny post implant that was inserted into the front of the ear, and its processor, which attached unobtrusively over skin via neodymium magnet. However, it could also run a small hands-on device. Freya had left hers in her locker while she worked out and turned off her implant's receptors temporarily, meaning she wasn't getting incoming messages pinging up in the corner of her vision – they were being logged instead on that hands-on device. Most Optiks only allowed you to turn off receptors for thirty minutes at a time, but Freya had long ago bypassed the standard installation settings, and since the fall of Albion laws about Optiks remaining turned on had been relaxed somewhat.

A lot of messages could mean any number of things, and few of them good.

"I was finishing up," she said, retrieving her towel and wiping the back of her neck as she headed for the changing rooms.

"Just going to leave me to put the weights away then?" Chalmers called after her.

"It's your gym, big guy," Freya responded without turning.

She opened her locker and retrieved her Optik's screen component, before turning on the implant itself. There was a message from her son, Andrew, superimposing itself directly across her vision once she focused on it. It said he'd gotten onto the linguistics course he had applied for at the end of his first year at Bristol Uni. That, and three missed calls from Wellend. One piece of good news then, and three bad.

She put the unwelcome possibilities to the back of her mind and phoned Andrew to congratulate him. He was excited – his first year at university hadn't gone exactly to plan, at least initially. There had been the stress of summer re-sits, and he had struggled living away from home for the first time. Freya had done her best not to let on that she'd had just as rough a time without him around. The fact that he had gone on to higher education at all though made her fiercely proud. It was the best way out, she was certain, the most sure-fire means of breaking the Bauer family cycle and avoiding ending up like her, with scarred knuckles, an Optik rammed with encryption and spyware, and a collection of fake IDs.

"Professor Silkener is running this course," Andrew told her enthusiastically over the Optik. "He's already said he'll consider being my supervisor for my dissertation next year."

"He knows a smart guy when he sees one," Freya said, taking a moment to enjoy her son's exuberance. "You'll have to take time out of your busy academic schedule to explain to me exactly what linguistics actually means though."

"You're bilingual, Mum, stop playing dumb," Andrew told her in German. She laughed, before a bout of concern reasserted itself.

"Are you all sorted for cash? Is your student loan still coming through?"

"Yep, I've got some saved up. Enough to mean I don't have to get a job at the student union next year."

"Then you're doing better than your mother. What about accommodation? Are those guys you're friends with still looking for a flat together? Harry and what's-his-face?"

"Yes, Mum. Stop worrying! I'm sorted."

A dull tone beeped in Freya's ear before she could respond. She scanned her Optik's heads-up display and realised she had an incoming call from Wellend. She dismissed it with an angry blink before resuming the conversation with Andrew, forcing herself to check her maternal instincts.

"It's my job to worry, kid. Your egg allergy hasn't been playing up, has it?"

"No, Mum! I've had it all my life, it's not like I've only just found out about it."

"OK, OK. Congratulations on getting on the course. We'll chat later and you can tell me more about it?"

"Sounds good," Andrew replied. Freya told him that she loved him before hanging up, then sent a terse message to Wellend.

I'll be there in forty. Stop calling.

She went through a stretch routine and had a quick shower before getting changed and heading out. Chalmers was preparing to lock up behind her.

"Trouble ahead?" he asked as she walked past, apparently noticing her expression.

"I'm looking forward to finding out," Freya replied.

A part of her wanted to leave Wellend to stew, but she avoided the temptation to head back to her flat before visiting him. In fairness, lately he'd been leaving her alone, giving her the distance she had requested. It had been a wild couple of years in London, with the rise and fall of Albion, the Zero Day bombings, and the ensuing crackdowns and countermeasures. DedSec had been busier than she had ever known, and a few close escapes – with the law, and with forces even more diabolical – had given her a moment of clarity. She had decided she wanted out, and she'd told Wellend as much.

Of course, leaving the world's most infamous underground hacker movement was easier said than done.

The worst of the rush hour traffic had worked its way through town by the time she left the gym, so she made good time on her scooter, making sure her digital cloak was activated, hiding her remote identity to anything that might be tracing her, from satellite imaging to drones and street cameras. It was a nasty, muggy evening, summer's last hurrah in the big city, North Islington grimy and perspiring in the close twilight. Drones whirred overhead, a counterpoint to the traffic on the ground. Most were food delivery services transporting evening takeaways, though a few commercial fliers were still up, and there was one newscaster that hovered over the entrance to Finsbury Park. Freya kept her helmet visor down, a lifetime of hard-earned experiences coupled with natural Bauer instincts. It was no use having a digi-cloak if someone on the street had physical eyes on her or snapped a pic. She also knew well enough that the facial recognition tech on even the courier drones wasn't only used to ensure the right goods were delivered to the right people.

She pulled up and parked outside Rajeev's corner shop, an unassuming store occupying a slender footfall between a tattoo parlour and a Jobcentre Plus, just off Stroud Green Road. She slipped her Optik's hands-on component out of the pocket of her yellow leather jacket, double-checking that it was dead, corresponding with the deactivated chip in her ear. It was her standard practice, but tonight it had the added bonus of meaning Wellend couldn't pester her anymore.

Sometimes she wanted to throw the device away, dig out the chip beside her ear, and go completely off-grid. She knew that was a fantasy. There was no such thing as "off-grid" nowadays. They were all logged down somewhere. Someone was always watching. Besides, an Optik with a full jail break and all the requisite DedSec installations – identity scramblers, a tracker null, fast uplink, and a clone interface – was invaluable. If it fell into the wrong hands it wouldn't just be her life at risk. It could potentially bust a good chunk of the whole system open.

She kept her helmet on until she was stepping through the shop's front door. Rajeev's establishment was unremarkable, a long, cramped space with teetering shelves ram-packed with goods, all under the store's harsh, buzzing lights.

It looked quiet tonight. That was good. Rajeev, a short, balding man in a stained paisley jumper, was behind the till when Freya walked in, her arrival announced by the tinkle of the store's bell. He didn't look up.

"Got any cookie dough mixture?" Freya asked him. He continued counting change, finishing sorting the till's trays and slotting it shut before finally looking up at her.

"We might have some in the back. Ajay!"

The exclamation was directed at his son, who was stacking shelves down one of the aisles.

"Come mind the front while I find some cookie dough for this lovely lady," Rajeev said, before adding to Freya, "It might be quicker if you helped me look. There's a lot of boxes back there."

Freya followed him through a narrow door behind the counter, into a storage space that was even more cluttered than the main floor. She made sure to shut the door behind her as Rajeev shifted a stack of boxes packed with biscuits. Beneath them was a small trapdoor.

"You're late," Rajeev said, stooping with a groan of effort and unlatching it.

"What's got Wellend so riled up?" Freya asked.

"Not my job to know, cookie dough lady, but I hope you find what you're looking for down there." He hauled up the covering, exposing a tight, almost vertical flight of stairs that led down into darkness.

"You and me both," Freya said, before beginning to descend.

Rajeev shut the door above her, and there was a horrible second of total darkness before a light flicked on automatically. Freya stepped down into the shop's cellar, a place as untidy as the storeroom above, but with the added bonus of being musty and a bit dank.

She worked a stack of pallets out from the wall, far enough to expose the damage done by what looked like a sledgehammer. A section of bricks and plaster had been smashed through, leading to a dark and uninviting gap.

Freya ducked into it, feeling a slight ache in her shoulders. She hadn't anticipated having to practically crawl around the depths of north London after today's reps. Wellend had better have a good reason for calling her in, especially since he hadn't for months.

More lights came on, illuminating the way ahead. She was in an old corridor with a circular roof and walls, white tiles faded to yellow. Arrows pointed both ways, twinned with signs indicating platform numbers or exits. It was an old Tube line, a branch of the northern Metropolitan from the 60s that had fallen into disuse and been sealed off.

London was a warren like that, a city with a Hades-like underworld of subways, sewers, basements, and crypts, running over, under, and sometimes even through one another. Expansions of the Tube itself were constantly unearthing everything from medieval plague pits to Second World War bomb shelters. And in among it all, amidst the underground empire of detritus, grime, and human history, DedSec made its nest.

She headed down the tunnel, her footsteps echoing in the dead space. At the far end a metal latticework gate was drawn over in front of an empty ticket booth. Faded posters were plastered on the façade showing the price of line fares alongside advertisements for museum exhibits, films and decades-old West End plays.

Above the booth, contrasting with the time-gnawed relics, was a modern semicircular security camera that gleamed like a cyclopean eye. Freya knew it wasn't the only piece of tech in the tunnel. The gate itself was fitted with both electronic sensors and scramblers that would alert those beyond to any live devices passing through, as well as frying said devices if they were left on and didn't possess the necessary digital handshake.

She paused in front of the barrier and blew the camera a condescending kiss.

There was a buzzing sound, and the thud of an automatic lock giving way. The gate clanged as it unlatched. Freya pushed it, grimacing at the squeal of rusting hinges, and stepped through. It banged shut and locked behind her.

Past the booth was a short flight of stairs. A thrumming sound echoed up from below. It was swelteringly hot now. Freya always got the impression that she was descending into the bowels of some ugly, ancient monster whenever she ventured into Wellend's lair. She unzipped the front of her yellow biker jacket.

The steps led out onto the Tube platform itself. The semicircular tunnel at either end had been bricked up, and most of the track had been layered over with timber boarding, extending the walk space and creating a boxlike chamber.

It was filled with signs of long-term occupation. There were a few commandeered old NHS bunk beds along the walls, outnumbered by rows of sleeping bags and, near the centre of the former platform, a communal area consisting of ratty sofas and a trio of mismatched coffee tables holding a TV, a kettle, a mini fridge, a toaster and microwave, and a scattering of books, laptops, and Optik burners, plus the obligatory tangle of wires and chargers. At the far end of the walkway a large power generator laboured continuously, providing the source of the thrumming and heat.

Often when Freya visited, the place was busy with DedSec activists and those close to the organisation, coming and going or hiding out, but it seemed most people had something better to be doing on a Monday evening than visiting the north London hackerspace –only a single person was present as Freya entered. He jumped up from one of the sofas and scurried over, a lean guy who hadn't quite yet thrown off the gangly awkwardness of late adolescence.

"Where is he?" Freya asked him. His name was Mike, a German kid and one of the more recent recruits who, from what she could pick up, was keeping a low profile while his flat was being thoroughly debugged following a brush with the authorities.

"In the office," Mike answered, scratching at his greasy, unwashed hair. "He seems stressed. Like, even more than usual."

Freya huffed. She knew there was no point in asking Mike what Wellend wanted with her. The kid didn't have that kind of clearance yet.

"Keep this until I'm done," she told him, and tossed him her scooter helmet. He caught it clumsily as she strode past, towards a metal door set in the flank of the platform's wall. It swung open as she approached.

Wellend, her least favourite freedom fighter, was waiting for her.

3
Proposals

Wellend looked tired, but that wasn't unusual. He was dressed in trackies and a Lacoste hoodie that looked like it had seen cleaner days. His usual stubble had grown out into a proper beard, and his locs were becoming straggly and unkempt.

"You look like crap," Freya told him.

"Don't," he responded, beckoning her inside. She entered.

The room was the old stationmaster's office. It had been repurposed into the nerve centre of the north London operation, with four PCs and a dozen monitors. Everything from mining cryptocurrency to maintaining surveillance – often via hacked feeds – was conducted here. Currently only Wellend was present. He sat behind the main desk, in front of a large map of London pinned up on the wall.

"Tea?" he asked.

"We going to be long?"

"Depends how willing you are to cooperate."

"I'll have an Earl Grey then," Freya said. "With milk and one sugar."

"You're an animal," Wellend said in response to such an idea before shouting to Mike. The kid stuck his head nervously round the door.

"Earl Grey, milk and one sugar, and a PG Tips, just milk."

Mike scurried off to make the brews. Freya doubted there were many members of DedSec that would have so obediently acted as literal tea caddies to anyone else in the organisation, but Mike was clearly still uncertain regarding his new life of hacktivism, and Wellend was taking advantage. He'd always liked making the new recruits run around after him. Hell, he'd even tried it on Freya, back when she had first been starting out. It hadn't quite worked out for him though.

"Going to tell me what's got you all bothered then?" she asked, taking an uninvited seat across the desk from Wellend and draping her leather jacket over its back. She watched him carefully as she did so, trying to gauge his mood. It was always good to know how far she could push him. She suspected he was trying to work out the same thing with her.

DedSec had no real hierarchy as such. Rigid command systems were anathema to such a loose group of underground rebels and agitators. Some, however, had a talent for coordinating the efforts of others. Wellend was one such person. He was in his mid-forties now, a little older than Freya, but still displayed the sort of deep, slow-burning commitment to the ideologies of individual freedoms and social justice that had, after years of running successful operations, left him more or less a respected top dog among those who considered themselves DedSec in north London. His charisma was always a big hit with the recruits and low-level informers, runners, and street cranks, and to be fair he worked himself and his fellow activists hard, not that he'd had much of a choice in recent years. It had been a deadly time for everyone involved in the movement. There had been losses, some of them long-term volunteers who had ended up behind bars, or worse. That was part of the reason Freya wanted out, and had told Wellend as much months earlier. She wanted to live to see Andrew graduate from Bristol.

"I've got a job for you," Wellend told her.

"Yeah, I gathered." Freya leaned back in her chair. "You blew my Optik up to get me here, but now you're being awfully cagey. How bad is it?"

"As bad as it gets," Wellend admitted.

"Then why are you asking me to do it?"

"Because you're the best one for it. I promise, I've looked for alternatives."

Freya didn't like where this was heading. It confirmed the bad feeling she'd had since realising Wellend was trying to contact her.

The door opened. Mike came in, carrying two mugs of tea and placed them down on the desk. Wellend watched him carefully until he had scurried out again.

"It's Germany," Wellend said after the door shut. "Or more specifically, Berlin."

"Yeah, bad start," Freya said.

"There's a group there that needs our help. They call themselves M-Bahn. They're to all intents and purposes the first branch of DedSec in central Europe."

"Good for them." Freya picked up the mug that looked like Earl Grey and blew on it. "What's that got to do with me?"

She was being deliberately obtuse. Berlin was her birthplace, but she hadn't been there in almost thirty years, and she had no intention of going back.

"We need someone competent, with local knowledge, to assist them as they find their feet," Wellend said. "You've got both of those bases covered."

"Competent is an interesting word choice," Freya said. "If they're just setting up, it'll be technical expertise they're after. You know I'm not one of your hacker nerds. Why would they need muscle? Unless they're already running foul of bigger, badder groups, or the authorities?"

"You wouldn't be going alone," Wellend said pointedly. "William would go with you."

Freya put the tea back down. Surprise gave way to anger. She looked hard at Wellend.

"Are you taking the piss?" she asked.

"No. You said what they'd need most was technical knowledge, and you're right. Will is perfectly suited for that. He's experienced, and he's fluent in German."

"He's also my arsehole ex-husband," Freya snarled.

"None of us are perfect, but together you're ideal for this. You're what M-Bahn needs."

"No. Absolutely not."

"It would be a dereliction of duty on my part if I didn't ask you both."

"Have you spoken to him already?"

"Not yet, not in full anyway. It's a work in progress."

Freya scoffed. She hadn't imagined Wellend would be this bold. He should have known better.

"You know I haven't spoken to him in four years?" she said. "Not since our son's fifteenth birthday. He hasn't even tried to get in touch."

"Then you'll have plenty to catch up on."

"I'm not doing it."

Wellend pursed his lips, looking at her. She returned his gaze fiercely, daring him to keep trying.

"Do you know what the current situation is in Germany?" he asked eventually.

"Changing the angle of attack won't work," Freya told him, but he carried on as if she hadn't spoken.

"The government, headed by the so-called Stability Coalition, passed the Defender Initiative last week. There were riots in the streets, and with good reason.

"None of my business."

"You remember Albion? You remember when the government here started surrendering authority to private security firms? We were one more faltering step from living in a totalitarian state. From civil war. Well now it's playing out in Germany, with their own version of Nigel Cass's shitheads."

Freya knew as much. She generally tried to ignore news from her homeland, but her mother remained invested and would regularly lecture her whenever she visited her adopted home in Hackney. A surveillance organisation with paramilitary trappings known as the Vertidiger – the Defenders – had come to prominence over the past few years, and the bill passed in the federal parliament, the Bundestag, by their political allies had legalised their spying and data-harvesting operations. People were calling it undemocratic, and they were right.

If a DedSec branch could grow out of Germany's fledgling resistance of hackers, it could do a lot of good. The Germans would have to do the heavy lifting, however, to be as homegrown, like all other DedSec efforts. DedSec was a movement, not an organisation. Even the idea of two UK activists being sent over to assist felt unusual. Wellend had often argued unsuccessfully for more coordination across the branches, so Freya supposed he considered this mission a priority.

She couldn't say it was a priority for her. She wanted out, and Wellend's pitch was only making her more determined to dump her DedSec responsibilities for good.

"I'm not going to Berlin, and I'm definitely not going with Will," she told him.

"You know, if I was doing my job properly, I'd try some sort of threat round about now," Wellend said.

Freya laughed. "Threats don't tend to work when I'm your best enforcer."

"Indeed," Wellend said, without humour. "So, what can I offer you instead? You want me to take your Optik off you? Dig out that chip? Wipe all communication footprint with us completely?"

For the first time since entering the room, Freya experienced a moment's hesitation. Wellend sensed it and pounced.

"You've been DedSec long enough to know how difficult it is to leave it all behind, especially for someone with your reputation. So I'll make you a deal, right now. Go to Berlin with Will, tick some boxes with M-Bahn, and when you get back you can hand in your Optik, metaphorically speaking. I promise that no one will interact with you again."

To her shame, Freya considered it. Then the anger, the same emotion that had gotten her through so many bare-knuckle and knife-edge moments, kicked in.

"I don't need you in order to leave this shitshow behind, Wellend, and I don't need your help either. This was a short one after all."

She stood up and picked up her jacket, her tea undrunk, then moved towards the door.

"Are you going to let Berlin become like London was a few years ago?" Wellend shot. "Because that's what's happening over there, right now. If I have to send William alone to stop it, I will. If you don't care about him, and you don't care what happens to the place that you used to call home, well, DedSec won't miss you."

Freya felt a powerful urge to shout at him. Instead, she swept open the door and snapped her fingers at a startled-looking Mike, who hastily pulled off his headphones and put down his gaming controller.

"Helmet," Freya demanded. He quickly leaned over the couch to pass it to her. She snatched it without breaking stride.

She almost expected Wellend to follow her, but he stayed in his lair.

That was the first wise thing he had done since contacting her. Knowing Wellend, it would probably be the last too.

William Fraser moved to close the tab he'd been working on and hesitated.

He was sitting alone in his office at home. Work for the day was finished, but he could feel the urge to meddle rising once more.

This happened too often. He was getting caught up again. But was that really so wrong? He had found himself wondering that more and more recently.

What he was doing was only natural. And it was all there, a few clicks away. Files that should have been private were easily accessed by someone like him, someone with the right software, the necessary know-how, the experience.

But was it the right thing to do? That was something he prided himself in asking. While the legal system of the United Kingdom of Great Britain and Northern Ireland may have ruled him a criminal, he did not believe himself to be such. Criminality was decided not by actions, but by motivations. If motivation and intent were pure, the concept of criminality was a hollow one.

Someone had once told him that he was overthinking it and

that he was wrong anyway. He was simply conflating actual justice with the warped and brittle construct that was this country's legal system. They were not one and the same. That much was true.

"Oh, I didn't realise you were in."

Will jumped and switched tabs, startled from the reverie he'd drifted into by his girlfriend, Samantha. She came into the spare bedroom that doubled as Will's workspace carrying a pile of laundry and smiling, though her expression took on a hint of suspicion as she noticed his jumpy reaction.

"All finished with work?" she asked.

"Just about," Will lied, pretending to scan his laptop's screen. "I'm going to head down and make dinner in a few minutes, if that's all right?"

He didn't really hear what she said. His Optik, lying beside the laptop, vibrated, twinned with the tiny pulse of his implant.

"Sorry if you're hungry, this won't take long," he added, smiling at Sam as she began to hang up the laundry on the rack they stored in his room. He mentally called up his Optik's interface as he spoke.

It was Wellend.

Going to have to try harder. Reach out to her.

Like it was that easy. Like he hadn't thought about doing that already.

But maybe he was overcomplicating things, as usual. There was only one way to find out.

He blink-closed his Optik's HUD and leaned back in his desk chair, stretching, paying attention to Sam in an effort to cover up his convoluted thoughts. She was a good judge of character. She'd be able to tell his mind was wandering, getting tied up and knotted in his past.

"Maybe we should go out for dinner sometime next week," he said. "It's been a while since we went on a date."

"You think you'll have time?" she asked. There was a little niggle there. Understandably so. He hadn't had many free nights recently. His work – as freelance accountant – had been busy, and his secret double life even busier. DedSec didn't get days off.

"I hope so," he told Sam. "Worst case scenario, a few more weeks and this backlog of reports will be cleared out. It's the inflation rates. Everyone wants their accounts checked. They're trying to squeeze every penny."

"Well, I'm glad you're getting regular work again," Sam said as she finished hanging up the laundry. There was still a hint of bitterness there.

"I'll make time, I promise," Will said.

"It's OK. I know things are crazy at the moment."

She didn't quite realise just how right she was. He was having to dedicate so much time to researching other matters. M-Bahn. Der Vertidiger. Other groups, or rumours of new groups like Reboot, or names like Erik and Kaiser. The German dark web was busy, twitchy, and distrustful, more so than he had known it when he had last mounted forays in that part of Europe. That had been years ago. Now it seemed worse, like a pot left to boil and bubble over.

He didn't want to get involved, to stick his hand in the pot, but there were incentives. There always were. Wellend knew how to get what he wanted. He just made sure he found out what others wanted, and made them an offer first.

"I'll go down and set the table," Sam said as she exited. Will took a moment, then went back to the tab he had been on before she came in.

"Leave it," he murmured to himself. He had enough trouble. He needed to take a step back. Adding family problems wasn't going to help.

He closed the tab. Then, mastering his disappointment, he mentally composed a message and sent it to Wellend via his Optik implant.

I'll see what I can do.

Freya got home a little after 9 PM. Mister Scruff was there to greet her with hungry yowls, the one-eyed rescue cat rubbing herself aggressively round her ankles as she closed the flat door.

"You and me both," she said, checking the entrance was locked before reaching down to fondle between the tabby's ears. He led her eagerly through to the kitchen, where she filled his bowl before opening the freezer.

She was too tired to cook, but thankfully she'd frozen a Tupperware's worth of bolognese after a batch session a few days before. The simple addition of some boiling water, salt, and spaghetti in a pan would suffice for tonight.

The meal prepared, she sat down to eat in front of the TV, switching idly between streaming services as she tried to find something to distract her. Mister Scruff attempted repeatedly to get at the bolognese mince but, warded away, eventually contented himself with curling up next to her.

She was just finishing when her Optik sent her a ping. She was tempted to ignore it, assuming it was Wellend, before recognising Andrew's avatar out of the corner of her eye. She accepted the heads-up display, a message from him superimposing itself onto her vision.

Still want to VR?

She cursed herself. She had been so morose following the

encounter with Wellend she had completely forgotten her earlier promise to her son.

She abandoned the dregs of her dinner and switched on her Optik's Virtual Reality mode. Without recourse to a camera, her Optik reconstructed Andrew's face on her display, twinning with his own implant to replicate his features and expression in real time perfectly. Well, almost perfectly. Freya still found an "uncanny valley" element to it, but it was little different from a pixelated video call. For a while she lost herself in their conversation, celebrating his triumphs and commiserating with the tribulations of uni life.

In truth, his experiences often felt totally alien to her. What was important was that he was doing well and continued to avoid the kind of life Freya led. He was one of only two males in her life that she trusted, and the other had a tail and was now curled up next to her, sleeping. If they were both OK, then so was she.

"You look after yourself, all right?" she told Andrew as the evening drew on and they began to wrap things up. He scoffed, making light of her mothering.

"I'm fine, Mum! It's Bristol, not Berlin."

Freya froze, enough for Andrew to notice even over VR rendering.

"Are you OK?" he asked.

"Yeah, fine," she said, pretending to look off to the side slightly. "Something on the TV, that's all. The news is shocking these days."

"That's why I don't watch it," Andrew replied.

"And that's why you're the cleverest of the Bauers," Freya told him. "Sleep well, kid. Love you."

"Love you too!"

She sat for a long while after Andrew hung up, her mind churning, before finally forcing herself to go to bed.

4
Full English

Will messaged Freya in the morning two days after her talk with Wellend.

Hey.

That was it. Even that made Freya angry. He could still be painfully awkward it seemed.

She left the message unanswered and went to her PT appointments, deliberately locking her Optik out so she didn't receive a ping when she got a new message. When she reactivated it at the end of her sessions, she had another message from him.

We need to talk.

She left it without any kind of response. Another day passed. He didn't try to call. A smart move on his part.

She wanted to ignore him, and everything Wellend had suggested. She didn't want this life anymore. She was out, or at least she had started hoping she was. Hadn't she done enough over the past twenty years?

She knew Wellend's answer to that would have been "no". DedSec's activists could never do enough, at least not in the eyes of people like him. Sometimes Freya thought he was a fanatic. He didn't care how many fellow activists were killed or imprisoned or had their lives eaten up by the strain of it all. What mattered was the cause – freedom, apparently. Freedom for all mankind. Or something like that anyway. It certainly felt very different from the sort of freedom Freya believed in.

Will's third message was the one that worked.

Don't ignore me.

He knew what he was doing, Freya could admit that much. The words, niggling in the corner of her vision, spiked her simmering anger into something more potent.

You've ignored us for the last four years, she replied, knowing he'd deliberately baited her.

You know I had to, came the reply.

"Bullshit," Freya snarled, causing two women to glance over at her. She was sitting on a bench in the gym's changing rooms, another class just completed. She had another coming up. She didn't have time for this, mentally or physically.

Will was following up without waiting for a reply now, the messages scrolling centrally along her vision.

You've spoken to Wellend. You know what he wants. It's a way out, for both of us.

Since when did you ever want out?

Longer than you might think. Let's meet and talk, like adults.

Another barb, designed to spike her into a response. She leaned back, forcing herself to cool off.

He knew how to push her buttons. But beneath the anger and annoyance, a part of her was tempted. She wanted to tell him how much of a useless father he'd been. She'd once dreamed about a confrontation, had even considered tracking him down before deciding it wasn't worth her time.

Besides, when someone like Will didn't want to be found, he

wouldn't be. He'd helped her to disappear too, enough times for her to know he was too good at it.

Snax, she wrote. *10 o'clock, next Friday. You're paying.*

The message was sent. He replied with a thumbs-up.

She stewed, wondering what the hell she was getting herself into, then realised she was at risk of being late for the start of her next session. She got up and tried to forget about it all for the next hour.

It was raining. Will was thankful of that. It meant he could wear his hood up without getting any funny glances.

He loitered outside a Tesco just along from Snax, a greasy spoon breakfast café that had once been a regular haunt when Freya and he had first been starting out. He doubted her decision to meet him there had anything to do with nostalgia. It was familiar turf, the best kind to be on when engaging in combat.

He had to avoid thinking like that. He wasn't here for a confrontation. He was here because it was the right thing to do.

Still, he was nervous. That was why he was vacillating outside Tesco instead of crossing the street and walking in. He was running late, not that that was unusual. He had no doubt Freya had been in situ within for at least the last twenty minutes. Another difference between them.

Man up, he told himself. This was the best chance he would get. A month in Germany, and he'd be out of DedSec and no longer worrying about the next potential brush with the law. He could enjoy an early retirement with Samantha. Maybe, along the way, he could even make it up enough with Freya and Andrew. No more checking tabs.

He glanced left and right, keeping his head down. The road was quiet, but commercial drones buzzed past overhead, creating eddies in the downpour. Cursing himself and his best intentions, he made a break across the street and into the cover of the breakfast bar.

Freya avoided the temptation to check her Optik. She was where she needed to be, and that was enough. If he didn't show, then he didn't show.

She had already ordered tea, and had it half-drunk as she waited, trying to straighten out her thoughts. She quashed any suggestion that she was nervous. Why would she be? Will was the past and deserving of nothing but her anger. He was also late, as usual.

She sat watching the street outside, a morning as grey as twilight. Rainwater streaked down the window to create an opaque world of dark, hurrying figures framed by the diffracted glare of red and amber lights from passing cars, playing counterpoint to the running illuminators of the drones in the air lanes above them. Dreary London, starting a precipitous descent into what looked like it would be a damp autumn.

Sometimes, it could be any city in the world. Sometimes, it reminded her of the only other city she had ever known.

One of the grey figures materialised at the café's doorway and came inside. He paused to pull down his sodden hood, but Freya had recognised him as soon as he stepped in.

William Fraser, a man she had once loved.

He smiled at her, and she raised an eyebrow.

Suddenly, she felt nervous.

"I hope this place is as secure as it was when we were last here together," he said, pulling off his dripping jacket.

"As far as I know," Freya said. The owner of Snax, while not exactly DedSec, operated in that nebulous grey zone that most definitely didn't find favour with the authorities. All sorts used the café as a meeting place, knowing that it would be free from bugs and regularly scanned for any touts masquerading as civvies. That was part of the reason Freya and Will had once been regulars. It sure wasn't down to the quality of the food.

"What you having?" Freya asked, tapping the greasy, laminated menu as Will sat down. She was doing her best not to go off on one right away, but her heart beat fast enough to bring back memories of the last time she'd been in a combat situation.

"Bagel, I think," he said, briefly looking at the list of options. "Doesn't look like the menu's changed anyway! How about you?"

"The usual," Freya said coldly.

This wasn't like her. She was being hesitant. Maybe that was for the best. A scene would be bad for both of them.

A bored-looking waitress took their orders. Freya sipped her tea as Will spoke. "Thank you for agreeing to this."

"I've agreed to nothing yet, besides eating a full English breakfast in front of you."

Will pursed his lips, then smiled awkwardly at the waitress as she returned with the orange juice he'd asked for. He'd gotten leaner since she had last seen him, Freya realised, and the stubble suited him. His hair was decidedly on the run now though, baldness creeping in at the corners.

She looked away, annoyed.

"So what's Wellend got on you?" she asked.

"Probably the same as what he has on you," Will said. "An offer of early retirement."

"Since when did you want to retire?" Freya asked him, giving in to genuine curiosity. He had always been one hundred percent DedSec. He had grown up a stereotypical tech-head, earning a degree at Leeds in computer science while hacking the university's systems to ensure he paid no student accommodation rent. He had fallen in with DedSec at the same time as Freya. They had been assigned to an early job together, and success had ensured further teamwork, earning a reputation as DedSec London's most effective duo. Between them they had run a host of successful big operations – the Rotherham heist, the leaking of the Kensington files, the activist jailbreak from the Albion facilities at Chatham. Before their last major job against DeLock Systems, a bounty of a million pounds had been put on both of their heads.

They had ridden the high of that wave for too long. At some point, boundaries had blurred. Youth, combined with repeated exposure to life-and-death situations, the thrill of hunting and being hunted, tended to do that. Sometimes she damned herself for ever letting it get intimate. But it had led to Andrew, so she couldn't truly curse the day she had met Will. Just the day he had left.

"People change," Will said, studying his orange juice. "I've done one job too many."

"You said that after DeLock," Freya pointed out, feeling dubious. The hit on the arms manufacturer DeLock Systems had also come the closest to disaster. They had exposed how the managing director, Hans Muller, had been siphoning weaponry into the criminal underworld across Europe. Freya earned two circular scars on her right side, old gunshot wounds, courtesy of Muller, who now served a life sentence based partly on evidence Will had managed to leak to the police.

While the sting had been successful, they both knew they should have died, and they ended up blaming each other. Will had made a mess of piercing DeLock's security, and Freya had found the escape route she had mapped out blocked and had improvised badly. In truth, neither of them had covered themselves in glory, but it was all well and good admitting that years later.

"DeLock was a turning point, but I couldn't quit then," Will said. "If I did it would have stayed with me."

"You decided to abandon your family instead," Freya pointed out. "Your work for DedSec was more important."

"Maybe we should both have stopped when Andrew was born."

Freya checked herself. She'd heard it all before. So had Will.

Their food arrived, a cream cheese bagel for Will and sausage, beans, bacon, eggs, and toast for Freya.

"What has Wellend told you about the job?" Will asked her, clearly trying to steer the topic back into the present. She spent a moment eating before answering.

"That it's in Berlin. That he's trying to help set up a possible DedSec branch over there, and we're going to be the boots on the ground. Not much else."

"That's the nub of it."

"You know more?"

"Only a little. I've got the specifics about what M-Bahn need help with. Some intel on the Vertidiger. They're some hard bastards."

"Is it true what people are saying? As bad as Albion?"

"Cut from the same cloth, for sure. Their leader, Erik Gerhardt, is ex German military intelligence."

"Doesn't sound like the sort of person I'd pick a fight with. Have you already accepted the job?"

"Pretty much."

"Did you know Wellend was asking me?"

"Yes. I told him you wouldn't like it."

"He should have listened to you."

Will bit into his bagel, apparently considering his response before speaking again. "The truth is, I'd feel better if we were both going."

"So sweet, I'm touched," Freya said, spooning beans onto her toast.

"It looks like it has the potential to get messy," Will continued. "What Wellend said is true. No one else is cut out for this job as well as we are. And if someone doesn't act, Germany's going under. It's already on the edge. The new laws, coupled with the rising, uncoordinated civil disobedience we're seeing–"

Freya set her cutlery down with a clatter, causing other people in the café to glance in their direction. She looked hard at Will, seeing him quail. His reaction caused her to take a second to gather herself, but she was done with holding back. It was easy to see where his interests lay, and it wasn't with her or their son.

"Where have you been for the last four years?" she demanded. "Four bloody years, Will. Andrew hasn't seen you since he was fifteen. He's going into his second year at uni now!"

Will glanced nervously at the neighbouring tables, clearly uncomfortable. Freya pinned him with her stare, her silence giving him no respite as she waited for him to answer.

"I had to go off-grid for work," he said eventually, voice low. "There were a couple of big jobs, and then it all blew up with Zero Day. You know how crazy the last twenty-four months have been."

"Don't bullshit me," Freya growled.

"It's the truth! I didn't want to risk bringing any harm down on you, or Andrew. Everything's been fraught. You know how it is. I'm pretty sure that's why we both want out."

"I know what you can do, Will Fraser," Freya said. "You could have contacted us without leaving a trail. You could have reached out anonymously. You chose not to."

Will didn't seem to have an answer to that. He laid down his bagel, unfinished.

"Is there someone else?" Freya asked, the question coming to her abruptly. The thought had occurred in the past. She could tell by Will's expression that there was.

"Yes," he said, then, after a pause, "how about you?"

"Not right now," Freya said tersely. "Is she the reason you've abandoned your son?"

"I haven't abandoned him," Will hissed, and there was an edge to his voice now. He met Freya's gaze properly, showing the spine she knew he possessed, when pressed.

"I've done more for him than you know, Freya," he said. "I think about him a lot."

"I'll be sure to let him know," Freya responded, matching the venom in his voice with her own.

"This was a mistake," Will said, fishing out his wallet and throwing a tenner down on the table.

"Glad you've finally realised it," Freya said, resisting the urge to ask him if he was running away again. It would do no good. She had made her point, had dug the knife deep enough.

Will left. Freya made herself finish her breakfast, thanked the waitress when she came to clear it away, and left a tip on top of Will's money. Then she sat for a while, calming down. She had hoped there would be a sense of closure, or at least satisfaction. But her words had left only a bitter aftertaste.

She got up and walked out.

5
Sauerbraten

A week passed, then another. Freya heard from neither Will, nor Wellend. She dared to hope that they had finally accepted that she didn't want to be involved. Still though, their words circled her thoughts, hunting her like a wolf pack in the wilds, shadowing their prey.

The weather was slumping rapidly, the air taking on a decided chill. The rain now seemed to fall with a vindictive sting to it. The leaves in Finsbury Park were showing autumnal shades.

Freya wasn't looking forward to the onset of winter, but then nobody was. Inflation and energy prices combined to produce an unholy assault on people's savings, and the volatility created by events across Europe weren't helping. A lot of good, honest folks were going to have to choose between heating and eating in the coming months.

Freya had laid up enough to get herself through, but she was hoping to take more classes in the gym in an effort to put some aside for her mother. Belinda Bauer lived in a tiny flat in Hackney, about twenty-five minutes from where Freya stayed, via scooter. The building itself belonged to a DedSec affiliate, who kept rents as low as possible for a few families connected to the movement.

Freya hadn't particularly liked the idea of her mother being involved with DedSec, even indirectly, but then Belinda had borne witness to a life of crime before Freya had even been born. Besides, housing in London was a nightmare, and Belinda's financial situation had been precarious ever since Thomas Bauer had gone back to Berlin and never returned. Freya knew there were times when it was best to accept a helping hand, and DedSec had long been offering one where her mother was concerned. It was one of the few places where they both felt safe, or as close to safe as they could ever really be.

The turning weather was an excuse for her to check in on her mother, but a part of her also wanted to tell her about Will and Wellend, to unburden herself and seek her advice. Another part, that stubborn streak Belinda had passed onto her, wanted to keep it all close to her chest. Conflicted, she phoned her after work one day, her Optik connecting to Belinda's house phone – Belinda was one of the few people left in London who didn't own an Optik herself, a mistrust of modern technology that, at times, Freya suspected she had partially inherited. Normally not owning one would come with a stiff government fine, but DedSec had helped ensure Belinda's noncompliance had not yet been noticed by the authorities. They organised a time, and she arrived – after making sure she wasn't being tailed and that her digital trace was clean – to the homely scents of sauerbraten filling the cramped flat. Belinda was listening to *The Bug* on the radio as she pulled a Pyrex casserole dish containing the meat from the oven, a welcome heat flooding the kitchen as Freya stepped inside. The recipe was marinated roast beef rump and potato dumplings, served on this occasion with sauerkraut. It was one of Freya's favourites.

"Right on time, as usual where food is concerned," Belinda said, smiling before closing the oven door. "You're in luck! I've had this sitting in the wine for four days. There was me thinking I'd get it all to myself!"

"As though you'd ever eat all of it," Freya scoffed. She was always worrying about her mother's weight. Compared to her daughter's tall, muscular physique, Belinda was small and almost painfully slender, a fact she assured Freya was entirely normal for her age, but which Freya still found disturbing. She remembered her grandmother, and how skinny she had been before passing away, back when they had still lived in Germany. A part of Freya associated her mother's slender build with declining health, hence the reason she so often urged her mother to eat more.

"I was going to give some of it to Helen," Belinda said, referring to the next-door neighbour. "You can take the blame when she asks about the lack of sauerbraten tomorrow!"

"I'm sure you'll rustle up something for her," Freya said as she helped her mother with the plates. Helen Dashwood was supposedly retired from her days as one of DedSec's most effective activists, though Freya suspected that was only half the truth. Nobody really retired, after all, and while most DedSec ops were on a need-to-know basis, word on the street was that, despite her age, Helen had been heavily involved in the recent chaos that had almost overwhelmed London.

"Maybe she'll accept leftovers," Belinda said, passing Freya the sauerkraut to begin doling onto two plates while she fished the cuts of beef from the wine, herbs, and spices they had been steadily absorbing for the better part of a week.

"I was going to take the leftovers home," Freya teased.

They talked for a little while about idle matters while plating the dinner, from the turning weather to Freya's gym classes. She sometimes had to remind her mother what she did, a conversation always accompanied by disbelief that people would pay so much just to be told to exercise.

"And it's legitimate work?" she asked Freya, as usual.

"My end is all legitimate," Freya reassured her. "The gym owner, I'm less sure, but you know how these things work. Don't ask, don't tell."

"Be careful," Belinda urged her. "I don't want you to get caught up with the wrong sorts, the way your father was."

"I'm always careful," Freya said. She knew what kind of "sorts" her mother was referring to. Thomas Bauer had run a relatively modest forgery business in Berlin but had eventually fallen foul of the city's most hardened criminals – mobsters, murderers and cartel kingpins. Freya didn't know the details – she doubted her mother did entirely either – but at some point, Thomas had pissed off someone serious. That was the night they had fled to London.

About a year later, Thomas had left to go back to Berlin. Freya still vividly remembered him telling her it was to settle some final business, and that he'd be back in a few days. Then he had embraced her, squeezed her tight, before letting go and walking out. Neither she nor Belinda had ever seen him again.

"I won't get caught the way Father was," Freya said softly, her voice tinged with bitterness. Belinda looked at her sharply.

"Getting caught and not acting wrongly in the first place are two different things," she said. "I failed you when you were younger, otherwise you wouldn't be caught up with these *gangsters*."

"DedSec aren't gangsters," Freya said for the umpteenth time, wondering at the fact she was implicitly standing up for the likes of Wellend. "They're trying to help. It's people like Helen next door who are holding this government to account."

"And who is holding the government to account back home?" Belinda demanded, stabbing a finger towards an old pile of *Die Zeit* newspapers stuffed into a rack on the corner of the kitchen counter. "I read the reports online with the tablet you gave me. That's all it's good for. This new legislation, these so-called 'Defenders'? No good will come of it. We know the price such authority demands!"

She was getting worked up, and Freya was beginning to feel the same. One of the big rules when going toe-to-toe with someone was not to fight them on their favoured ground, and lambasting Freya about her homeland was Belinda's most familiar turf. She forced herself to embrace her mother who, after a second, returned the hug.

"Let's eat," Freya said. Belinda accepted the change in subject graciously enough. They both sat and began to tuck in.

"How is your boy?" Belinda asked.

"Doing well. He got into a good course for next year."

"He staying out of trouble?"

"As far as I can tell."

"You're his mother, I'd hope you can tell!"

"He is. He's a good kid. Not like me."

Belinda grunted noncommittally. There wasn't much debating that Freya hadn't been a good kid, but in retrospect that seemed inevitable. The death of her dad and adjusting to a new, difficult life in a strange city had seen her go off the rails. There had been a slew of ill-advised, petty crimes, nights spent in police cells, scraps and scrapes with rival gangs. Then DedSec had come along. That had changed everything. At first, Freya had felt as though she was atoning for her youth by doing good via the movement. Nowadays, she wasn't so sure.

"And what about the useless man Andrew calls a father?" Belinda demanded. She had never shied away from expressing her negative attitude towards Will, a fact that had been uncomfortable when they had actually been together, but which was now a welcome addition to Freya's own thoughts on the matter.

"He got in touch recently," she admitted, not wanting to go into any more detail. "But yeah, useless as ever."

"Kill him," Belinda said.

"That might be a bit much. But I've thought about it."

Belinda swallowed some sauerkraut and chuckled.

"He's not worthy of you, my daughter."

"So you've said, frequently. Seems I should have heeded my mother's advice."

Belinda made an expansive shrugging gesture.

"I told you when you met him, he may be good with all these gadgets and computers and… electronics –" she said the word with some vehemence "– but he's not like your father. There was a man who could provide for his family. Provide and protect."

"Until he couldn't," Freya said without really meaning to. For a moment, Belinda looked stung.

"He died trying to see us safe," she said quietly. "Someday the animals who murdered him will face justice. Not the pathetic justice supplied by the law, but a real reckoning."

Freya had heard it all before. Ever after all these years, her mother burned with bitterness and remorse. Freya shared it, had grown up with it. Sometimes it felt like all she had ever known. She sometimes wished she knew who had done it. Who had ordered the hit. As a teen she had fantasised about going back to Germany and finding them. That felt like a childish idea now, though sometimes Freya still found herself indulging it, even all these years on.

"I have something for you," Belinda said abruptly, rising from the kitchen table with the dinner only half-eaten. Freya watched her warily as she rummaged around in a drawer, wondering just what her mother intended to give her. After a while she let out a satisfied grunt and returned to the table, carefully placing a small square of glossy paper beside Freya's plate.

It was a Polaroid photograph, dog-eared and worn, featuring Freya around the age of nine. A school photo, uniformed up, pigtailed, beaming at the camera. Seeing it felt like a stab in the gut.

"Think I should grow my hair out like that again?" she asked, instinctively trying to mask the unexpected emotion of seeing her childhood self. A time before London, before the existence she had constructed here. A life she had often tried to forget but had never quite managed to let go of.

"That photo was one of three taken before your father left for the last time," Belinda said, unmoved by Freya's half-hearted effort at humour. "One was left behind in our home when we escaped Berlin. Your father carried the other with him when he went back. I wish I knew what became of it."

Freya felt an overwhelming urge to tell her mother about Will and Wellend and Berlin. She checked herself, deciding against it after all. What good would it do? It wasn't connected to her past, not directly. It was the spectre of the city, hanging over her. Worrying her mother with it would do no good, she decided. It was her burden to bear.

"I wish I was as cute now as I was back then," she said, sticking resolutely to levity, no matter how shallow it felt. "It would probably make life a whole lot easier."

"If you need help with anything, you should tell me," Belinda exclaimed, giving Freya a look only a mother was capable of. She knew well enough to back down quickly.

"I'm fine. I just miss the freckles, that's all."

They finished their dinner, talk drifting to the rising cost of bills. Freya helped her mother do the washing up while making her promise to let her know if money was getting too tight. Belinda made some noncommittal grumbles before heading to the door with Freya. She stopped her as it opened.

"Wait," Belinda said, going back to the table and returning with the little Polaroid. "Take it. Please."

"Why?" Freya asked, unwilling to even touch the photograph. It was too redolent with memories, too heavy to be added to the weight she was already carrying.

"It was sitting in a drawer for years," Belinda said. "Forgotten. It shouldn't have been. It should be remembered, and there's a better chance of that if you have it than if it goes back where I found it. So please. For your mother."

Freya accepted it reluctantly, slipping it into the slim rear pocket of her workout tights.

"Phone me when you get in," Belinda said, kissing her daughter's cheek.

"I will," Freya reassured her, before setting off down the stairwell.

As she was leaving the flat block, she almost walked into a short, elderly woman wearing a knitted turtleneck jumper, a drab paisley skirt, and black tights. She had square, black-rimmed glasses on, seemingly too stylish for someone of her age, and short grey hair. Her name was Helen Dashwood, the DedSec legend.

"Hello dearie," she exclaimed as Freya came up short. "Haven't seen you in a while!" She carried a cat box two-handed, the feline visible through the slats, glaring up at Freya. "Just back from the vet's," the elderly Londoner explained. "Marmaduke's been having liver problems."

"Let me have that," Freya said, taking the cat carrier one-handed and beginning to lug it up the stairs she had just descended. She offered her other arm to Helen as well, helping her up.

"Been visiting your mother?" Helen asked, accepting the assistance. "How is she?"

"Well, Miss Dashwood," Freya said. "She's planning on having you over, but don't tell her I said! I may have eaten all the sauerbraten that was stewing for you."

Freya couldn't kick the habit of calling Helen "Miss Dashwood". The old DedSec stalwart had been one of the main reasons she had stuck with the movement after first joining. She had gotten Freya on the so-called straight-and-narrow after the near-fatal turbulence of her disrupted teenage years. She was one of the few people Freya felt she still owed something to.

"Well, you'll have to come and visit me and bring the ingredients, and you can make sauerbraten for me in person," Helen said as they arrived at her door, the little old lady smiling up at Freya. "I'll trade you for a Sunday roast."

"I think I'll take you up on that, Miss Dashwood," Freya replied, returning the smile and setting down the cat box. "Goodnight."

6
Wolves

Chalmers said something Freya couldn't hear. She set down the dumbbell she'd been using and took out her earbuds.

"You OK?" Chalmers asked.

"Yeah?" Freya responded questioningly. It was getting late, but there were still a few punters on the treadmills or stretching out on the side lines. Freya had finished her last class and had been getting some reps in early before closing time, something she'd been doing with increasing frequency. It helped get some of the aggression out. Helped her forget the stress that felt as though it was building with all the slow, powerful inevitability of a runaway train.

There had still been no word from Will or Wellend. That hardly helped now though. The relentless wolves were still circling in her mind, snapping at her conscience, her peace. She hoped time would drive them away, but memories of her past now only seemed to be growing stronger.

"Just checking up on you," Chalmers said, holding his hands up. "It sounded like you came down pretty hard on Abby earlier, that's all."

Abby was one of her PT customers. She was a conscientious

hard worker usually, and was really starting to get in shape, but lately her form had been dipping. Earlier, Freya had reminded her to maintain her high standards.

"She just needed a bit of a pep talk," Freya said.

"Is that what you call it?"

"Was there a complaint?"

"No. I just overheard you."

"Maybe don't eavesdrop on your employees then?"

Chalmers's expression hardened. Freya found herself welcoming it.

"What's your deal, huh?" he demanded. "You've been acting out lately."

"Acting out? Like a child?"

"Yes, like a child. Snapping at your clients. My clients. This is my gym. Your attitude reflects on me, and all my other employees. Wind your bloody neck in."

Before she'd even realised what she was doing, Freya was on her feet. Chalmers grinned dangerously at her, hands on his hips, not backing down.

"I think it's about due for you to take a time out, Freya," he said. "Don't come into work until you sort out whatever it is that's got you so wound up."

"You're really going to suspend me?"

"Well maybe you should punch me and see if it'll change my mind?"

Freya glared at him for a moment before making to storm past. He held a hand up though and stopped her, before bending over and picking something up.

Freya realised it was the photo her mother had given her. It had slipped out of her pocket when she had stood up. Chalmers offered it to her.

"Nice pigtails," he said.

She didn't reply, taking the photo and walking to the changing rooms.

She sat for a while, looking at the old picture. Her anger cooled, leaving behind something cold and hard. She realised abruptly that she had come to a decision. What she had been going through wasn't going to change anytime soon, not unless she took action.

Sometimes you couldn't outrun the wolves. You had to fight them. Freya had never much enjoyed running anyway. Fighting, on the other hand…

She put the photo in her wallet. Then, riding the sudden conflagration of fiery resolve, she triggered her Optik and sent Wellend a message.

I'll do it.

Mister Babić had four minutes to live.

He didn't know it yet. Der Gespenst enjoyed that aspect of the hunt. It made him feel powerful, to be so utterly in control of another man's destiny. Life and death, in his opinion the essence of godhood, was his to command.

The Ghost was not close to Mister Babić, but he was watching. He had worried that his steadily advancing age – he had noted, if not celebrated, his fifty-fifth birthday a month before – would limit his job opportunities and thus curtail his pleasures. It was one thing to find himself chasing down a target, or worse, grappling with them in a moment's intoxicating, deadly embrace while he was in his prime, but to do so now would be to risk disaster.

Three minutes to live.

That would no longer be a danger with the wonderful

advancements of human technology at his fingertips. There were so many ways to kill now without having to even go outside. As he had gotten older, he had found himself embracing the more laid-back methods of murder. Using drones, or hacking and overloading a target's Optik, frying their brain. It removed the dangers of personally pursuing and overtaking his victims. That was a young man's game.

He was currently sitting in a hotel room, laptop open, a high-resolution view of the sky lane above the A115 gliding past. It was raining lightly and there was no reason to go out into it. No reason for him to seek Mister Babić on his doorstep personally.

Two minutes to live.

He was using what he called a *wespe*, a wasp. It was, officially, a K-17 Hermes type commercial goods drone, the smallest available. Just slightly larger than his splayed hand, it was used to carry purchases like new Optiks or other small valuables on premium deliveries. The only modification the Ghost had made to the drone itself was the remote camera he had mounted on its back. Of course, the package itself was something special too.

He had worried that such a method of operation would remove the thrill of moments like these. After all, he had long ago ceased killing because of financial incentives. It was not a job. It was a passion, an addiction. He craved it, more than his cigarettes, more than anything. But it was not the physicality. He could do without that. The rush that came with each life-and-death encounter was equally rewarding whether he looked his target in the eye in person, or electronically. Realising that truth had come as a huge relief.

One minute to live.

He didn't have to control the drone manually. The address had already been implemented, and it now followed its own directional programming. Its facial recognition technology would also ensure it only made its "delivery" to Mister Babić – if there was any uncertainty on that end, it would confirm his identity via his Optik, which the Ghost had already taken a clone of and downloaded to the drone's system. It was quite sophisticated. The Ghost found it a delightful toy.

Number 2 Bettinastraße. Time was up for Mister Babić.

The wasp's presence pinged the apartment's front door alarm automatically. At the same time, the Ghost's own Optik notified him of an incoming message. He felt a potent stab of frustration. Now was not the moment for a distraction. But there was only one person who had access to that means of contact, and he would begrudge him the interruption.

He kept his focus on the laptop screen, finger gliding over the keypad. The front door of 2 Bettinastraße opened, revealing the target. Antonio Babić, a heavyset, balding man who had thought Berlin a safe haven after a lifetime spent pulling strings in the Croatian underworld. He was the sort of man who knew well not to personally answer his front door to an uninvited guest, but he was too old to suspect the threat carried by a tiny buzzing drone.

The wasp was automated to find Babić, but it was not automated to kill him. That requirement the Ghost retained. He had allowed drones to take the kill-shot themselves in the past, but had found himself feeling bereft, the rush of the moment stolen. It was one thing to take his pleasure remotely, but whether it was a trigger of a gun or the button on a keyboard or Optik retinal display, it had to be his finger, and not the enslaved will of an artificial program, that felt nothing, knew nothing, could do nothing beyond what it had been told to do. Without this connection he was truly transformed from orchestrator to mere spectator.

Mister Babić's face filled the laptop screen, surprised and annoyed. He hadn't ordered anything. The Ghost supposed that made this a gift then.

He pushed the button on his keyboard.

The box slung beneath the drone was made to look like the package for an Optik, but it held something far deadlier. It punched a single shot clean through Babić's forehead. He dropped immediately, sprawling across his front step, dead before he had even realised the danger he was in.

The Ghost let out the breath he had been holding, a slow, shuddering exhalation. He still remembered when he had done this for money, when he had tried to convince himself it was some sort of job. It had long ago stopped being that.

He sent the drone on its way, letting it drop into the nearby Hundekehlesee lake. It was entirely disposable, easily replaced. The police would not try hard to recover it. The man killed was no friend of Germany's new authorities.

The Ghost opened a chat window and sent a quick message.

Mister Babić has received his package.

There was a double-tick to show it had been received, but no reply. There never was.

Only then did he allow himself to check his Optik, blinking open the HUD that superimposed itself on his vision.

He read what he had been sent, several times over. At first, he could not believe what it hinted at. Surely the sender would not joke about something such as this? Perhaps he was mistaken? Perhaps he was interpreting the message wrongly? But the Ghost was rarely wrong.

Slowly, he closed his laptop and leaned back in his chair. Then, he began to laugh.

7
Orders

In the end, Wellend's briefing was remote, held over Optik-linked VR and hosted by Bagley. Freya sat on the sofa in her flat and checked in.

The VR space itself was a simulation of Wellend's cramped Tube office. Will wasn't present as Freya logged in.

"Let me start by saying thank you for accepting the job," Wellend said.

"I did it for myself, not for you, or DedSec," Freya replied. "I decided it was time I went back."

"I suspect you'll find Berlin much changed," Wellend pointed out.

"It's going to say the same about me. So why aren't we doing this in your office? The real one I mean?"

"It's easier to keep the details of this mission contained. What I'm about to tell you and Will is highly sensitive."

"I'm not some sort of SIRS government spy," Freya said scornfully. "This isn't 'my mission, should I choose to accept it.'"

"Regardless, I'm not taking any chances. We need this to go

right. No leaks. Bagley is the only other remote program I'm using for this."

Will's avatar materialised in the cyberspace.

"Sorry, sorry," he said. "Just got back in my flat. I thought I had a tail past Crouch Hill Tube."

"And did you?" Wellend asked pointedly.

"Nah. Had to take a few false turns to be sure though."

Such nervous energy had once set Freya on edge. She avoided the urge to greet Will. She wasn't here for him, and she intended to make that abundantly clear.

"Let's get started then," Wellend said. "Activate Bagley. Freya, I know you have him blocked. He's hosting the files for this. You'll need to review them before you go to Germany."

"You know me so well," Freya said testily. Bagley was the AI system that DedSec in London relied on as an overarching assistant and Fixer. That would have been fine, but the digital program had quite a personality, one that grated on Freya endlessly. Since going partially off-grid, she had taken great delight in blocking all Bagley updates.

Hello again, Miss Bauer, the artificial intelligence said in her ear after she had blink-deactivated the inhibitor on her Optik's HUD, the voice realised as smooth Received Pronunciation.

"Don't even try your sass, Bagley," she snapped. "I'm not here for it."

Don't worry, Wellend here has my complete attention.

"As you know, the group you're contacting call themselves M-Bahn," Wellend said, ignoring Freya's outburst and sending a series of files via Optik to the pair. Freya blink-opened the first. An image of the actual Berlin subway M-Bahn logo – a white "M" in an orange circle – appeared overlaid with the old CND "peace" symbol.

"To all intents and purposes, M-Bahn is DedSec Deutschland," Wellend continued. "Given time, we hope to help M-Bahn grow, and provide mutual assistance in much the same way that our UK activists now work frequently alongside our American friends. Spread the movements, spread the love, and stop the march of totalitarianism across Europe and, eventually, the world."

A worthy sentiment, Bagley said. *If I had hands, I would applaud, politely.*

"So, they're not just a bunch of script kiddies?" Will said. "It's quite the grand strategy."

"Well, a group as loosely affiliated as DedSec needs a bigger picture to work towards, otherwise we'll have members wasting their efforts," Wellend said even as Freya exchanged a glance with Will. "M-Bahn have the potential to be another piece of the puzzle, and they fall at an important time. The rise of VERT in Germany poses the same threat to the rest of Europe as Albion did over here."

"VERT, the Vertidiger?" Freya wondered aloud.

Jawoll, Bagley said.

"Exactly," Wellend replied. He sent a video showing a recording of ominous troopers in grey fatigues and black combat kit, heavily armed, walking down the pavement. Another followed, of VERT troopers detaining and beating two men at the side of the road before hauling them towards a waiting armoured vehicle.

They look like they know how to party, Bagley said drily.

A third video, grainy and seemingly from an undercover camera, showed VERT troopers spread out along a firing range, taking shots at distant targets. A fourth was a shot of a cordon of troopers with helmets and riot shields stamped with "VERT", then a series of patrol cars that looked more suited to a warzone than the streets of one of Europe's capitals.

"Their leader is one Erik Gerhardt," Wellend narrated. "He did twelve years in the German army, including six in Afghanistan working with German military intelligence. After that he joined the police, where he worked as a detective for a decade. A few years going solo with private military contractors, and now he reemerges as the founder of the Defenders. He's already got powerful patrons in the Bundestag, including Meyer, the current federal minister of justice, and Claud Schapps, the leader of the authoritarian party gunning for votes at the forthcoming elections."

"Erik sounds like a bastard," Will said.

Seconded, Bagley added.

"He is," Wellend said. "If authoritarianism is a boot, he's the spiked heel that does the crushing. They're the spawn of the worst aspects of the last century reimagined with combat boots and drones instead of jackboots and tanks, though they've got a few of the latter as well. The Vertidiger, also known as the Defenders, are a private surveillance and security firm that have jacked themselves into the mainframe of the German government. They're offering quick solutions to sticky problems. Near-unrestrained data harvesting, oversight of the actual police force, and increasingly, the ability to detain whoever they like.

"The current party in power in the German parliament have elections coming up, and they think the public mood is in favour of these sorts of things, despite increasing civil unrest. Perhaps because of it. The biggest fear is VERT are abusing the situation to crack down on activist and change-advocating groups like M-Bahn or even the progressives in the Bundestag. Between them and the parties backing them, they're going to send the country back to the Cold War era, or worse."

"And M-Bahn are supposed to stop them?" Freya asked,

finding the idea dubious. The picture Wellend painted was bleak and confirmed all the fears her mother had regularly expressed.

"M-Bahn won't stop them, no," Wellend responded, to Freya's surprise. "The people are going to stop them. But first they need to realise what bad news VERT are. M-Bahn are going to help show them."

"An information campaign then, basically," Will mused. "What're the specifics?"

"At a basic level, making Erik and VERT look like the shitheads they are. M-Bahn are coming up with flyers, posters, videos. Hacking corporate and government websites to display them would be a first step. On a more vital and elaborate level, they hope to get into VERT's own communication channels and undermine the copy of CTOS 3.0 they're using to string their surveillance-gathering together. The parties backing VERT in the Bundestag are changing the playbook as quickly as possible to give them more sweeping powers, but there's no doubt whatsoever that VERT are currently breaking dozens of laws, mostly regarding incarceration and use of force. There's probably much juicier stuff on secret record as well. Start digging that type of dirt, and the progressives in the parliament will have a real chance at pushing back and getting VERT struck off. It could turn the tide of the elections."

"I take it that's where I come in?" Will surmised.

"Yep. M-Bahn show potential, or else we wouldn't be extending this helping hand, but they don't have our expertise yet. Specifically yours, Will. Get their tech up and running, give them practical advice. Then, if the situation allows, see if you can help them crack VERT. If not, we gave it a shot. I understand there's only so much either of you can do, and that I'm asking a lot of you."

Wellend the Conciliator, Freya's least favourite version of the DedSec veteran. He tended to become that way only when he had already gotten what he wanted.

"Bagley can help, I'm assuming," Will said.

Afraid not, sweet William, Bagley said. *Germany doesn't agree with my constitution. Too much sausage.*

"Commercial Bagley AIs are banned in Germany, as of last month," Wellend said by way of explanation. "We've been trying to see if our DedSec version functions, but so far it seems like a full lockout, and we've yet to develop a reliable workaround."

"At last, some good news," Freya said.

I'm also set for sunnier climes, Bagley added. *I'll be leaving dear old Blighty behind for a while too.*

"He'll assist you with further planning and preparation over here," Wellend said before the AI could elaborate. "But once you've crossed the Channel, you'll only have each other. That's another reason why I wanted both of you on this one."

"And what am I supposed to be doing while Will mucks about with laptops and Optiks?" Freya asked. "Just beating up anyone who tries to stop him?"

"Something along those lines," Wellend said. "You have local knowledge, even if it's been a while since you were there."

"Yeah, I get it, I'm DedSec London's token German," Freya said, allowing her bitterness to show.

"And you could be the difference between Will getting out of there in one piece, let alone at all," Wellend said. "I told you, you're the best candidate for the job."

"I feel like I'm going to get pretty sick of hearing that soon," Freya said.

"If everything goes to plan, your involvement will be minimal," Wellend said. "Close protection while you scope out the situation in the first few days, but M-Bahn should have security of their own."

"Who are the main players, then?" Freya asked, still not liking what Wellend was saying. It felt to her as though he was edging around an apparent lack of information where M-Bahn were concerned.

"Like DedSec proper, there's no single head honcho," he said, sending Freya and Will a trio of pictures, each of a different individual.

"But these are their main movers and shakers. Revolver, Teuton and Luther."

He highlighted each person in turn as he spoke. Revolver was a man wearing a long, dark leather jacket and a flat cap, sitting on the bank of what looked to Freya like one of Berlin's canals. Teuton was a tall woman with raven hair and a fierce expression. She was dressed up in boxing gear, ringside, slicked with sweat. Luther, a male, was altogether less noteworthy – a bespectacled, balding man in his late forties or early fifties, dressed in a T-shirt and jeans and smiling from a seat in a café. He looked like a university professor on a day off.

"I have more detail on each of them, which I'll transfer to you, but they all check out," Wellend continued. "Revolver and Luther are the brains behind the movement, while Teuton is in charge of security and operations."

"Sounds like my kind of girl," Freya said, looking at Teuton again.

I'd love to see you both fight, Bagley said.

"Bet you would."

"You'll get on, I'm sure," Wellend said. Freya couldn't tell if he was being serious, or deadpan sarcastic.

"What are their specific capabilities, digitally speaking?" Will asked. "Are we going to be supplying any hardware?"

"Again, I'll get the details to you in due course, but in terms of the latter question, yes. I have some gear already earmarked for you to take over. Nothing that will raise suspicions at the airport though. Once you've reviewed the specifics you can request anything else you think is lacking, and I'll see what I can do. I've already called in quite a few favours on this one."

"Speculate to accumulate," Will said. "I take it once we're over there we'll have minimal contact with you?"

"You should be able to set something up once you've met with M-Bahn," Wellend said. "I'll be waiting to hear."

"And just how are we meeting them?" Freya asked.

"That, I'm still working on," Wellend admitted. "It will be finalised over the next few days, along with tickets and new IDs."

"Do you know where their hackerspaces are?"

"No. That's one level of security they're not yet comfortable with sharing. A pickup point will be communicated with me."

"A digital handshake would be good," Will added. "Something secure at both ends."

"Agreed," Wellend said. "Ask Bagley, and he will download what you need. Password for the encrypted files he's holding is 52blacKFox-338. They're time sensitive and copy-locked, so they'll disappear this time next week."

"Why?" Freya asked.

"Security," Wellend replied tersely.

"Looks more like you're eliminating anything that leads back to you," Freya pointed out, wondering if she had hit a nerve.

"We're DedSec, that's how we work," Wellend said. "Any further questions?"

"Is this really the last one?" Freya said, changing tack. "The last job. Because that's the only reason I'm doing it. I hope I've made that clear. After this, I don't want any contact with you, or anyone else with DedSec affiliations." She shot Will a look for good measure.

"I know," Wellend said. "And I understand. It's not what I want, but I respect it."

Freya rather doubted that, but she decided she had pushed him enough.

"That makes this goodbye," she told Wellend.

"It does. Thank you for all that you've done down the years. I know there's a lot of people who appreciate it. That goes for both of you."

"Don't make it weird," Freya said.

"Then I'll just say good luck," Wellend replied. Freya's last view in the meeting was of the M-Bahn logo, before she left the room and cut off her Optik's connection.

8
Hunter's Hall

The Ghost was summoned, just as he had expected.

The place he was to attend was not far from the site of his last killing. Emil Kaiser was a wealthy man, and owned several properties in Berlin, but at the moment he was staying in his villa in Grunewald, a leafy suburbia of mansions and chalets scattered between lakes and the forest on the city's south-western edge.

The villa itself was called Jägerhalle – Hunter's Hall. It was a three-story building with timber walls painted white and a steep, long roof built from red, clay, beaver-tailed tiles. Its construction was not quite vulgar, but neither did it have the statesmanlike grandeur of the proper mansions that flanked it beyond its carefully cultivated grounds. Kaiser, despite his name, was not truly old money, and that much was readily apparent.

The Ghost caught the S7 bus to Grunewald and walked the last fifteen minutes, deliberately taking a route that passed by Bettinastraße. Sadly, the street itself was still cordoned off by the police, which meant he didn't get an up-close view of the ripples his little killing had caused. He enjoyed standing at the taped cordons, feigning the look of a shocked bystander and watching as detectives and forensics did their work. Sometimes he wished he had been a policeman.

He wondered how many of the police were killers in their spare time.

There was no sign of the Vertidiger at the street, only regular law enforcement. That was as he had predicted. Babić was not a man VERT considered valuable. His case would remain unsolved.

He passed by and announced himself at the gateway into the villa. It was not the sort of place the Ghost would have lived, though he was sure it was to Kaiser's taste. Men like him had appearances to keep up.

He trudged up the gravel driveway, lined by oak and ash trees, fighting the urge to light a cigarette as he went. His lungs were getting bad now, and even this short walk left him out of breath. Still, it was too late to stop now. That was something he had come to terms with a long time ago, round about the time he realised he didn't actually kill for money.

The Ghost emerged at the end of the drive. A footman showed him inside. He removed his shoes at the door. One of Kaiser's strange habits. The Ghost had never questioned them. He had plenty of his own.

Inside the villa, Kaiser's interests were readily apparent. The general order of the day was white and minimalist, but this was offset by the decor, which consisted of taxidermied animals, trophies, and all manner of exotic paraphernalia. As the Ghost passed down the entrance hall, his feet padding silently on the cold, white tiles, he cast his eyes along the old spears and bows, the pelts and the sightless, severed heads of antelope, bison, and boars that decorated the walls. There was a more vulgar air here, but it felt affected, as though the owner was consciously presenting himself in a style that others would find distasteful.

Beyond the hall was a square lobby room with a glass ceiling. In the centre was a whole, taxidermied elephant, dominating the space, its head slightly upturned and long, ivory tusks gleaming. Doors led left and right, and a twin staircase arched up on either side, leading towards a landing that overlooked the space, the long-dead elephant facing towards it.

The footman led the Ghost up the left-hand staircase and onto the landing above the elephant. Double doors awaited him, guarded by a meathead in a suit. He knew that any other visitor, even Kaiser's friends and relations, would have already been searched twice, both physically and electronically, by the time they got this far into the villa, but he had not been subjected to anything like that for many years. Kaiser knew that, if the Ghost wanted to kill him, he would. Taking security measures against him was a waste of time.

The doors were swung open. The Ghost stepped into the office beyond, a large room that overlooked the back of the house and its grounds. A triangular window showed a vista of hedges, trees and ornaments, dominated by a small bush labyrinth with a life-sized statue of the Minotaur at its centre, and a stone fountain set before it.

The office space itself mirrored the rest of the villa. A rug made of bear skin, complete with head and paws, lay underfoot, while the skins of tigers and lions adorned the walls alongside their owners' heads. There was a series of old percussion cap hunting rifles, inlaid with silver, and several stands of spears and tribal shields. There were no books.

A desk occupied the far end of the room, heavy mahogany, its varnished surfaced chipped and scratched. Behind it sat Emil

Kaiser, dressed in a white suit. He leaped to his feet as the Ghost entered, smiling warmly.

"Welcome, old friend, welcome," he said, rounding the desk and shaking the Ghost's hand vigorously. He was a short man, battling the onslaught of age in his own way. The tautness of his face, the fullness of his hair, the even whiteness of his teeth all spoke to money spent attempting to hold back the tide. Wealth acquired from a lifetime of murder, extortion, robbery, and drug-dealing had been spent on making Emil look younger. To the Ghost, he looked more like a doll, artificial and stiff in his little white costume.

"I hope my last message did not interrupt you," Kaiser said, gesturing to a chair across the desk from his own. "I take it the stir I'm reading about on the news is your handiwork? The neighbourhood is all aflutter."

The Ghost confirmed nothing but offered a polite smile. Kaiser knew better than to press further – while he had been the Ghost's most constant patron down the decades, there were plenty of others he had worked for. The hit on Babić had had no connection to Kaiser or his empire.

"Shall I have some refreshments brought?" Kaiser asked as he moved back to his own seat before the triangular window. "It's a little cold out there for lemonade now. Coffee perhaps, or hot chocolate?"

The Ghost declined, as he always did. He suppressed his eagerness. He knew Kaiser liked to tease.

"I see by your message that there have been… developments," he said carefully.

"Developments indeed, my friend," Kaiser said, steepling his fingers. Even with his expressions half ruined by plastic, the smugness on his face was apparent as he continued to speak.

"The trail is not as cold as we feared. An interested party has contacted me with new information. They have a location."

"Where?" the Ghost asked. The word was cold and hard, a contrast to Kaiser's excited levity.

"London," Kaiser replied. The Ghost felt a spike of annoyance, bordering on embarrassment.

"So the reports about DeLock were true?" he asked, scarcely believing they had been able to conceal themselves there for so long.

"So it seems. She was the one who brought down Muller. She's set back my plans by years, just like her traitor father. I shall upload the details to your Optik momentarily."

"And who is this 'interested party' you speak of?"

Kaiser smiled, the expression hollow.

"DedSec," he said.

"DedSec? Unlikely allies, surely? They're the ones who have been hiding her."

"Even more than you might think. I have found that gang of do-good hackers quite useful of late."

The Ghost had heard of DedSec. The nebulous hacker organisation, more a disconnected movement it seemed, occupied a grey space in the criminal underworlds of the US and UK. Their angle appeared to be political agitation and the targeting of corporations rather than more traditional acts of criminality. They had been involved in the recent ruckus in London, and there were rumours they were expanding into Europe.

"Who in DedSec found them?" the Ghost, in a moment of weakness, asked.

"You should know better than to ask, my friend. Suffice to say we now know the location, and the multiple false identities, of

Thomas Bauer's surviving family. The man who wreaked such misery on my family shall at last pay with his own."

Despite the Ghost's caution – almost disbelief – he felt a fierce thrill. He had harboured ambitions of being the one to find Thomas's wife and daughter, but Thomas had hidden them well before his foolish, short-lived return to Berlin. The years had slipped by, and the trail, as Kaiser liked to say, had gone cold. It remained a decades-long frustration to the Ghost. They were the only targets he had failed to reach, the only contract he had not yet completed. Kaiser, who had first ordered the hit long ago, had remained similarly invested, for personal reasons.

"Give me their new names and locations, and they will be dead by tomorrow night," he told Kaiser.

"Patience, old friend," Kaiser responded. "I have something more elaborate planned."

The Ghost fought to hide his anger. Kaiser loved his games. Normally he was happy to indulge. It kept matters interesting after all. But this had become too important to him down through the years to entertain foolishness. It was an obsession for them both.

"I hope you are not thinking of employing someone in my stead," he said.

"Oh, such a betrayal would never occur to me, Gespenst!" Kaiser exclaimed. "But I need more from this than three quiet hits. I need a public execution. And it needs to be here, in Berlin."

The Ghost frowned.

"Explain," he said. Few would have dared take such a tone with Kaiser.

"You know as well as anyone that the escape of Thomas Bauer's wife and child has undermined my standing for years," Kaiser said, losing his jovial edge. "Especially given his involvement in what happened to my own wife and daughter. That was before her involvement in destroying my gunrunning operation via DeLock became common knowledge. The hierarchy of the world we inhabit is never static, and certainly never certain. There have been… authority issues lately, here in Berlin. Newer players of the game less deferential towards their betters."

The Ghost had heard as much. Kaiser, while long-established as a crime kingpin, didn't command the same respect he might have done. Many events had undermined his standing, but it had all stemmed from his seeming inability to wipe out the Bauers – or so he believed. If Thomas's offspring really was behind the Muller hit, that only confirmed Kaiser's obsession. There was a general sense among central Europe's mobsters that his star was now clearly waning. The Ghost, of course, did not concern himself with such problems, unless Kaiser gave him a contract. Like all good hitmen, he operated outside the boundaries of the various crime empires, affiliated with Kaiser, yes, but independent.

"Lessons need to be relearned," Kaiser carried on. "And the remnants of the Bauer family will provide the perfect demonstration. The daughter, Freya Bauer. She will be coming to Berlin. I am having her delivered to me. She will be made an example of."

"What about the mother?" the Ghost asked.

"The artifice I am using to lure Freya will not be effective on the mother, but one is enough. This is where you come in. You will go to London, and you will kill her. Freya will serve a purpose once she is here in Berlin. She will be killed in front of my rivals, and they will know that Emil Kaiser always gets what he wants, eventually."

"It will be… less satisfying to kill only one personally," the Ghost said. He hadn't yet admitted quite how his "work" had changed in recent years, how he had embraced the thrill of murder over the supposed priority of monetary gain. The concept of only slaying the mother left him incomplete. The sensation of it would be sullied. For a moment he panicked, as he considered the void left by the fact that he had never been able to wipe that family out might remain forever if he wasn't directly responsible for all their deaths.

"You will find more than just the mother in London," Kaiser said. "Freya has a son now. Andrew Bauer. He is nineteen, a student."

That changed things. The Ghost had considered the possibility of offspring down the years. The job would not be complete until they were all annihilated. A vengeance over two decades in the making.

"The son must perish as well," Kaiser said, voice cold and hard now. "What that family did to mine, it can only be fully expunged when the name Bauer is no more."

The Ghost thought about it for a while. Three generations. It was a tantalising prospect. There were few things he had craved more down the years than finding and finishing Thomas Bauer's legacy. He had never once thought it would prove as difficult as it had been, but finally, the hunt was drawing to a close.

"Will you do it, old friend?" Kaiser asked him. The Ghost nodded, slipping a cigarette from his pocket.

"I'm going to fulfil a promise I made to a dying man," he said.

9
Assurances

Freya told her mother she was going back to Berlin in person.

Belinda sat for a while at the kitchen table, silent, expressionless.

"I'll be careful," Freya said in a self-conscious effort to fill the void, the words feeling weak.

"You will find the man who killed your father," Belinda replied, her voice hard.

Freya had been thinking the same thing. In the years since the murder, she had wondered just who had been responsible, but whenever she had considered trying to delve into that dark, deadly underworld her father had inhabited, events conspired against her. Now they were doing the very opposite – sending her back to the city where he had been killed. Still, a part of her tried to rationalise her decision by focusing on the job she had been given. Ignore the wolves prowling around her.

"No, it's nothing to do with that," Freya began to say, but Belinda carried on over her.

"You will find the man who killed your father, and the one who paid him to do it. This is the reckoning. It has been long in coming."

"There will be no reckoning," Freya said, trying not to lose her cool with her mother. "It's just a job, like any other. DedSec business."

"Your father said it was just a job," Belinda said, tears in her eyes now. "And he also said he would be careful, and he never came back to us."

Freya felt a sudden tightness in her own chest. She moved round the table and embraced her mother tightly.

"I do not want to lose you both," Belinda said, voice muffled. "But it has to happen. His vengeance has waited too long."

Freya held her a moment longer before stepping back, holding Belinda at arm's length. She had heard all this before. The idea of finding Thomas's killer haunted Freya's mother – truth be told, she thought about it regularly as well. Sometimes she would slip into the memories of him leaving, and the news that had reached them second-hand, via the newspapers, of his death. Months of sorrow and uncertainty had followed, months that had left scars. It was only when she had grown up that Freya had come to appreciate how hard Belinda had worked to keep herself and her only child safe. Revenge, however, had always seemed out of reach.

"It's not vengeance," Freya said firmly. "It's a job, and it's not related to anything in the past. We still don't even know for sure who ordered the killing, let alone carried it out."

"You cannot go back to that city and not seek recompense for what is taken from us," Belinda said, turning fierce.

"Berlin didn't kill Dad," Freya responded. "Right now, 'that city' needs our help. You've said it yourself. You follow the news. It's all going to shit over there. The Defenders taking control. The government amending federal laws. A DedSec in Berlin can push back against that. I'm going over there to help them."

"Alone?"

"No. But you know I can't say who else is involved."

That was a lie, but it was difficult enough telling her mother she was going back to Germany, let alone that it would be with her good-for-nothing ex. That would make her really fly off the deep end. She'd probably buy tickets to come too.

"Do not trust them," Belinda said. Freya laughed.

"Don't worry, there's not much chance of that."

Belinda took her hand and squeezed. "I mean it! Trust nobody! I believe your father did, and it was the death of him."

"I'll be careful," Freya reiterated. "And it's going to be my last job as well."

To her surprise, Belinda scoffed. "I doubt that, my dear. The kind of work you do never really ends."

The statement was chilling in a way, and matched up well with Freya's own fears, but she brushed it aside.

"This is as good an opportunity as any. I've had enough of the cause. Almost, anyway."

"We shall see. How long will you be gone for?"

"Perhaps a month. That should be long enough to get them properly up and running."

"There will be a reckoning," Belinda said, looking Freya in the eyes. "I just pray that at the end of it, I still have a daughter."

Freya had feared the meeting would go like this, laden with the weight of the past. Belinda had enemies of her own, tied to the work Thomas had done. Her mother understood what it meant to triple-lock the door every night and keep a rucksack with supplies handy at all times. That had been true even before Thomas's death had left her looking out for herself and Freya. There was always the fear the past would finally catch up. That, besides the proposed visit to Berlin, was what Freya put her mother's moroseness down to. She was always watching her back, but now doubly so.

"Be careful of Emil Kaiser," Belinda added. "He's still alive, and that means he'll still be hunting us. He'll know when you're in Germany."

"We don't know Kaiser was behind the hit on Dad," Freya said, trying to brush aside her mother's relentless concern. She was aware that Thomas had been working for Kaiser at the end, but despite some attempts in her teenage years to find more evidence, the identity of who had ordered her father's death remained conjecture. Freya didn't want to be dragged into that pit now. She knew from bitter experience that it was bottomless.

They talked for a while longer, before Freya said goodbye. They hugged, and Belinda reminded her how proud she made her, and how proud she would have made her father. Freya choked back a rush of emotions. Now was not the time.

"Do you still have the picture?" Belinda asked on the doorstep. For a moment Freya was nonplussed. Then she realised what she meant.

She fished out her wallet and showed her the corner of her childhood photograph.

"I think you were right after all," she told her mother. "I think it's good I keep it. Maybe it'll bring me luck over there, or something."

"You and I both know there's no such thing, Freya Bauer," Belinda said with a sad smile. "Keep your wits about you. When it starts, you'll need to be ready."

Freya waited until her mother had closed and locked the door. Then, instead of heading downstairs, she crossed the landing to the front door of the flat opposite. After knocking softly, it opened.

Helen Dashwood smiled warmly and gave her a hug. Freya wondered at how frail the woman felt.

"Well, isn't this a lovely surprise," Helen said. "Brought me some replacement sauerbraten I hope?"

"Sadly not this time, Miss Dashwood," Freya replied, feeling a pang of guilt.

"Well, I'll expect some strudel next time," Helen said, waving her inside. "Come for a cuppa have you? I'll stick the kettle on."

The flat's interior was the image of a retired British pensioner's home. The carpet was dark brown, the wallpaper a yellowing shade of sepia, and cushions, rugs, and doilies proliferated. There were photos up on the wall of Helen with her children and grandchildren, as well as snaps with uniformed colleagues in days gone by, back when she had worked as a police engineer. The curtains were half-drawn, and a golden light suffused the room as the setting sun slipped between them like liquid.

There were also cats, at least two in sight, and the strong scent hinted at many more.

Freya knew that was all an illusion. Helen Dashwood was as hardcore as they came, a fact that anyone who made it through the multiple locks on the door at the back of the living room would quickly realise.

Freya had been through on a couple of occasions, and discovered a hideout of bare metal and processors and thick bundles of cables, a lair filled with computers, Optiks, and half-disassembled drones. It was a tinkerer's paradise on par with any DedSec hackerspace. From there, Helen indulged the secret favourite pastime of many a retiree – sticking it to the man. With a degree in BioRobotics and former employment with the law, there were few members of DedSec who could say they had achieved as much down the years as Helen. Her current project, from what she had mentioned to Freya, was developing software that caused a drone's facial recognition programs not only to fail to identify a person by their appearance, but to trick them into thinking it was someone else. The doddering pensioner viz crazy cat lady was all an act.

"Visiting your mum?" Helen asked as she walked through to the kitchen.

"Just saying goodbye," Freya answered, settling herself down on the couch next to a sleepy-looking ginger tom.

"That serious?" Helen called back over the rising rush of the kettle.

"Just a temporary parting," Freya replied. The tom nuzzled against her leg, and she scratched between his ears, eliciting an appreciative purr.

"One sugar or two?"

"One please."

The kettle clicked off, and there was the rattle of a teaspoon in one mug, then another. Helen reappeared moments later, carrying them both, steam wafting lazily from the pair of brews.

"Big job, is it?" she asked, setting one mug down on a doily on the coffee table in front of the couch. "Not had one of those in a while!"

"Count yourself lucky," Freya said, thanking her for the tea. Helen settled herself into a well-worn armchair opposite with a grunt and a crack of old bones.

"You wanting out?" she asked.

"Thinking about it."

"Nothing wrong with that," Helen said, looking at Freya thoughtfully while blowing on the top of her mug. "Otherwise, you'd end up like me. Celebrating your eightieth birthday dodging the coppers down Lambeth Walk."

Freya laughed despite herself. She had been hearing Helen's stories for years and, unlike most old folks, she was fairly sure there had never been a single repeat. Even since retirement, her experiences with DedSec had been wild.

"How's things with you then?" Freya asked, taking a sip from her mug. "Is Jasper still fighting the good fight?"

"Old bugger takes after me, doesn't know when to quit." Helen grinned. Jasper was one of her cats, a battered old Persian who could have given Mister Scruff a run for his money in a scrap. Last Freya had heard he was at the vet's.

"Everything all right with the flat?"

"Can't complain, not when everyone else's rent is going up and mine isn't. Funny that."

"Wish I could call in favours like that," Freya said, shifting to better accommodate the tomcat as he clambered fully into her lap. "In fact, that's mostly why I'm here."

"I'm all ears," Helen said, her gaze discerning behind the thick lenses of her glasses. "You know my door's always open to you, and your family."

"That's what I was going to ask about, actually," Freya said. "You were right when you said I've been given a job, a big one. It's back in Berlin."

Helen whistled through her false teeth.

"That big, eh? Who's put you up to something like that? Reckon I can guess…"

"Yeah," Freya shrugged. "Wellend. And guess what. I'm supposed to be partnering with Will on it."

"He's bold, is our Wellend," Helen said. "I always liked young William though. It's a shame you two didn't work out. I see him sometimes. Not out and about, of course, but online. Still seems to be up to his own tricks, but ain't we all?"

"Unfortunately," Freya said, trying not to sound too disgruntled.

"So have you accepted it yet? This job?"

"Pretty much."

"And what does it entail?"

Freya knew Wellend had expressly forbidden sharing such information, but she wasn't one of his errand-runners. She needed backup on this one, and there was no one better placed to provide it than Helen Dashwood.

"There's a branch of activists setting up in Berlin that Wellend fancies could be the first proper DedSec branch on the continent," Freya said. "Calling themselves M-Bahn."

"Funny name, that."

"It's after the city's subway. I'm guessing they're based somewhere near it. As a group they've got legs, but they need more help if they're going to become a proper force, something that can help hold back the rising tide over there."

"I've heard the news, looks nasty," Helen said, nodding. "Lot of crackdowns on protests and dissent, both cyber and in-person. There's been loads of chatter online about, what's this group called, the Defenders?"

"Yes, der Vertidiger," Freya said.

"Sounds like Albion with umlauts."

"The name doesn't have umlauts. Wellend's right insomuch as they have to be stopped. But who knows if this new group are the ones to do it."

"I've not heard of them," Helen admitted. "There's a few other groups operating over there already, Bulwark, Reboot, and the like, but they're small. A few prominent members get banged up by any of these new laws, and they're pretty much finished."

"Hopefully they can start working together," Freya said. "I

guess that's what we're expected to help with. I'm just the muscle though. Will's heading it."

"Sounds like you've not really been told what you're getting into," Helen mused. "I can dig around, try to paint a bigger picture for you. When do you head off?"

"Not sure, probably less than a week. I was going to ask if you could do something more though."

"Don't you worry, dearie," Helen said, smiling. "I'll look after Mister Scruff. And I'll keep an eye out for your finger and thumb."

Finger and thumb was Cockney rhyming slang for "mum". Freya smiled, relieved.

"She's… conflicted about me going. Understandably. It could be a while before I'm back, probably a month. I'm not sure how much I'll be able to get in touch, certainly not over a standard Optik, but I can probably reach you more easily via Will."

"Of course," Helen said. "I'll see her right until you're back."

"And if I haven't asked enough already… could you check in on Andrew too? Just once or twice. He's just gone into his second year at Bristol. I think he's still finding his feet."

"I'll have him round for a cuppa if need be," Helen said. "He'll be all right though. Young men like that adjust quickly, especially when they get used to the student lifestyle."

"Thanks, Miss Dashwood," Freya said, heartfelt. Helen had always been there for her. She was as dependable as an old English oak, and as tough as one too. Freya didn't like to imagine where she would be without her guidance.

She was about to make her goodbyes at the door when Helen checked her.

"You sure about this?" she asked, taking Freya somewhat by surprise. "Sure about going over there? I imagine that's going to be difficult for you."

"It is," Freya admitted. "But maybe it's what I need. What Mum needs too. It's been hanging over us our whole lives. It's why I'm the person I am today."

"I've got a hunch that it's going to be more dangerous than Wellend is letting on."

"Well, it usually is."

"You look out for yourself then. And Will. Don't be too hard on him!"

"No promises there," Freya said.

Back at her apartment, Freya VR'd Andrew to tell him she was going away. He seemed at once crestfallen and confused.

"This has something to do with your other work, doesn't it?" he demanded. Freya had shielded him from her other life down the years, but there was only so much she could hide. She was thankful she had been able to convince him it wasn't something he wanted to become involved in.

"I thought you said you'd finished with the shady stuff?" he pressed.

"I'm just going to visit my aunt," Freya replied. "She's very sick."

"Pull the other one, Mum," Andrew said with a hint of anger. "Can you at least say where you'll be going?"

"Berlin."

"You're going back to Germany? Seriously?"

"I've given it a lot of thought," Freya said, wondering why she felt so guilty, and acted so defensively, towards her own son. "It's the right thing to do."

Even to her, that reasoning sounded terrible. She couldn't properly articulate the choice she'd made, only that she had.

"Does Grandma know? Was it her idea?"

"She knows, and no it wasn't. I hoped you could stay in touch with her while I'm gone. I know you've got your studies, but maybe give her a call, or even come through if you've got a spare weekend."

"You're going to be gone that long?"

"About a month. Communication will be difficult, which is why I'm asking you to step up."

Andrew looked less than thrilled, but he nodded.

"Doesn't really go with the territory here at uni, having a gangster for a mum," he said bitterly.

"They're good people I'm trying to help," Freya said, giving up on the weak aunt story. "Someone has to."

Andrew didn't look convinced.

"It's going to be dangerous," he said, a statement rather than a question. "Germany is on the news apps almost every day. Who are you going with?"

"I won't be on my own," Freya said. "What is it you always tell me? Don't worry?"

That drew a wry smile, at least.

"I'll bring you something back from Berlin," Freya told him.

"Just bring yourself back in one piece, Mum."

"I will. Promise. I love you so much. Stick in with your studies!"

"I like that the advice about my studies is what you're finishing this on."

"What can I say, I'm all about practical parenting. I love you! Is that better?"

"I love you too, Mum."

Freya hung up and swore. She hadn't told him about Will. Why? She had bottled it, choked. A moment of cowardice. In truth, she hadn't known what to say.

It was best to put all that as far back in her mind as possible from hereon in. She had a job to do.

She checked her emails. One had been forwarded from Wellend. An airline ticket, Stansted to Berlin, leaving in five days. The return was open-ended.

10
Questions

Helen stopped typing and flexed her hands. The weather was getting progressively colder, and it showed up as a dull ache in her fingers. Frustratingly, working at a keyboard was no longer as easy as it had once been.

She wouldn't let that stop her though. Freya Bauer's decision to reach out to her had been fortuitous. Since the chaos of Zero Day had subsided, Helen Dashwood had experienced an unaccustomed lull in activities. She was almost beginning to worry that some of DedSec's bigger players were starting to deliberately leave her out of the game. It actually felt like she was retired.

A part of her wondered if it was time to let go. She had already accepted that she couldn't defeat the march of time. The stiffness, the pains, the forgetfulness – many had fought it before, but none had won in the end.

Every time those thoughts surfaced, she dismissed them. Death was inevitable, decline less so. The fire within her still burned bright, sometimes brighter than ever. Technology still fascinated her. Justice and freedom remained dear to her. She was still determined to do her part, to build a better future for the young ones.

If the Queen had worked up until the day she had died, then so would Helen Dashwood.

She went and brewed a mug of tea and returned to the room hidden at the back of her flat's lounge. This was her own private hackerspace, a concealed haven rammed with laptops, a PC, a hub, Optiks, tablets, and more. Right now it lay in near-complete darkness, the only illumination coming from the one laptop she had up and running.

She settled back in, sipped the tea, and waited. She had hoped to ask Bagley for intel about the planned operation, but he was off-grid – inter-DedSec chatter claimed he was now on the other side of the world, tying up loose ends after the rogue AI incident earlier in the year. She had reached out to an old contact instead, one scheduled to come online soon. Then, she would see what they were really up against.

There had been something amiss about what Freya had told her. She was a good sort, and Helen had watched her grow from a scraggly, scrappy kid to a hard-working, hard-hitting young woman, and then a mother, wrapped up in the trials and tribulations that came with raising a child alone.

Helen had more than a passing maternalistic streak towards Freya, and she had been glad when Freya had come to her seeking her help. She hadn't felt needed for a while now. She had already come up with contingency plans for keeping an eye on Belinda Bauer, and getting her to safety if need be, but watching out for Andrew would be trickier. She would work something out though; she always did.

Still, there was the looming sense that something wasn't quite right. Freya had seemed furtive when describing the reason for her return to Berlin. A job, concocted by Wellend, apparently unconnected to Freya's past life, yet requiring her involvement. Helen had done a lot of DedSec ops of her own, had been an activist almost all her life, and something just didn't sit right about this one. Even if Freya had been keeping the details from her, there were too many coincidences.

So, just as she had promised, she began to dig. Who were M-Bahn? On the surface, it was difficult to say, though that wasn't a surprise. Even with the notoriety DedSec and similar, lesser hacker groups had gained in recent years, it wasn't as though they plastered their membership or activities regularly across any old search engine. Helen knew the best places to look, though, as well as the best people to ask.

It hadn't been long before alarm bells had started to ring. A deep web forum about progressive activist work across Europe had included a thread about efforts in Germany, which had visibly devolved into a raging argument between various posters about whether M-Bahn were a legitimate group, or whether other longer-running efforts like Reboot were more genuine. Helen had been noticing more and more chatter about that group in particular. They seemed young and inexperienced, but increasingly active. An admin had locked the thread.

There were also a few articles from the German press, passing mentions to minor hacker crimes committed against banks and one media hub, and a single longer thinkpiece that named M-Bahn as the latest in a rising wave of what it derided as "spoiled youths" who were supposedly spitting in the faces of their elders by defying the state. There had been no further elaboration about where M-Bahn had come from, though, and what specifically they were up to.

Helen's laptop pinged. Her contact was online and typing.

Good evening.

Helen greeted them in turn, and used the twinned pair of safewords to show she wasn't under duress, with the contact replying in kind.

You said you could tell me more about M-Bahn, Helen wrote.

Perhaps.

That wasn't especially encouraging. Helen took a sip of her tea, then wrote back.

What's the situation with M-Bahn and the other groups in Germany?

Not good, came the reply. *Nobody knows much about them. They've come out of nowhere in the last year or so.*

That suggested one thing to Helen. She typed and sent her reply.

Do you think they have a powerful backer somewhere? Someone wealthy and connected?

It seems like it, the contact sent back. *But I don't know who. There are theories.*

Theories are always good, Helen said, trying to encourage the contact. They seemed furtive, another damning indictment of M-Bahn's legitimacy.

It took a while for the reply to come back.

Some say they were set up by one of the far-right parties in the Bundestag, or even VERT, to try to agitate for the new laws. A false flag, to give legitimacy to the authoritarian movement. Others think they're just a criminal front masquerading as activists.

Have you heard about links between them and DedSec London, Helen typed.

No.

Are M-Bahn working to establish a DedSec presence in Germany?

No.

Helen considered her next question, but she didn't get time to ask it. The contact had disconnected.

"Oh Freya, what have you gotten yourself into?" Helen murmured. This was the sort of thing she had feared. Those who worked under the name DedSec did so to help the oppressed and fight back against tyranny, but it was all too easy for individuals or groups with less noble purposes to adopt the mask of DedSec to meet their own goals. If that was what M-Bahn were doing in Germany it was the last place Freya should be going to.

She finished her tea, got up stiffly, and carried her empty mug from the secret room through to the kitchen. All the while, her thoughts were turning over.

It felt as though her suspicions were correct, but in terms of understanding exactly what was going on, she seemed no closer. Right now what she knew was of no help to Freya or her family. She needed to go deeper. Or, alternatively, she needed to open a different line of questioning.

Wellend. Helen had never much liked him. He had always struck her as too hard-bitten. Becoming jaded by the struggle wasn't uncommon, but as far as she could remember he had always had a ruthless streak. He reminded her of some of the detectives she had dealt with down the years, both during her time with the police, and since her shift to less strictly legal practices. He tended to be uncompromising, almost radical in pursuit of the cause. That made him dangerous, but she knew other DedSec members respected his willingness to do what needed to be done. Zero Day and the events that had followed immediately afterwards showed how much of a life-and-death struggle they were all caught up in.

Was Wellend hanging Freya out to dry? What would he have

to gain from that though? He had to know more about M-Bahn. He had to know what he was sending Freya into.

She needed to get close to him, but their paths rarely crossed. Thankfully there were a few others she trusted to help who were better placed with Wellend than she was, and one in particular that she had in mind.

She was an unlikely friend, perhaps, but they had worked together well in the past. A reunion was overdue.

After filling the cats' bowls, Helen blink-triggered her Optik and made a call.

Will apologised for the third or fourth time that day.

"I told them to stop springing things on me last minute, but this job is a big one," he added, yet again. Sam just shrugged, a sure sign she was furious, but doing her best to contain it.

"I don't understand why you can't say how long you'll be gone for," she said.

"It'll be about a month."

"That's a really long time, Will!"

"I know! I'm sorry!"

This was what he had feared. After months spent trying to ease off on his DedSec duties, it was now difficult to justify being gone a month for "work". And to be fair, Will didn't blame Samantha. He'd be pissed off as well.

"If I do this then I'm first in line for promotion," he lied. "You know the firm are being hit by a lot of redundancies now. It's a tightrope."

"I don't believe you," Sam told him bluntly.

Will tried to muster further excuses, but Sam kept talking.

"I also don't really care. You told me you were going to put all this behind you – whatever it is you really do when you're not actually in the office – but here you go again. Thinking you can swan off and leave me with less than a few days' notice."

"Sam–" Will began to say, but she had him bang to rights. Her face flushed with anger, she turned away, her voice now low and hard.

"You go. Go right ahead. I may not still be here when you get back though. And if I am still here, you're going to explain it to me. All of it. Or it really will be the last time you see me."

Will had to hand it to her, she knew how to deliver an ultimatum. Stung, he simply nodded.

"I will sort this out," he said after a few moments of bitter silence. "You deserve better. I'm sorry."

"Stop saying you're sorry," Sam snarled, turning back to him. "Just promise. Promise you'll tell me the truth from now on."

Will sighed. He wasn't always very good at telling the truth. Still though, he had to try. For Sam. For their future together.

"I promise," he said. "This is the end of it all. And when I get back, I'll tell you all about it."

There was a knock at Helen Dashwood's door.

The elderly Londoner set down the sock she had been darning and got slowly to her feet. Then, she made her way over to the door, and opened it.

"Hello, dearie," she said.

"Hello, nan." The woman on the other side grinned.

She was in her late teens or early twenties, with round glasses, dyed red hair, and a headband with stylised cat ear accessories. Incongruously, she wore what looked like a school uniform – green tartan skirt, white shirt, and a dark green and maroon tie – beneath a studded black leather jacket and a satchel replete with peace and rainbow badges.

Her name was Harriet Parks, one of the few people still alive that Helen had any respect for. Despite her tender years, she was a ferociously good operator, both online and in a physical sense. They had both been intimately involved in the Day Zero fallout, and had done several jobs since.

"Come in, come in," Helen said, waving her inside. "You get here all right?"

"Took the Tube, regretted it," Harriet said, popping bubble gum in between the two statements. "Where's the good stuff?" she added, gazing around the flat.

"Try the kitchen," Helen said with a slight smirk. Harriet let out a squeal.

"Perfect," she said, fishing her Optik's hands-on component out of her leather jacket's pocket as Helen joined her.

Helen's collection of cats clustered round a trio of bowls, enjoying their lunch. Harriet squatted down nearby and snapped a flurry of photos, then what looked to Helen like a video that only lasted a few seconds, to which she expertly began adding colourful, cartoony text and cat emojis.

"Cat videos are still all the rage online," Harriet explained, taking more photos. "An evergreen form of content, aren't they, cutie?"

The question was directed at one feline, Roger, who broke from the feeding pack and wandered over in curiosity, nuzzling against Harriet's leg.

"Roger's always fancied himself a bit of a celebrity," Helen said, as the cat purred. Harriet scooped the cat up and took a selfie with it. "Don't worry. It isn't location-tagged."

"I loved the last cat compilation video you posted," Helen said.

Harriet shot her a grin. "Of *course* you follow me. I'm going to work out which account is yours."

"You'll need luck for that, young lady. Cuppa?"

"Yes please! Mind if I go straight through?"

"Go right ahead, dearie."

Helen had first met Harriet during the chaotic events surrounding Zero Day, a couple of years before. She had immediately identified with the young woman's spirit – or vibed with her, as Harriet liked to say. When it came to interacting with technology, she had that youthful, cutting edge, the kind that Helen needed if she wasn't to fall behind.

For her own part, Harriet seemed fascinated with Helen. She had never taken her at face value, assuming that she was a doddery old woman out of touch with the world, left behind by the rapid technological shifts of recent years. She was too smart to fall for that ruse. She loved hearing Helen's stories, of years spent undermining unjust authority.

They had done a number of jobs together and had found themselves to be an effective team. Nobody suspected a highschooler coming in to report a mugging with her granny, or a uni student helping an old lady with her shopping. Phone tapping, bugged premises, identity theft – in the wake of Zero Day they'd struck a series of blows against the paramilitary law enforcement group Albion in particular, helping speed along its demise. When Helen needed help, Harriet was the first she called on.

Harriet deposited Roger back by his bowl and walked to the bookshelf by the window, slid a copy of the third edition of the 2011 *Digital Evidence and Computer Crime* off the shelf, and opened it. The middle pages had a small space hollowed out, big enough to hold the key within. She removed it, returned the book, and walked over to the door in the back of the living room.

Beyond it lay London's smallest hackerspace. The laptop

Helen had primarily been using to investigate M-Bahn was still running. Harriet pulled over one of the room's two wheeled chairs and slid her own laptop from her satchel. She cleared a space for it on the tech-cluttered desk and plugged it in before booting it up.

"So it all went according to plan?" Helen asked as she came in with two steaming mugs, carefully setting them down beside the laptops before closing the door to the little cubbyhole. Harriet removed her bubble gum and stuck it next to her laptop's trackpad.

"I think so," Harriet responded, thanking Helen for the tea before sitting down with her. "But there's only one way to find out. I was going to transfer this via Bagley, but he's unreachable. In India, apparently, tracking down possible other AI activity. I've downloaded it to my Optik instead."

Helen activated her own HUD, monitoring the transference of data directly onto the laptop. The day before, Harriet had visited Wellend, and stayed overnight at the North London Tube hackerspace under the pretext that the police had been sniffing around her flat. She and Wellend weren't on particularly good terms – she didn't tend to take on any of the jobs he put up – but she had managed to spend long enough in his office to swap out his charge pack for an identical one. Identical, but for the fact that it contained a cloning scanner and a transmitter that would copy the software and data of any device Wellend plugged into it. Harriet had picked it up on her Optik while she'd still been at the hackerspace and had transferred it to the USB.

"So, what have we got?" Helen said as Harriet pulled over the room's other wheeled chair and settled in beside her. The light of the screens underlit their features – old and young, side-by-side – as Helen entered the passcode and opened the cloned package.

"Let's see," she said, locating and opening the necessary folder. Harriet grinned. It was full.

"Bingo," she murmured.

"Don't like bingo, too many old people," Helen said. "This looks good. Very good. Well done, young lady."

It was unlike Wellend to make a mistake, but it was easily done in a place he had thought secure. In Helen's experience, no one was immune to being caught out. From phishing scams to high-level bank fraud, everyone had the potential to make a mistake eventually. You just had to help them into making it.

Of course, spying on fellow DedSec felt wrong – it was for reasons like these that so much of the movement maintained their anonymity even from each other – but if Helen's hunch was right, then Wellend had forfeited the right to call himself DedSec. When someone went rogue, they had to be called out, or the damage they could do might prove worse than the efforts of the authorities or rival hackers.

Besides, if he planned on hurting her friends, he'd deserve everything that was coming to him.

She began opening files. It looked like the cloner had worked. Whatever Wellend had recently charged, the device had copied its contents and successfully decrypted over half of it.

"This is going to take a while to sift through," Harriet said, adjusting her glasses. "I'll transfer it to you so we can work on it together."

"We might need more tea," Helen said thoughtfully.

"Coffee for me," Harriet said. "It's going to be a long night."

PART TWO

RATS

11
Homecoming

Darkness was beginning to fall when Freya returned to the place of her birth. She watched Berlin's lights gleaming like a mirrored constellation below her as they descended towards Brandenburg Airport, laid out in the lengthening shadows. The sight filled her with equal parts fear and anticipation. She had spent a long time thinking this place was home, and then hating it. It had murdered her father and driven her and the rest of her family out. She remembered her mother's words.

No point in getting wound up, she told herself. Worrying wouldn't help either. She was committed now. Short of hijacking the plane, she would be landing in Germany. She had to focus. She had a job to do, nothing more and nothing less. She tried to tell herself that was the reason she was here. Not revenge. She didn't know who had killed her father. Regardless of her mother's instincts, there was no approaching reckoning.

The disembarkation process seemed interminably slow. She hadn't flown for a while, and remembered now that she had always disliked it. There was no control, something she prized.

Will eyed her as he got out of his seat further along the cabin.

They hadn't selected seats next to each other – as far as the cover was concerned, they were work colleagues, not partners. Which, thankfully, was entirely the truth.

There was a pause at the baggage carousel in the terminal as Will waited for his suitcase to be unloaded. Freya preferred to travel light with only a backpack. She could buy whatever she required. Will, however, preferred home comforts, and had needed the space for various unassuming electronics he would doubtless put to use after they made contact with M-Bahn.

"Good flight?" he asked as they waited.

"I was on the same one as you, you tell me," Freya said absently, her attention on the crowd around the baggage-laden carousel. She was instinctively scanning them for threats. The truth was she had been wound tight ever since boarding. After months, she was back in the thick of it. From now on vigilance and care were everything. She had no time for idle chatter, not out in public.

Will said nothing more, hauling his suitcase off the runners when it juddered slowly round.

There was no trouble at border control. That was as Freya expected. DedSec-supplied identifications weren't mere back-alley forgeries. It helped that the scanning systems were fully automated nowadays. There were multiple layers of plausibility built into the Optik ID's biometrics. Freya had only had to memorise a few key basic lies about her supposed identity on the off-chance that there would be a spot check by the German customs service, the Bundeszollverwaltung, but it seemed they were having a night off.

The airport itself held no memories for her, its layout unrecognisable after thirty-three years. The last time she had been here had been in the dead of night. Her father had roused her from her bed and told her that they were leaving immediately. A surprise holiday. Such a surprise, apparently, that she could only spend a few minutes packing. It seemed her mother hadn't liked surprises, as she had spotted her crying through the door into her parents' bedroom.

That holiday had turned out to be a long one indeed.

They exited the terminal building, a chilly, unwelcoming autumn wind slicing at them and causing Freya to pop her yellow jacket's collar. Her heart raced. This was where it started to get dicey, out in the open and beyond the boundaries of the airport's security.

She checked the corners and angles without making it obvious, a subtle half-pace back and to Will's left. For his own part, he was likely more concerned with making contact than worrying about potential assassins. His suitcase rattled where its wheels passed over the flagstones at the terminal's taxi rank. It made Freya uncomfortable.

Will had the hands-on device of his Optik out, and Freya could tell from the glazed look in his eyes that he was reviewing data. He prowled along the length of the taxi rank, Freya forcing her attention to lock on to their surroundings. The queue was busy with the recently arrived flight, harried-looking families or businessmen and women exuding exhaustion and annoyance as they looked for transport into the city centre.

A few of the taxis had their reserved lights on. Will stopped beside one. Freya noticed his Optik's hands-on device had pinged.

The driver slid his window down. He was a big man, jowly, but relatively young.

"Mister Carter?" he asked.

"That's me," Will lied, using his fake ID. He spoke English too, just for effect, rather than switching to German. "Can you take us to the nearest subway station?"

"My pleasure," the driver said. "Let me help you with your bags."

He popped the door and the trunk, moving with Will round to the rear of the car. Once there, he scanned over Will's physical Optik device with one of his own, presumably running a digital handshake. Freya sized him up briefly. Not a threat, at least not one she couldn't handle. From Will's body language, it seemed like they'd successfully made contact.

She watched the street over the top of the cab's roof, shooting occasional glances along the road at passing traffic and up and down the rank. A lot of movement, but nothing out of the ordinary. The suitcase stowed, Will got in the back. Freya waited until he was inside before doing likewise, trying not to make it too obvious that she was watching out for them both.

The taxi driver began to pull away. Will frowned and held up his Optik device.

"Scramblers?" he demanded, sounding slightly angry. Freya blink-checked her own heads-up display, and found it inactive, frozen.

"In the taxi sign on the roof," the driver confirmed, indicating there was tech up there that was playing merry hell with Will's device. Freya checked her own and found it similarly inoperable.

"Necessary, I'm afraid, to shield us from observation," the driver went on.

"And to stop us from contacting anyone," Will pointed out. "What's your name?"

"Termite," the man said. "And I take it you're Key and Feline?"

Those were their underground names. It felt strange to Freya to hear her own again. She'd been starting to hope she had left it behind.

"We are," Will confirmed. "I assume M-Bahn are ready for us?"

Termite didn't reply. Instead, he took a sharp left down a side street and began to speed up.

"What're you doing?" Freya snapped, immediately on alert.

"Trouble," Termite said curtly, looking in his wing mirrors. They had been customised to include an upper angle that gave a view of the air lane used by drones passing above the street. "We might have a tail."

"We've just left the terminal, and I didn't notice anyone there follow us," Freya said. She had checked as they had pulled away.

"It's a drone," Termite said, taking another hard turn that pitched his passengers hard against their seatbelts.

Freya tried to get a view out of the rear window, but she couldn't see much of the air traffic. A car behind them hit the horn.

"You're going to attract more attention driving like this," she told Termite, speaking German. "If a drone has locked us, we need to get under cover."

"That's where I'm going," Termite said.

The supposed taxi driver ran a red light, then turned off into a multi-storey car park. They rolled down a ramp, heading down the way, until they came to a floor that was almost completely deserted. Despite the plethora of free spaces, the taxi pulled in next to one of the only other vehicles present, a Skoda Kamiq.

"Out," Termite said. They exited. Freya was on edge, not liking this one bit. It stank of a setup.

A man exited the Skoda, wearing a bulky respirator mask that had been crudely spraypainted red. From a glance, Freya established that he was unarmed. That didn't make her feel much better.

"This is Tex. He'll take you the rest of the way," Termite said.

"Evening, boys and girls," Tex said, voice coming out as a rasp. "I'm going to recommend you both mask up, then get in the back and keep your heads down. It's busy out there tonight."

Will looked at Freya. She could sense his unspoken question. Termite had provided the correct digital script for M-Bahn, but now they were into the unknown, entirely in the hands of others.

Freya nodded. It was always likely that this would happen. They would have to take their chances, roll with the punches if need be. Improvisation was one of the things that made her an able bodyguard.

She pulled her mask from her backpack. Everyone in DedSec owned one, each one personalised. They were standard equipment for anyone looking to avoid having their face logged on 300+ cameras a day. Freya's was made from moulded plastic, shaped like a cat's face, with a triangle painted over one eye. It was a tribute to Mister Scruff. Will's was an old paintball visor, still spattered with red, blue, green and yellow hits. It was strange seeing him in it again. It had been years since they had been on a DedSec op together.

Will hefted his suitcase into the rear of the Skoda, and they both clambered into the back seats, Freya noting the number plate as they did so. It was a lenticular, changing numbers depending on the angle it was viewed at, a trick that would help throw off any artificial systems watching them.

Tex climbed in the front and started the engine.

"Welcome back to Berlin," he said in English, though his accent was definitely local. "Now get your heads down, please."

"We're masked," Freya pointed out. "And I'd rather see where we're going."

"Suit yourselves," Tex shrugged. "But things might get bumpy if we're tailed."

"Understood."

They pulled out of the car park. At some point, Termite had already vanished.

Whatever had been following them before appeared to have either given up, or failed to ID their new mode of transport. They passed through Adlershop and onto the 96a, the lights of the city rolling over them. Freya did her best not to let her mind wander, not to consider how her past was catching up with her present. She had to remain sharp.

The route they were taking didn't fill her with confidence. She had been trying to work out the most likely location of M-Bahn since Wellend had first brought them up. Presumably the setup was similar to the hackerspace in north London, but Berlin's subway system was far less convoluted, with fewer forgotten or disused lines. Still, there were a few stops she thought they might make, but didn't. Her unease grew with each one they drove by.

"How far is it?" Will asked eventually, seemingly sharing her thoughts, though she considered it unwise to let on to their unease at this stage.

"Not far," Tex said, a stock answer if ever there was one. "Please excuse my manners, I should have asked how your flight was."

He was still speaking English, but Freya replied in German.

"We're looking forward to a good night's sleep," Freya grunted.

"You and me both," he said, also switching to German. "But I'm afraid the place we're going can get quite loud."

They came to the corner of Treptower Park, another subway stop she had earmarked as a potential hideout, but carried on by it to the Elsenbrücke, crossing over the Spree. Freya felt an unexpected chill as she did so. Neither she nor Belinda knew many details about her father's death, but newspapers at the time had described his body being found floating in the Spree, the river that flowed through the heart of the city. Those same dark waters now gleamed with reflected streetlights, cold and uninviting. It felt as though the city had no wish to see her back.

They crossed the bridge and turned left then right, sticking with the 96a until they turned off towards Comeniusplatz park. Another subway passed, and something in the car pinged.

They took an abrupt right turn. Freya didn't like that at all.

"Company?" she asked sharply.

"Yes," Tex answered, his tone terse.

"The drone from before?"

"No. Worse."

Freya twisted to look out the rear window. She saw immediately what had spooked their driver. Two bikers in black leather, almost side-by-side. One's helmet was painted with a skull, the other's with neon blue flames that seemed to shift and flicker beneath the street lamps. They were right on them, and beginning to split to pull up on either side.

"Who are they?" Freya demanded as Tex sped up, the engine starting to roar. "VERT?"

"Unlikely," Tex said. "Now please be quiet while I get us out of this."

Freya had no intention of doing that. She looked at Will. "Got something that could help?"

She could tell from the moment's silence before he responded that he was scanning through his Optik's display.

"Possibly, but you're going to have to turn off that scrambler."

"If I do that, they'll be able to hit our systems," Tex said.

"And I'll be able to hit theirs," Will retorted. "You want us to trust you, then trust us. Kill it."

With obvious reluctance, Tex hit a series of dials on his

dashboard. Freya's vision was overlaid by a message from her Optik saying it was rebooting and back online.

Traffic forced one of the bikers to drop back, but the skull-helmet was now alongside the back door. Freya considered throwing her door open, but Tex swerved before she could reach for it, throwing them both hard against their seatbelts.

"You're not going to lose them like that," Freya pointed out. Skull-helmet had anticipated the move, and was about to pull up alongside again, while their friend was now right behind. Freya was just glad none had pulled a sidearm yet.

"We just have to outrun them," Tex said.

Tex ran a red light, the sound of blaring car horns whipped away in an instant. The bikes stayed right with them. There was another sharp turn and a hideous moment as they briefly mounted the pavement, Freya's stomach lurching.

Her Optik pinged. A red warning superimposed itself on her vision, telling her that a malicious program was attempting to hijack her implant's systems. Were it not for DedSec-installed security measures, they would have been able to access her data.

"They're trying to break into my Optik," she said, blink-activating a series of countermeasures.

"That's just a by-product," Tex said. "They're trying to hack the car. My steering is locked."

More of the vehicle's advanced systems began to chime.

"Will?" Freya said urgently.

"I'm working on it," he said, one hand on his temple, a sure sign he was processing a lot of data on his own Optik.

Freya turned to check on the location of the bikers, and found herself staring into a leering skull visage. The lead pursuer was closer, now right alongside her. Death itself, come for her.

The moment lasted only a second. Without warning, the biker

swerved onto the curb, scattering pedestrians before colliding with a lamppost. Freya looked out the back window in time to see the same thing happen to the second biker, sudden loss of control resulting in a crash with a bin that sent rubbish flying.

"These new smart engines really are a liability," Will said smugly. "Apparently a manufacturer was told to include a failsafe that allowed the police to switch them off if a suspect was using one to get away. And anything the police can do, DedSec can do better."

Freya permitted the moment's smugness. She scanned her Optik. The warning had disappeared.

"We all good?" she asked.

"Looks like it," Tex said after checking his steering. "Guess you *are* the real deal, huh?"

"Who the hell were those two?" Freya snapped. "I want answers."

"You're about to get them," Tex said as he turned into a side street. "We're here."

Freya looked around as they pulled over. It seemed like another unassuming side street.

"We walk the last few minutes," Tex said. "Masks off now. They'll only attract attention."

Will looked at Freya, and she nodded. Still playing along. They pulled off the masks. Freya didn't much like wearing them anyway. She found them stifling, especially when things turned physical. This still had the potential for that.

Tex ditched his own mask, revealing a pale, youthful complexion, studded and accentuated by dark kohl smeared around his eyes. His hair was long and lank. He gave Freya a nod, as though acknowledging actually meeting face-to-face.

They set a brisk pace down the street, the wheels of Will's

suitcase still clattering uncomfortably. Freya cast a glance back, but there was no sign of their former pursuers.

It was only as they turned the corner that she realised their destination. It certainly wasn't what she had anticipated.

Helen dozed off in her chair at about midnight. Harriet had half a mind to try to get her to bed but knew if she woke her the old campaigner would insist on continuing. Besides, Harriet had found what they were searching for.

There was a message log, a thread between Wellend and someone anonymous recorded as "Askari". The log itself had been deleted but not the individual messages, and the cloner had been able to reconstruct much of it. Wellend had tried to cover his tracks, but he hadn't anticipated the level of scrutiny Helen and Harriet had brought to bear. There wasn't much online that the pair of them couldn't access when they combined their abilities.

Harriet scrolled through the log, her heart starting to race as she realised this was what they had been hunting.

Wellend had been a very naughty boy.

And that meant Helen's friend, Freya, was in grave danger. Her, and all her family.

Carefully, she woke Helen.

12
The Mountain Grove

Ahead of Freya and Will lay a towering structure, a solid block of 1950s Stalinist architecture flanked by open scrub ground. Its name was the Berghain, and every Berliner, hell, probably every kid in Europe, had heard of it.

"We didn't come here for a night out," Freya said sharply to Tex.

"Don't worry, we're not here to party," Tex said, before adding, "yet."

"This is where M-Bahn is based?" Will asked.

"What, you thought M-Bahn would have burrowed a hackerspace out beneath some subway tracks?"

It was true that, regardless of the name, nothing specific had been mentioned in the briefings about the Berlin subway. It wasn't helping Freya's mounting suspicions though.

The Berghain was the most famous techno nightclub in the world. It had been built in the 1950s as a heating plant, its name a portmanteau of the two Berlin districts it sat between, Kreuzberg and Friedrichshain. On its own, the word itself meant "mountain grove". Its three floors and basement had been associated with raw, mind-bending hedonism for over two decades.

Freya had never been, but she had dabbled in London's techno scene when she had been younger and had heard all the stories. Getting in was difficult, borderline impossible for anyone not German or not a true member of the scene. Taking photos or videos inside was forbidden. The bathrooms had questionable locks, and no mirrors, so that partygoers were spared the indignity of witnessing themselves at some of the highest and lowest points of their lives. The basement housed so-called dark rooms, where carnal desires of all kinds were indulged.

It was also said that only half of the building was actually in use. Freya suspected they were about to find out just how true that story was.

They passed the long queue stretching away from the front doors. There were countless articles online giving supposed tips on how to pass the opaque, secret rules the bouncers set for entry. Wear dark or unassuming clothes. Don't talk, especially not in any language other than German. Act casual, and know which DJs were performing on the night. Even then, there were no guarantees about entry. Unless, it seemed, you were Tex.

He led them along the line, hundreds of eyes staring at the unlikely trio – Freya doubted anyone had tried to get into the Berghain with a suitcase before, let alone actually made it inside. Tex seemed unconcerned though. Ahead of them, the noise from the club began to swell, the pounding beats reaching out into the chill night.

They arrived at the front of the queue, cutting in. Wisely, those directly behind said nothing.

Several disinterested bouncers blocked the entrance, the walls behind them scrawled with graffiti. One stepped forward, a heavily-tattooed man with nose and lip piercings and a silver beard and hair.

"Hello, Sven," Tex said. "Busy night?"

The bouncer shrugged, casting his eye briefly over Freya and Will. Then, after a moment's thought, he nodded.

"Wait here for a moment," Tex said to them both, leading them around the bouncer and between his onlooking cohorts. They stopped at the last one.

"Bags," he said, nodding to their backpacks and Will's unwieldy suitcase, but Tex waved him away.

"I'm vouching for them," he said. "The bags are fine."

The bouncer shrugged, like it wasn't his problem, and turned back towards the door as though they weren't there anymore.

"Stay close to me at all times," Tex told them, before waving them through into the nightclub.

Ahead, the music surged.

Teuton dragged off her skull-marked biker helmet and swore viciously.

The handover hadn't happened. Everything had gone wrong the moment the targets had gotten into that taxi outside the airport. Now they'd made it to the Berghain before she could, and that meant they were beyond her reach, for now.

She called Luther via her Optik.

"Reboot got to them first," she said. It was Luther's turn to curse.

"Where are they now?" he demanded.

"The Berghain."

"So get in there and get them."

"You want me to bust open Reboot's headquarters? I thought Askari said they were off limits until VERT got involved?"

"It's a nightclub, Teuton," Luther said slowly. "Go for a fucking dance."

It was gloomy inside. Freya and Will passed by a small ticket booth, and found themselves in an entrance hall, big, cold and brutalist. The wall directly ahead was tiled, displaying artwork of a series of windswept black, white, and grey vistas that spoke of loneliness and desolation, though the majority of the tiles seemed to be missing. There were people milling about, most from the queue who had just been permitted inside.

A set of suspended steel stairs lay at one end of the hall. Tex took them up, the metal beneath them vibrating with the insistent beat that was shuddering the air. Will hefted the suitcase, Freya staying behind, ready to bundle him aside at a moment's notice. She had expected to go downwards, into the Berghain's infamous basement, rather than up. Then again, nothing else tonight had gone as expected either.

The noise grew ever louder. They passed onto the next floor. There were more people here, revellers, drunk or drugged or both, most of them coming and going from a set of doors that, judging by the primal blast of techno music and the burst of strobe lighting they emitted, led onto the Berghain's main dance floor.

It was a sensory assault. Freya knew she would have enjoyed it once, but those days were rapidly receding. Worse, it made the job she'd come here to do much more difficult.

The stairs continued though, and so did Tex. Freya felt a moment's relief. Ensuring she kept an eye on Will in a place like that would have been impossible.

They passed up through the old, careworn building, until they finally came to the end of the metal spiral. A door awaited, this one closed. Tex banged the side of his fist on it, twice.

Freya noted the camera, set into the wall on their right. She also spotted the symbol that had been spraypainted onto the door. It was the standard power/standby symbol, a circle cut through at the top by a short horizontal line, except that line then pierced a crude rendering of a skull that had been added into the middle of the circle.

Freya took in the macabre tech symbol before there was a scrape, and the door was hauled open.

"Late," the figure on the other side of the door grumbled. He had piercings, a black goatee, and a blue spiderweb tattoo over his right eye and temple. He looked Freya and Will up and down without expression.

"There were drones up," Tex said. "Termite's going the other route."

"Whatever," the man said, then moved aside. Freya got in front of Will before he could enter, making sure she went through the door first.

The room was almost as large as the entrance hall downstairs. Like everything else it was mostly stark concrete and exposed electrical cabling, a trio of bare lightbulbs dangling in a row from the high ceiling. They swung almost imperceptibly with the endless beat from downstairs, but the sound was muffled here, relegated to more of a constant, indistinct background noise.

There were more people in the room. One experienced glance gave Freya a figure of about two dozen. Most looked like their only source of clothing and accessories was EXOMOD, all leathers, spikes, and neon accessories.

This was a hackerspace, not so dissimilar from the north London hideout, though not in the location she had expected. It seemed busy, which seemed to bode well for a fledgling cell, if they could all be trusted.

"We're looking for Luther, Revolver, or Teuton," Freya said, addressing the room.

There was no answer. The tension in the air was palpable.

Freya realised they had to get out.

As she turned to Will, one of the assembly spoke up.

"They're not here," she said.

"Then we're leaving," Freya replied, shooting a look at Will. He'd already set his suitcase down.

"No, you're not," the woman said. There was a thud behind them as the one who had shown them in closed and locked the door.

Mentally, Freya cursed. From the taxi scrambler and the chase to this, she knew she shouldn't have entrusted Will with making first contact. Something, somewhere down the line, had gone badly wrong, and now they were in at the deep end.

"Who are you?" Freya asked the woman who'd addressed them, trying to buy time as she worked out an exit strategy. In the distance, the music on the club's dance floor rose to a crescendo before dropping powerfully.

"My name is Leona," she said. She was Black, tall, and almost painfully skinny, with dark hair piled high on her head. Her features were as slender and delicate-looking as the rest of her, her dark skin accentuated by a small tattoo on her temple, a circle joined to a line that curved like a fishhook. Freya was confident she could take her. Her two dozen friends might be a bit much though.

"This isn't M-Bahn, is it?" Will said, clearly thinking along the same lines as Freya.

"No," Leona admitted. "We're something better."

She gestured at the end of the room's long table. "Take a seat. We've got a lot to discuss."

Freya weighed their options. From what she could see many

of the room's occupants were armed, and weapons covered the table, automatic rifles as well as sidearms, some looking freshly printed. None were close to the length of bench Leona had indicated for them to sit at. There was the door at their back, and another at the far end of the room, though that would require them to get past everyone in between. There was a trio of slender, tall windows looking out into the city's nighttime skyline, but they were far too high up to try those. The first floor might be doable as a jump; this one definitely wasn't.

The odds weren't good from where they stood, but it all depended on their own location and that of the others in the room. That meant they could change rapidly. They just had to stay alert.

"You've got a lot of explaining to do," Freya told Leona, while making a tiny, subtle gesture to Will, pinkie and thumb extended and the other fingers clenched. They'd been in situations like this before and had long been proficient in passing on their intentions under observation.

This one meant *wait for my signal.*

They walked to the table and sat close to its head.

"It's been a necessary deception," Leona said, seemingly missing Freya's gesture as she sat down across from them. As Freya had hoped, the rest of the room shifted too, most of the occupants moving to surround the table. The one with the spiderweb tat who had let them in was among them, leaving the door they had entered through less closely guarded.

"You seem to know who we are, so you have us at a disadvantage," Will said. Freya was happy to let him do the talking. He was good at that, usually. She had her own job to do. One of the onlookers had a 9mm in his waistband and was almost within touching distance.

"You're DedSec, so you'll understand if introductions are limited," Leona said. "Identities tend to come at a price."

"You're not DedSec too then," Will surmised. Freya suspected he was doing what she had done and stalling for time. "We thought we were meeting with M-Bahn."

"We aren't M-Bahn, and M-Bahn isn't DedSec," Leona said. "Luckily for you, we decided to hijack your encounter with them."

The one with the pistol shifted a little further out. Freya kept her cool. No point in getting frustrated in situations like this. Frustration got people killed. There would be another opportunity. Patience. Her heart raced, but her hands, which she had laid on the table, were steady.

"How did you manage that?" Will asked. "M-Bahn gave us the handshake program over a fully encrypted channel. Assuming they didn't send it to you too, how were you able to mimic the digital signature in the taxi?"

"Why would we tell you that?" Leona asked.

"Call it hacker's courtesy."

"You're thinking too much along the lines of software encryption," said a thickset man with a shaven head and neck tattoo standing behind Leona. "How secure was your connection on the ground at your end?"

"So you've got someone inside north London DedSec," Will surmised, sounding genuinely surprised, and with good reason. Freya felt a sense of alarm as she realised the implications. Someone in Wellend's hackerspace had physically gotten into the communications between them and M-Bahn and had shared the meetup signature.

Leona looked annoyed, as though she hadn't intended to share the information, but her own poker face quickly reasserted itself.

"Much like DedSec, we've got friends all over," she said. "Our name is Reboot, and Berlin belongs to us."

Freya recalled talk about Reboot being a preexisting hacker group based in Germany. Will, unsurprisingly, seemed to know more.

"So this is where Reboot is based," he said, gesturing at the room. "Must be difficult to get work done, but I'm guessing you all enjoy the 'scene.'"

"It's more of a home to us than a lot of the places we grew up," Leona said.

"What is Reboot?" Freya asked. More time-stalling. Another of the onlookers had shifted their stance, and while this one didn't have a sidearm visible, she did have an extendable baton hooked to her studded belt.

"Another of Berlin's hacktivist organisations," Will said. "One of the smaller groups."

"Small, but growing," Leona said, stung. "You already know we have friends in many places. Including London."

"What about friends in M-Bahn?"

"We don't affiliate with M-Bahn. No good activist does."

"And why is that?"

"Because they're not who they pretend to be. You've been sold the idea they're DedSec Berlin. That is false."

"Then who are they?"

"A front created by a local crime lord, Emil Kaiser."

Freya looked hard at Leona. She knew Kaiser's name, as did Will. He was infamous in the German criminal underworld, one of the most established and long-lasting gangsters in the country. His name had also been connected to her father. Thomas Bauer had been his primary supplier of fake identities for a while. Belinda had told Freya several times that she believed he was the one who had ordered Thomas's murder.

"Why would Emil Kaiser create a false DedSec-like group here in Berlin?" Will asked.

"To weaken the legitimate movement," Leona said, her voice taking on a fiercer tone. There was passion there, Freya could see. She empathised with that at least.

"Both of you know something of Berlin," the black-haired woman continued. "You will know of the troubles we face here. We believe Kaiser is in league with VERT. They plan to create a threat to national security, M-Bahn, a false flag that will allow VERT to further tighten their grip on the government and civil society."

"We also think Kaiser wants you," the burly man behind Leona said, looking directly at Freya.

"Why?" she asked, playing dumb, even though she was in turmoil. This was what she had both feared and hoped for. Her past, entangling her future. Just what her mother had hinted at. A reckoning. Perhaps she had been right. Perhaps Emil Kaiser had been behind her father's death after all.

"You probably know better than us," Leona said. "But you're known to us, Freya Bauer. Known in Berlin. People haven't forgotten how your family hurt Kaiser. They know that he's been hunting you all this time and failing. The most important thing right now is that M-Bahn don't receive your assistance, or the legitimacy that affiliation with the real DedSec can provide. That is why we had intercepted you. We'll also be taking the contents of your suitcase. Reboot needs every advantage it can gain if we're going to stop VERT from taking control of this country."

The woman with the baton hadn't moved away. Below, the incessant pounding of Berghain's glorious techno rose to another crescendo.

"I was tired lugging it about anyway," Will said. "Look, we're not really interested in getting involved in a hacker war between two groups, so maybe you could just drive us back to the airport?"

As he spoke, Freya took one hand off the table and drew the other closer to her, flicking a signal to Will as she did so. Forefinger and middle finger extended for a fraction of a second, finger-guns.

Get ready.

Leona didn't answer Will, instead asking an abrupt question of her own, looking at Freya.

"Will you teach us?"

Freya frowned.

"Teach you what?"

"What the signals you've been signing to your partner mean."

"You're making a mistake," Leona said. "Put the gun down, and we can continue to talk. If you don't, you won't be leaving the Berghain."

"I beg to differ." Freya waved Will towards the door. He edged back, baton extended, knowing well enough that he had to do exactly what Freya instructed in situations like these.

"If you come after us, even if you catch us, this space will be compromised. Let us go quietly, and we won't make a scene. We're not here to rat you out."

"We can't let you help M-Bahn," Leona said.

"If what you said is true, we won't be," Will interjected. "But forgive us if we want to find that out on our terms."

The man Freya had a grip of groaned and squirmed. Freya dragged him, with some difficulty, nearer the door, then stepped back from him with the weapon still aimed at him.

"Not so much as a twitch," she snarled at everyone else, as Will unlocked the door and stepped through. There was a painfully tense moment where Freya was left confronting the whole room alone, and then she stepped backwards through the doorway too. Without looking at Will, she spoke.

"Run."

13
Disaffected

It was even worse than Helen had feared. The whole job was a setup. Wellend had delivered Freya into the hands of some very bad people.

She reread what Harriet had found on Wellend's cloned files one more time, wanting to be absolutely certain. It was all laid out, though, in the chat logs, and in receipts of payments received. Wellend was funding his end of DedSec's operation using blood money, paid for delivering Thomas Bauer's daughter to Germany.

"We need to warn Freya," Harriet said.

Helen hesitated. "She seemed to want to avoid contact. I'd consider reaching out via Bagley, but he's now tied up elsewhere, and besides, he'll be blocked in Germany. We're going to have to risk reaching out I think."

She blinked on Freya's number, calling her Optik.

"No answer," she said after a while, pursing her lips. That wasn't a good sign. She sent a series of brief messages, telling her to get in touch.

"We've got to put a black hat on Wellend," Harriet said. "Make everyone else aware of what he's doing. We don't know who it is that's coming after the Bauers either, but he must. Maybe we should pay him a visit."

"Not a good idea, not at this stage. As soon as he realises we're on to him he'll get the word out. 'Askari' will be notified, and Wellend will probably blacklist us as well. We'll have the whole of DedSec running against us, at least until we can publicise this data. Even with the intel we've gained so far, we don't know if anyone else we might otherwise turn to might be backing him. We've got to be smarter than that, or Belinda will be compromised as well, and we won't even make it out of London, let alone get across to Bristol to help Andrew."

"It feels wrong though, letting Wellend get away with it," Harriet said bitterly. "Who knew he was a rat?"

"That's the problem with rats, especially in a city like this. You know they're there, you just hardly ever see them. Wellend isn't the first, and he won't be the last. We'll get him, we just need to be patient."

Harriet still looked unhappy at the idea of sparing Wellend. Helen tried to focus her mind. The next few hours in situations like these were critical.

"Securing Freya's family has to be our first priority," she told her. "If the worst has happened to Freya, we need to see them safe."

"Right now, the middle Bauer is on her own."

Freya and Will pounded down the metal stairs, the music of the main floor rising to meet them.

Freya's thoughts were like a knife, unsheathed and cutting. Going all the way to the bottom of this flight was too risky – it would take too long, and give Reboot time to intercept them.

Besides, she didn't fancy getting through the phalanx of bouncers at the door.

That only left the dance floor, halfway between them and the ground. After that it would be a case of more improvisation. Nightclubs had to have fire exits.

Will was in front of her, so she'd have to direct him rather than lead the way.

"Left here, into the main hall," she bellowed over the techno. Thankfully he heard her, turning at the landing leading into the Berghain's cavernous heart. He paused for a second, panting, to let her take the lead.

She ran through the doors.

It was akin to being punched in the face. According to legend, the sound system used on the main dance floor, the Funktion-One, only ever operated at ten to twenty percent output. That was difficult to believe. It wasn't just an assault on Freya's ears – she could physically feel the music slamming through her body, beat after beat. It was at once painful and thrilling.

There was no time to adjust. Before her lay the Berghain's central hall. It was a high, vaulted space, its centre demarcated by double rows of pillars, like a grand throne room. Overhead the ceiling was disrupted by a series of air vents shaped like inverted pyramids, their flattened tips pointing down towards the great mass of bodies underneath. Both the pillars and the vents were marked up with graffiti, the all-seeing eye, slogans in German about freedom and expression, and, in at least two places, the skull-and-circle sign of Reboot.

Freya doubted most of those in the hall knew what the latter meant. The place was ram-packed with revellers, sweating and gyrating, wild or dead-eyed, lost in an unending celebration of primality. On a less fraught night a decade earlier, Freya would have exulted at walking in on such a sight, and would have thrown herself into its heart, to let the currents of the crowd and the rhythm of the speakers carry her wherever they pleased.

Tonight, however, she would have to forge her own path.

She considered pulling the pistol and shooting into the ceiling, but decided a mass stampede would hinder them rather than help. Besides, she wasn't even sure anyone would hear a gunshot.

A quick assessment showed that there were neither windows nor obvious exits on the nearest side of the dance floor. She could see the Berghain's tall, slender windows all along the far wall, however, through the flashing strobe lights and over the heads of the crowd. That was where they had to make it to. Putting a thousand or so bodies between them and Reboot's immediate pursuit would be good too.

"Mask on," she shouted at Will, having to use the hand signals again. Many of the partygoers had their faces covered, sporting everything from simple black masquerade masks to rubber party shop animal heads to ornate custom jobs with LEDs and movable parts. Tex had seen their own masks, but no one else here had. Right now they needed every possible advantage.

She pulled on her Mister Scruff covering, adding to the claustrophobia and the sweltering heat as she forced herself into the crowd. Will grabbed on to her shoulder.

There was a technique to moving through packed clubs. It was all about finding the pockets of space that existed between groups of friends and exploiting them, rather than trying to push through and break people apart. A little bit of pressure, a deft touch, could do much to pierce even the densest crowd.

That was in theory, but in practice it was a messy business. In the first thirty seconds Freya was half drenched by spilled drinks and took a flailing arm to the mask. She did her best to stay in control, not lashing out. A fight with randoms here would be as fatal as being caught by Reboot.

The music changed, the DJ presiding over the great rite from the stage segueing towards the next song. Function's "Disaffected" began blasting out, the synthesised sounds followed by a blaze of strobes, a brutal oscillation between light and dark.

It coincided with the sudden disappearance of Will's grip on Freya's shoulder. She turned immediately, knowing how instantly someone could disappear into a crowd like this.

Will was still there, but so were two men who were grappling with him. Judging by their attire, they were Rebooters. Clearly, Leona had already put out a call.

Freya lunged at them through the jostling crowd. One sensed her coming and turned, angling a punch at her gut. It connected poorly though, and Freya took it, bringing her own fist up and cracking the man's jaw. He reeled back into the press of people, and Freya lunged on into the second attacker, who had Will in a headlock.

He was a big brute, but the attempt at restraint left him defenceless against a short, sharp left hook.

Will ripped himself free from the man's grasp, but by then the first to come at Freya had flung himself back onto her.

Around them the crowd had started to push away, the natural reaction to a brawl developing in a congested space. A circle was beginning to form around them. Freya didn't really want that.

She let loose on the guy swinging at her, a forearm blocking his clumsy haymaker while she jabbed him in the gut, kicked him between the legs, and elbowed the back of his neck when he doubled over. The blazing strobes were making everything more difficult, the wildly oscillating light and dark interfering with landing a clean blow, and the music made her skull ache and pound, but she couldn't stop. She had to finish this quickly.

Will had finally made himself useful, kicking the legs out from under the second Rebooter. He raised his foot to bring it down on the man after he'd hit the sticky deck, but Freya snatched his collar and dragged him away.

"We've got to move," she shouted, pointlessly, as she couldn't even hear her own voice.

The fight had at least served to clear them a bit of space, even if it had well and truly drawn the attention of the whole Berghain down on them. Freya waved her commandeered pistol in the air for good measure, helping ensure that, even in the midst of the dance floor, with people wildly intoxicated or high, a path opened up in front of them towards the far wall.

Freya ran, pulling Will along for fear that someone else in the crowd would snatch him. She was dimly aware of people shoving their way towards them through the press on all sides.

Two of the oncoming figures – bouncers – burst through into their path, but Freya barely had a chance to check Will before others came out of the crowd, two males and a female.

Freya recognised the woman, who made a curt gesture to her two companions, from Wellend's presentation. They set about the bouncers, grappling with them as the woman signalled to Freya to follow her.

It was Teuton, the M-Bahn enforcer. Freya felt no relief, only the unwelcome realisation that it added another variable to an already fraught situation.

She didn't have a chance to weigh up their options, because more Berghain reinforcements came charging through the rapidly disintegrating dance floor. The music abruptly cut off as well, leaving Freya's ears ringing.

The M-Bahn woman, Teuton, was grappled by a tattooed brute. She broke his nose with a sharp blow of her elbow, but he clung on, trying to throw her to the floor.

Freya knew they didn't have time for this. Even if M-Bahn had belatedly found them, and even if they could be trusted, it didn't look like they stood a better chance of getting out with them.

She dragged Will through the developing melee, which now appeared to have spilled into the milling crowd as well, drawing in strangers and random clubgoers. Freya waved her pistol, finding it to be the only thing that kept everyone else away.

They made it past the pillars and out into an open space just before the far wall. As she had feared, the bottom sections of the Berghain's tall, slender windows were bricked up. There was a fire exit though. It was guarded by another bouncer who saw Freya and Will coming. He was unarmed and could do nothing but raise both hands and back off when Freya brandished her stolen sidearm.

"Kick the door open and step away," she bawled at him. He didn't do anything to the door, but he did back up, which gave Will enough space to get past and slam open the exit's release bar.

A set of metal stairs awaited, on the Berghain's outside, leading down onto the street next to the club's beer garden. They thundered down them, leaving behind the uproar that had gripped the nightclub. The DJ began to say something over a microphone, but the words were indistinct to the pair as, panting, they made it down to street level.

And found themselves facing a drone.

It whirred not far above them, an unmarked, unarmed chase unit with dual motors and a single, central red optic, glowing red, a bit larger than a shoebox in size. As they moved to the left, along the street, it started to follow them.

"I've got this," Will said, the darting of his eyes telling Freya he had his Optik's HUD up, no doubt to remotely hack the drone.

"Nope, no time," Freya growled, and shot the thing. She didn't know who it belonged to – presumably Reboot – but she was in no mood to play cat and mouse anymore.

Her shot clipped its left rotor, causing it to veer away, though whether it was because she'd damaged it or because its remote controller was recalling it, she didn't know.

"Keep going," she urged Will, pushing him along the street. She could hear shouting and the ringing of feet on the steel stairs of the fire exit behind them.

They sprinted into the Berlin night.

14
Trust Issues

Freya wasn't familiar with the area around the Berghain, but she knew it was close to the Spree. She didn't want to be caught between the river and their pursuers, so she went in what she vaguely thought was the opposite direction, northwards.

The only positive was the late hour meant only a few drunkards wandered away from the club, and the light traffic meant they could bolt straight across the Strausberger Platz.

"There's a park… further ahead and left…" Will huffed, blinking as he struggled to keep going. A map superimposed itself into the corner of her vision, an aerial shot of Berlin with the expanse of greenery highlighted.

A moment later she saw the actual entrance ahead of them. It was an unassuming iron gate set into a graffitied, derelict-looking brick wall that bordered onto the street. There were trees beyond it though. She recognised it.

She reached the gate and tried it, unsurprised to find it locked.

"Up and over," she told Will, gesturing at the top of the gate. It was only slightly above head height, and they cleared it without much difficulty. Beyond lay a dark pathway, flanked by well-kept trees and hedges.

“No time to stop,” Freya said.

“Do you know where we are?” Will asked as they set off at a jog, struggling to keep up as Freya began to stride out.

“Yep,” Freya replied.

The pathway led to a stone structure reminiscent of a Roman or Greek temple, serene in the night amidst the parkland greenery. It was the church of Saint Peter, and what looked like a parkland was actually a well-kept cemetery, rows of headstones lying beyond the trees and hedges on either side of the central path.

“Here.” She grabbed Will and steered him off to the right of the church itself. They stood alongside a row of headstones, doing their best to hold their breath and listen, but there were no sounds of a pursuit. They yanked off their masks, Freya welcoming the cold air on her face.

“We can’t stay here–” Freya began to say as her heart rate gradually levelled out, but Will held up a hand, checking her.

To her surprise, he dropped the hands-on device part of his Optik in the dirt and brought the heel of his shoe down on it. There was a crack as the screen split in half and its light went out.

“Why?” Freya asked.

“Likely compromised,” Will said, still panting, leaning against one of the taller gravestones. “The handover, with the taxi. They’ll have hacked the physical component when I exchanged the handshake. Reboot, listening to us, tracking us. They’ll know we stopped here. We need to keep moving.”

“I was planning on it,” Freya said. She checked the pistol’s safety and slipped it into her jacket.

“There’s a much bigger park about a ten-minute walk away,” she said. “The Volkspark. We can hole up there until morning, figure something out.”

"Agreed."

"We should mask up again. You ready?"

Will nodded, and with their identities covered, they set off, taking the cemetery's rear gateway into a side street. They walked briskly, alert for any sign of pursuit, whether on the ground or in the air. However, besides the occasional car that drove past, Berlin slept.

They made it to the Volkspark, an expanse of greenery about a kilometre square. It was dark in amongst the foliage, and the going was slow and awkward, branches snapping and snagging. Once they'd worked their way in deep, Freya came to a halt.

"This will do," she said. Will gratefully pulled off his mask and sank down, his back against a tree trunk.

"Well, that was horrific," he said.

Freya didn't respond immediately. She turned, putting Mister Scruff back in her pack. She was angry, still running off the buzz that escape and evasion had given her, pissed off that it had all gone so wrong so fast. She should have known.

"We should never have come here," she said.

"It's certainly looking that way," Will admitted.

"I'm contacting Wellend, and then we're going to the airport and getting the first flight out."

"Sounds like a plan. Give me a second."

Freya turned to him in the dark.

"Why? You're using your Optik?"

"Call me petty, but I'd rather the suitcase I left behind, filled with hardware that can connect back to DedSec, didn't fall into the hands of a random hacker group," he said. "Especially one that just tried to kidnap us."

"You've got a way to stop that?"

"The suitcase is locked," Will explained. "I'm sure they'll be able to crack it, but I doubt they'll have managed it yet. By the time they do, a heat-burster I left in one of the CPUs will have fried the circuits of everything I brought. I can use my Optik connection to trigger it."

"Fine," Freya said gruffly. Will went silent for a few moments, presumably blink-calling his suitcase.

"That should be it frying as we speak," he said.

Freya checked her own Optik while he was at it and realised she had missed messages. They were from Helen Dashwood. As soon as she saw them, a sense of foreboding crept over her.

There were two missed calls, both around the time when they'd been in the Berghain, followed by two texts.

It's a trap.

Don't trust Wellend.

Freya swore softly, then more vehemently.

"What is it?" Will asked, sounding alarmed.

"It's a setup," Freya spat, her thoughts racing. "Wellend's hung us out to dry."

"What? Why? How do you know?"

She sent the messages over to Will's own Optik display with a blink.

"Not very helpful," he said.

She was on him in a flash, hand to his throat, pinning him back against the rough bark of the tree.

"What did you know about all this?" she snarled. "Who put you up to bringing me here?"

"No… one…" Will choked, grabbing Freya's wrist in a vain attempt at loosening her grip.

"Bullshit! Why did you and Wellend work so hard to convince me to come to Berlin? He enlisted you because he thought you could get through to me. What did he offer you?"

Will made a gargling noise. After a supreme battle, Freya managed to force herself to loosen her grasp a fraction.

"I… told you what he offered," Will hissed sarcastically. "A way out of all this. I only know what you know. We're supposed to be linking up with 'DedSec Berlin.'"

"I'm not sure there is such a thing," Freya said. "And considering someone back in London told this Reboot group we were coming, my trust is at a premium right now."

"It says not to trust Wellend. I'm not bloody Wellend. I've no idea what he's up to!"

Freya let go, still standing over Will.

"It would be stupid of me to trust anyone right now," she pointed out.

"I know we've had… issues, Freya, but I'm not trying to get you killed," Will answered acidly, rubbing at his neck. "If I were going to betray you, I just might have done it when we were completely surrounded by Reboot."

Freya grunted and turned away.

"That would be assuming it's Reboot you're working with," she said, looking out into the dark undergrowth of the parkland. She needed answers, but the possibilities seemed endless right now. It was like fumbling in the pitch black for something that didn't want to be found. It could be anywhere.

"Maybe Wellend tipped off Reboot," Will said.

"Perhaps," Freya answered, still thinking. "Maybe what Leona said was true. M-Bahn are a front for Kaiser."

"Kaiser, the gangster," Will added. "All the chatter I've read online makes him sound like the sort of guy we definitely don't want to get involved with."

"True. He was a rising name in the crime world even when I was a kid."

As she spoke, she called Helen via her Optik interface. Right then she was the only person Freya trusted.

Thankfully, she picked up right away.

"Helen. What the hell is going on?"

"Something bad I'm afraid," the Londoner replied. "How secure is your connection?"

"Not very. We've just had to fight our way out of a nightclub. We were picked up by someone other than M-Bahn as soon as we arrived."

"That might have been a stroke of fortune," Helen said. "I'm not sure M-Bahn are all you were led to believe."

"What do you know?"

"Our mutual friend in London seems to have spun you a lie. I'm not sure why just yet, but he seems to have delivered you to Germany in exchange for rather a lot of money."

Freya felt herself being gripped by a dark and burning rage. Things were beginning to make more sense now. She had been played for a fool. Even worse, it seemed as though the spectres of the past were stretching out to grab her.

Stark reality momentarily quelled her anger, as she realised that she wasn't the only one in danger. If her father's killer was trying to exterminate the Bauers, Belinda and Andrew would be in the crosshairs too. And now she was in Germany and unable to help them.

"You've got to get in touch with my family," Freya told Helen.

"Don't worry dearie, I have that in hand," Helen replied. "You'll understand if I can't go into details, but I'm going to make sure they're all safe. Myself and a good friend are on the case. I don't want you to worry about them. Focus on getting out of Berlin and back here in one piece. Then we can do something about that mutual friend I mentioned earlier."

From anyone else, Freya would have still fretted, would have demanded further assurances. But knowing Helen was going to see her mother and son to safety was as close to a relief as she would dare admit.

"One more question," she said. "Is Will in on it?" As she spoke, she looked down at her former husband. It was too dark for her to read his expression, but she could see the tension and anger in his posture.

"We've not uncovered anything to suggest that," Helen said. "He's probably the only friend you have right now east of Dover."

Freya considered that briefly, then thanked Helen and hung up.

"If you don't trust me then feel free to leave me," Will said bitterly. "I'll make my own way."

"I do trust you," Freya admitted, deciding it was time to go all in. What Helen had said was true. At that moment Will might be the only one she could count on in Berlin. And while she knew well enough how to make it on her own, sometimes it was still easier with two.

"Change your T-shirt and jeans, then dump all the other clothes from your backpack," she told him. "Plus anything else you don't think you'll need within the next twenty-four hours. We're cutting our holiday short."

Helen hung up and exchanged a glance with Harriet.

"Well at least they're not dead," Harriet pointed out.

"Right now they're not the ones I'm most worried about," Helen replied. In truth she had feared the worst when Freya hadn't picked up initially, but it seemed like she and Will had gotten out, and right now there wasn't much more they could do for her.

Her family were a different matter. If Freya was now in Berlin and on the run, the part of the plot they had unearthed involving Belinda and Andrew Bauer would now also be underway. Whoever "Askari" was, he had made Wellend divulge the locations of both Freya's mother and son. Wellend had given them up without asking any questions. The inference was pretty clear. They were both in danger, as of right now.

"I'll go over and speak to Belinda," Helen said. "She's a tough one. Knows the score. I should be able to convince her, and then we'll move her to one of the safe houses. One not on Wellend's radar."

"I've got one in mind," Harriet said. "Will she go right now though, without Andrew?"

"We'll need to convince her we're getting Andrew to safety as well," Helen said. "Which we'll have to, if I'm to ever look Freya in the eye again. I'm going to call him."

Harriet looked pensive for a moment before speaking again.

"Maybe leave it for now. I might have had an idea. A way we can draw out whoever is coming for him without putting him in danger. Well, not too much danger anyway."

Helen looked surprised, but she smiled.

"It almost sounds like a plan involving live bait, dearie."

"At least at the start," Harriet said, returning the smile. "It's going to be more like catfishing."

15
Checkpoint

The sun rose as Freya and Will prepared to set off again.

They had changed clothes. There was no reason not to try to switch up their appearance, and the time spent in the Volkspark had left them muddy and dishevelled, which hardly fit the look of two casual tourists. Their jackets were the only things they couldn't replace, and Freya opted to keep them – putting her commandeered pistol in her backpack kept it out of easy reach, and she wasn't foolish enough to want to shove it down her waistband.

She was tired, but she knew better than to dwell on it. Stopping after an adrenaline rush inevitably brought on a low, and keeping active was the best way of riding it out. She focused on their priorities. Right now, they involved getting to the Berlin airport.

There were four ways of doing that. The first, on foot, would take far too long. The second, hitching a lift, would be impractical in central Berlin unless Freya pulled her gun, and that sounded like a terrible idea. The third, getting a taxi, she didn't fancy given Reboot had picked them up at the airport posing as one.

That left the bus. Risking using her Optik, Freya located an airport service not far from the entrance to the Volkspark. It would take them via the middle of the city, but it was still faster than catching connecting buses that took a more direct route.

"All set?" she asked Will as they left the park. He nodded. That was good enough.

Freya was still angry with Will for convincing her to come here. She was angry with herself for agreeing. Most of all, she was angry with Wellend. The bastard was a traitor. She had never particularly liked him, but neither had she ever thought so low of him. She kept replaying their most recent interactions over and over, trying to work out if there was something she had missed, a hint or tell. She had spotted rats in DedSec before. She was an enforcer, not a tech-head like Will. She should have sensed something was wrong.

At least Helen had. Getting her involved had been the best choice she had made in a while. Andrew and her mum were still at the back of her mind, but she was experienced enough to hold those concerns at bay. Helen would take care of them. What she had said was true. Right now, it was about getting herself and Will out of Berlin.

They walked out of the Volkspark. Traffic was steadily building as the morning wore on, and there were more pedestrians too. Getting through the city without drawing attention was becoming steadily more unlikely. Freya told Will to trigger their masks' facial recognition scrambling tech anyway, courtesy of Helen. It would be no good if VERT or anyone else got physical eyes-on, but for automated surveillance it should let them slip by.

One street over, while waiting at a set of traffic lights, two bulky armoured vehicles rolled past. They were matte grey, and their flanks were stamped with the white letters "VERT". Freya engaged Will in casual conversation, pretending not to notice them.

"So those are the Defenders," Will murmured after they had passed, watching the two combat transports growling away down the street, incongruous surrounded by civilian traffic. "Looks like they're getting set for World War Three."

Freya said nothing. VERT were the least of their worries right now. It was all about staying under the radar.

They made it to the bus stop. There were a few other people waiting already, tourists by the look of it. That was a relief. They almost blended in.

The bus came, and they boarded. Freya immediately sized up everyone around them. There was a young Polish couple, a family of either Americans or Canadians, and several individuals sitting or standing silently, most of them with headphones on or looking at their Optiks, eyes glazed or darting. None did more than glance at Freya and Will. That in itself didn't mean much, but she was confident there was nobody on the bus she couldn't take in a fight.

It drove off, towards the heart of the city. Freya signalled to Will to stay standing, and they grabbed the bus's overhead handholds.

The experience of being on the run together wasn't new for either of them, but doing it in Berlin was. London had been so familiar. They had both known the streets, the alleyways, the bus and Tube routes, where the safe houses were located. Contingencies had abounded. They were aware also of how the authorities operated – the MET, SIRS, Albion, all with their own protocols and jurisdictions, all battled and overcome many times. There had been plenty of close scraps too, but they had been fighting on home turf, as Freya liked to say. The odds were good.

Not so here. At that moment, Berlin could have been on Mars for all the familiarity Freya felt. The recollections of life as a young girl didn't stack up with what she needed to know in the present. The local police, the local gangs, VERT, her knowledge of their strengths, techniques, territories were all gleaned from little more than Wellend's briefings, none of which she could even trust anymore. All she had was Will. The two of them were adrift in the unknown, with only their wits and good fortune to get them home.

The bus stopped at Schützenstraße, just up from Checkpoint Charlie, the Cold War interface-turned tourist honeypot on Friedrichstraße. Now they really were in tourist central. More piled on, filling the bus with suitcases and a multitude of different languages.

One figure stood out. Freya clocked him as soon as he got on board, and shot Will a warning look.

It was a BPOL grunt, a member of the federal police, decked out in navy blue gear and a beret. He was armed, but more importantly, he had an Optik device out. As Freya watched he began requesting the IDs of locals and the passports or Optik tags of travellers, scanning them.

"That's not great," Will said under his breath in German.

"English," Freya replied softly. "Just going to have to trust what we've got."

She fished out her Optik device – which would pass on her false identity – and glanced briefly at herself in the reflection of the bus's window. She'd definitely looked better, even with the change of clothes, and there wasn't much she could do about the mud on her shoes, jacket or backpack.

"Just be ready," she told Will.

"Put your Optik back," he said. "Look more clueless."

He was right. Freya returned it to her pack quickly.

The officer worked his way steadily down the bus, exchanging pleasantries as he checked identifications. It said a lot about the state of Germany that this was even happening, Freya supposed. At least it wasn't a VERT trooper.

The man reached Freya and Will. She saw him look them both over, a fractional hesitation before he smiled professionally.

"Identification?" he asked in English.

"Oh, yeah, of course," Freya said, also in English. It wasn't difficult to mask the vestiges of her Berlin accent. She'd spent her teens in Hackney and Tottenham and Islington, more than enough to pass as a Londoner.

She retrieved her Optik again, checking a few wrong pockets beforehand, and allowed the policeman to interface with it.

"I forgot my hands-on device, but you can interface with it still," Will said with an apologetic shrug, also speaking in English. "I'm guessing we still need to go through this at the airport?" The officer didn't reply, his smile remaining fixed, then disappearing as his eyes flickered, scanning through the data being transmitted.

Freya caught a green tick appearing on the small screen of the policeman's own device. Thank God. It didn't mean much though. The policeman didn't look satisfied. He scanned their Optik signatures again, before reluctantly breaking the connection.

Freya waited to see if he carried on to the next passengers. As she had feared, he moved past all of the remainder without checking them, going instead to the driver.

"Hold the bus," she overheard him say in German.

"I've got a timetable to keep to," the driver complained. "If I don't get to the airport when I'm meant to my supervisor will lose it."

"Not my problem," the policeman snarled.

He stepped off, and Freya saw his mouth moving as he patched through to someone via his Optik's audio. He was making a call.

"We're going to have to go," Freya said urgently to Will. He nodded.

"Middle door?"

"Yes. Now."

Will pushed his way through the packed bus to its central doors, then pressed the release. There was a beep, and they clattered open.

"Don't wait for him to notice," Freya said. "Just run."

For the second time in little more than a few hours, Freya found herself dashing through the streets of Berlin. Surprised tourists hurried to get out of her way, and she heard the shout of the policeman behind them.

It wasn't the worst place to try to make an escape, but the crowds on Friedrichstraße were a double-edged sword. They slowed them down, but also helped obscure them from pursuit.

They raced past Checkpoint Charlie, a heap of sandbags around a small booth, surrounded by people taking selfies with reenactors in US and Soviet military gear. Judging from the expressions, some thought Freya and Will were part of the act as they pounded past, followed by the policeman.

"Left here," Freya shouted to Will as they passed onto Kochstraße. They entered an alleyway, where Freya abruptly stopped. Will had to double back, looking frantic.

"What're you doing?" he shouted.

Freya didn't answer. The policeman came pounding round the corner and almost ran right into her.

She had the pistol out. The man froze.

"Don't move," she told him in German, then carefully shot him in the foot. The report in the confined space made Freya's ears ache. The man yelped and went down on one knee.

"Now we can go," she told Will.

They set off again. Freya had been trying to work this one out from the moment she had spotted the policeman. Northwest, towards Berlin's central train station? Or south, towards the 96, one of the main arterial roads out of Berlin?

One led even deeper into the city, and that meant more crowds, more surveillance, more security. The other would require a bit of luck and the successful thumbing of a lift or stealing of a car.

"We're going south," Freya said as they went. "Catching a ride and giving ourselves some breathing space."

She took Will in the direction of the Landwehrkanal, knowing vaguely where she was. The layout of the city was the same, but some of it was difficult to recognise, especially here in the centre. There were more electronic screens and billboards than she remembered, advertising everything from pharmaceuticals to political slogans for the upcoming elections. There was also a general air of dilapidation that Freya didn't recall, though perhaps that was due to the rosy memories of youth. Bins overflowed with refuse, and there was more graffiti, including the skull-and-circle of Reboot. The air had a cold, hard bite to it, and the general vibe would have been unwelcoming even if she and Will weren't desperately trying to get out.

They had just crossed the canal, the bridges busy, when Freya spotted a face she knew.

It was Teuton. She stood on the corner of the adjoining street, dead ahead, staring back at her. There was a split-second of mutual recognition, before Freya grabbed Will and pulled him off towards the nearest alleyway.

"Running time," she said. To his credit, Will did so without asking questions.

Freya had already had her reservations, but Helen's phone call had made it clear. M-Bahn and its leadership couldn't be trusted.

They didn't get far. Two men blocked the alleyway, both hard-faced thugs. They were the ones Freya had seen in Berghain, who had ended up in a scrap with Reboot's foot soldiers. She was about to draw her pistol, extremely thankful that she'd kept hold of it, when a voice called out behind them.

"Stop."

They both turned. Teuton approached. Even without the information gleaned from Wellend's briefing, Freya could tell from the way she walked that she was a kindred spirit. She was M-Bahn's enforcer, her build solid, her eyes cold. She was even taller than Freya.

"There's no need to make this messy," she said, stopping and raising her hands. She wore fingerless biker gloves. Freya suspected the knuckles were reinforced.

"We're M-Bahn," Teuton continued. "We're here to get you to safety."

"Nothing personal, but we'd feel a lot safer with just the two of us right now," Freya said, her heart starting to race. If this was all a setup as Helen had claimed, M-Bahn were the last people they wanted to get picked up by. They were as bad as Reboot, if not worse. They were probably working for Kaiser.

"Whatever Reboot told you, they were lying," Teuton said, as though reading her thoughts. "You came here to help us, didn't you?"

"I'm not getting in a debate right now, sweetheart," Freya said sharply, pulling the pistol. At least that checked Teuton's advance.

"Stop trying to play us for fools," Will piped up, though he kept looking nervously at the two brutes who had initially barred their path. "This is either a setup, or it's damn close to one."

"Don't make this more difficult than it needs to be," Teuton said. "We're only trying to help."

Freya was spared the need to tell her what they thought of her help by a shout that came from behind Teuton. She spun round just as another voice bellowed.

"VERT! Get your hands in the air!"

Instead, Teuton went for the pistol Freya now realised she had concealed at her back.

There were a series of thumping reports that Freya recognised as the discharge of rubber bullets. One of Teuton's henchmen in front of them cried out and dropped, clutching his leg. The altogether more fearsome discharge of Teuton's pistol followed as she returned fire.

"Go," Freya shouted at Will, charging the M-Bahn thug who was still on his feet.

"Face against the wall," she screamed at the thug, her own sidearm levelled. The man was wise enough to do so, hands splayed against the stonework. Freya hustled Will past him, and they broke into a run again as there were more shots, and a cry of pain, from behind them.

"This has really gone to hell," Will huffed.

Freya didn't waste breath replying.

The alleyway was littered with overflowing rubbish bins that they were forced to dive around. Freya aimed for the light at the end of the tunnel, until it abruptly darkened.

There were figures there, advancing on them, their silhouettes impossible to identify.

Front and behind, they were trapped.

16
Drop-In Art Session

"Nope," Freya growled, coming up short in the alleyway. Will collided with the back of her and bounced off.

"Door," Freya snapped, turning towards an entrance to their left. She booted it in and hustled inside, sidearm held low in both hands, aimed at the floor.

It was a kitchen. A pair of harried-looking chefs looked up in shock, frozen at their stations.

"Sorry," Will said breathlessly to them as they stormed past and burst through a set of double doors and into a restaurant space. It was busy with lunch goers who gasped or scrambled up from their tables. Will collided with one party, overturning their food with a crash of shattering plates.

"Come on," Freya urged with adrenaline-charged fury, once more having to grab Will and haul him through the mess. She shoulder-barged her way out of the front doors.

Once out, she looked left and right, trying to rapidly assess the situation. This street was running parallel with the alleyway, so should have seen them clear of the trap, but no such luck. There were two of the matte grey combat vehicles stamped with VERT insignia to the left. One was coming in their direction while the other had pulled over and was disgorging a team of grunts in grey and black riot gear. Some bystanders had their hands-on Optiks out and were taking it all in, while the wiser ones had begun hurrying in the opposite direction.

Freya was about to do the same, but too late. One of the dismounted VERT troopers had spotted their ungainly exit from the restaurant and was shouting.

She smacked Will on the shoulder and pointed across the street at another alleyway. This one had a set of fire escape stairs.

"Up," Freya instructed before they bolted across the roadway ahead of the oncoming VERT vehicle, ignoring the other cars that came up short with a screech of tires and a blaze of horns.

The dismounted VERT grunts began to fire at them. A rubber bullet cracked off the roadway just in front of Freya and ricocheted up to ping off a lamppost. More thrummed by, until they reached the temporary safety of the alley.

They thundered up the stairs, Freya's thoughts racing as quickly as her heartbeat. She had already scanned the street to check the rooftops were continuous, but going all the way up was a last resort. It was the surest way to find yourself stranded during escape and evasion, and besides, up there was drone territory.

They took a second-floor fire exit, emerging into a long, somewhat dingy hotel corridor.

Ahead was an internal stairwell, set alongside a pair of elevators.

Up or down? From her glance earlier, it had looked as though the hotel's entrance led out onto the same street they had just come from. There would be a back door, but finding and accessing it could take time.

"Why don't we hide in one of the rooms," Will panted as he caught up. "There's dozens!"

"We can't go to ground here," Freya growled. "They'll lock this place down, then go room to room until they have us. We've got to keep moving."

As though to emphasise her point, she caught the sound of iron-shod boots ringing on the fire exit stairs.

Up. It might have to be the roof after all.

"Just stay with me," she told Will brusquely before leading him into the stairwell. They climbed, Freya's thighs burning from the effort of the multiple ascents. Will wasn't doing well, a panting, sweating mess. She urged him on.

They reached a door that read "Roof Access – Staff Only". She kicked it open, sweeping out onto the roof beyond, gun raised.

The space was empty, a flat expanse studded by ventilation chutes and rank with weeds. They were high up here, and the wind was cold and cutting. Freya took a moment to get her bearings.

The space beyond the immediate roof to their right was open – the alleyway with the fire exit – but to their left there was only a short drop down onto the top of the neighbouring building.

Freya led the way to it. "Watch your footing," she told Will after leaping down. The central portion of the roof they were now on was flat, but it fell away to tiled slopes on either side, and there were no rails or barriers. The weeds underfoot were treacherous, and there were several skylights in a row ahead.

The sound of police sirens rose from the street beneath. The noose was tightening.

The next roof was a little higher than the one they were currently on, but not entirely beyond reach.

"Boost me," Freya said. Will cupped his hands, and she slipped the pistol into her jacket, stepped up and lunged, managing to get a fingerhold on the ledge above and haul herself up. She was becoming increasingly thankful for her Monday night workouts.

She got herself up onto the ledge, then rotated on her belly and reached down with both hands for Will.

"Jump," she called. He did so, managing to snare Freya's wrist. She hauled on him, teeth gritted, relieved he was still as skinny as when she had first met him. He managed to get a grip on the ledge too, and she heaved him over by the scruff of the neck, like a lioness with a wayward cub.

"Got to keep going," she panted. Both of them were struggling now. There was no time to stop. Make or break.

Freya had just found her feet when she heard the sound she had been dreading. An incessant, whirring buzz. Will gave her a knowing look. Before either could speak, the drone hovered into view, appearing up over the left-hand edge of the latest rooftop.

Freya didn't know the specific build, but it was clear from the colour and branding that it was a VERT counterterrorism drone. It was a bulky thing, with large twin rotors, shielded sensors, a mic, and an underslung weapon, in this case a rubber bullet launcher. It swept up to a fixed spot just above the roof and began to rotate to face them, buzzing like some great plastic and steel insect.

"The vents," Freya shouted, gesturing to the concrete chutes that studded the rooftop as she drew her pistol. Will dived towards them, Freya following while opening fire on the drone.

It didn't have quite the same effect as it had on the smaller surveillance unit she'd driven off outside the Berghain. Her shot merely sparked off one of its reinforced rotors, glancing back down onto the rooftop.

The drone returned fire. Rubber filled the air around her. She threw herself down into a skidding fall, her boots connecting with the base of the vent and bringing her to a halt in cover next to Will as a salvo of non-lethal rounds battered off the rooftop behind her.

"It'll circle round to get an angle on us, be ready to move when it does," she panted. The only blessing was that it couldn't be carrying much in the way of ammunition. One more burst, maybe two, and then all it could do was track them.

"Give me your Optik," Will said urgently.

Freya shot him a look. "Why?"

"I don't ask you questions about running, so don't ask me questions about Optiks," Will shouted, frantic now. "Just give it to me!"

Freya passed him the device. He seemed to be linking it to his own remote Optik.

"You are surrounded," blared a voice in German over the CT drone's microphone "Lay down your firearms and come out with your hands up."

Considerately, it repeated the command in English. More importantly, Freya heard the pitch of its rotors change. It was coming around.

"This is going to take a minute," Will said. "I've already tried to jam it, but it didn't work."

"We don't have that long," Freya responded. "It's coming from our left. Move right with me."

They edged around the ventilation chute, Will glancing between his phone and the sky. Freya caught the edge of the drone, and hustled Will into cover as another rubber bullet, just a single round this time, bounced past.

"I'm downloading what I need," Will explained. "It'll stop it!"

Freya didn't have time to lambast him. Right now, she was all out of ideas, besides keeping the chute between them and the drone. Abruptly, even that fell through. She looked up, and realised it was rising over them, getting an angle where they would have no cover.

"Just hurry." She moved off to one side and standing up. All she could do now was distract it. "This has all been a big misunderstanding," she shouted, then shot it again. "Or maybe not."

The bullet did as much damage as the last one. She stared down the barrel of its launcher, trying to recall the lethality statistics for being hit by rubber rounds.

Suddenly, Will was in front of her. He held her commandeered Optik device up like an exorcist with a crucifix. The drone dipped lower, practically on top of them now, the whirring of its large rotors eclipsing everything else. But it didn't shoot them.

"What… did you do?" Freya asked. She tried to access whatever Will had downloaded, but that part was now locked to her.

"Took a gamble," Will answered. Keeping the Optik up, he edged towards the neighbouring roof, grabbing Freya's wrist with his free hand to keep her close.

"It's been modified, but the chassis of that drone is the standard type five CT drone model used by most western law enforcement agencies," he went on, still moving cautiously. "I have access to software that makes this Optik's hands-on device appear on its scanners as a friendly piece of hardware. Another VERT drone. It used to work on the drones in London before the latest CTOS update closed the back door on it. I've read online that Erik Gerhardt doesn't trust CTOS 3.0, so I took a gamble that this particular device wouldn't be operating up-to-date CTOS protection. It wasn't. Whatever it's running on, it's still susceptible to this particular trick."

Freya was suddenly glad Will was with her.

"About time you did something useful, instead of just getting dragged about," she said. "We need to make it across to the next rooftop, then down."

"The drone's operator will be able to override the weapons lock and fire it manually," Will said. "But they'll need codes and authorisation for that. It'll take them… probably another ninety seconds."

"Then what are we waiting for?"

Together, they turned and ran.

Ahead was a sloping slate roof. Freya wasn't entirely certain they could make it up the angle, but they didn't have a choice. She pocketed her pistol and hit the slope at full tilt, throwing herself forward. Will did likewise, struggling with the Optik still in one hand.

The momentum carried them both halfway up. Freya scrabbled against the cold slates, hurting her fingers, her shoes slipping desperately. She lunged for the edge of the next roof, Will half-falling next to her, both on all fours.

Freya barely made it. Before rolling over, she lashed her arm back and snagged Will.

Just in time. The drone shifted to keep them in its sights but didn't advance.

Freya and Will dropped into a square space, but this one was devoid of cover. No ventilation, no stairway doors, just a hatch. That, and a large skylight in the centre, divided into sections by metal struts and slightly raised up from the roof's level.

She moved to the edge of it and looked down. Below was an open room, figures moving around its edges. Freya tried to make out what they were doing – seemingly, all looking at the walls. Will crawled up beside her.

"Art gallery," he said.

That made sense. Freya realised there were paintings. More importantly, there was a bench in the middle of the room, and it was currently unoccupied.

The drone was now back above them, and probably seconds from being fully armed.

"Please don't tell me you're about to –" Will started to say, but Freya had no time. She dragged him into the central section of the reinforced skylight, drew her pistol and aimed directly down.

"Jacket up," she said.

"This is getting ridiculous," he said, pulling his hood up.

With what she suspected was her last bullet, Freya shot the glass between their shoes.

It gave way with a crash.

At the same time, she heard the whump of the drone's underslung launcher, discharging.

She fell, that horrid, gut-wrenching sense of dislocation lasting seconds, and hit the padded leather of the bench in the middle of the art gallery, alongside Will and a hail of broken glass. She felt slashing pains in the back of her skull, her thigh, and the back of her hand.

For a second all was confusion. She fought to breathe, trying not to give in to panic, uncertain yet as to whether she had broken anything. She was aware of screaming, and the crunch of shattered glass.

Will was still beside her on the collapsed seating. He bled from the scalp, and his jacket had been torn in multiple places by the hail of shards they had fallen through.

Freya's was much the same. She got to her feet. Blood ran from her injuries, and they hurt like hell, though neither were as bad as her thigh, where a piece of glass was still impaled.

Snarling, she hauled the shredded jacket off and used it to

pull out the glass in her leg before tossing it aside. Blood welled up, but it wasn't as bad as she had first feared. It had missed the artery.

Everything around them was chaos. The metal struts of the skylight had ensured only the central portion they had been standing on had given way when she had shot it, meaning those around the edge of the room, where everyone had been gathered, had avoided the worst of the deadly rain. Nevertheless, the place was in turmoil.

The exits were rammed. To their credit, several bystanders came towards them rather than try to push their way out. One elderly man offered Freya an arm to lean on. They thought it had been an accident.

She had lost her grip on the gun, and spotted it lying under the broken bench. Not much use now. Will had retrieved her Optik device, and a quick glance confirmed her link was unbroken, though he looked stunned and the blood from his scalp gash was blinding him in one eye.

Despite it all, they couldn't stop.

"Thank you, sir," Freya told the man helping her, and likewise a woman who was assisting Will in getting to his feet. "You should get out though."

The man nodded. Freya moved to Will's side, making him look at her with his one good eye.

"Good to go?" she demanded. She saw his vision focus properly.

"I think I twisted my wrist," he said, holding up one arm.

"As long as your legs still work. Come on."

Keep going. That was the only thing that was going to get them out of this. Sheer, bloody-minded determination. Freya had always been good at that.

She led Will, hissing with pain as the movement exacerbated her leg injury.

"You're limping," Will pointed out.

"Thanks, Sherlock," she responded, turning left along another gallery that was rapidly emptying. An alarm rang. Blood poured down the back of her neck from the head cut, warm and cloying. Will clutched at his own scalp with his one good hand as they went.

They emerged into what appeared to be the art gallery's front foyer, a set of stairs ahead of them leading to the front doors and a ticket booth. No way out there though. Armed VERT troopers were already hustling in, fighting against the tide of people.

They spotted Freya and Will. One shouted at them to stand still, the other raised his rifle, a G36, and fired. The bullet – a real one this time, not rubber – ripped through a painting on the wall just to Freya's left.

"Oh, now they're serious," Will said. Freya grabbed him and doubled back out of the line of fire.

They reached a set of stairs and descended, with mounting pain, to a rear door. Freya realised she was leaving a blood trail. Her leg went numb.

Don't stop. Don't stop.

Out, through the door. Sunlight hit her, and the smell of refuse. Another back alley.

Except this one was full of VERT troopers.

She stumbled to a halt with half-a-dozen G36 rifles pointed in her face. There were more on the other side of the alleyway, and the thudding of boots from behind announced yet more grunts closing in through the gallery.

"Hands against the wall," one of the VERT troopers bellowed, waving furiously. "Right now!"

Instead, Freya just sat down where she was, and swore.

It was over.

"It's over," Teuton panted via her Optik, double-checking back along the side street that there were no more signs of pursuit.

There was silence on the other end of the connection. Teuton had expected another diatribe from Revolver or Luther and had been primed to respond just as angrily. This was the third time the target had slipped away from her. She would not make the same mistake again.

The next time she met Freya Bauer, regardless of orders, she was going to kill her. It was the least she owed her.

"Askari wants to see us," said the voice of Luther over the Optik. "All of us, at the villa."

He sounded far more concerned than angry, and Teuton understood why. A meeting with "Askari" wasn't what any of them wanted right now.

At least it wasn't just her that was going. That was bad news for the other two.

"When?" she asked.

"Two hours from now."

"He thinks I can make it halfway across town in two hours with half of the damn Defenders looking for me? They've got the target!"

"I know, we picked it up on the street cams. Just get to the Tempelhof safe house, get a change of clothes, and get on a damn bus. And for God's sake don't be late. That's the last thing we need."

Luther hung up before Teuton could respond. She hissed with frustration. Then again, maybe Luther was wrong.

Maybe a meeting with her father was in order after all.

•••

Freya and Will were cuffed and hustled into a VERT jeep.

"Not ideal," Will grunted. He had hissed when he had been handcuffed, his injured wrist responding badly to the restraints. It was a struggle for Freya to ignore the pain of her own wounds. At least the gash in her thigh appeared to have clotted.

"What the hell are we going to do now?" Will asked. He sounded as hopeless as Freya felt, but she let her anger fire her.

"It wasn't my idea to come out here," she said.

"Yeah, well I didn't exactly anticipate things turning out like this!"

"No speaking," a VERT trooper sitting in the front of the jeep snapped. Another reached in while the rear doors were still open and tugged a black bag down over Will's head, before moving round to the vehicle's other side.

Freya's world went dark.

17
First Impressions

It was difficult to say how long the journey took, though Freya did her best to count the seconds. This wasn't the first time she had been snatched and hooded. Counting out time was a good way of staying calm, and it helped combat the disorientating sensation of being driven while blind.

She got to approximately twenty-five minutes before she felt the jeep come to a halt. The doors opened and hands grabbed her, manhandling her out. She clenched her teeth as the pain in her leg surged, forced to keep up with the pace of those leading her.

There was the scrape of a door and the unintelligible squawk of a radio set. She was shoved forward, her feet scuffing off an uneven, hard floor.

"Chair," said a voice. "Sit."

She was turned around and planted on the seat. Her hands were uncuffed, but only to be restrained once more around the chair's back.

"What do you think you're doing?" she demanded in English. "You can't do this to me. I'm just on holiday."

The ruse was probably pointless, especially considering, if she really had been an innocent tourist, she would have been acting in a far more distressed manner. Still, there was no incentive to come clean just yet.

There was the sound of boots and the noise of a door followed by what she took to be a locking buzzer. Then silence, abrupt and unwelcome.

This was exactly what she had been hoping to avoid. Falling into the hands of VERT was bad news. She would have to fall back on contingencies she had laid out before coming to Berlin, and most of those involved some degree of negotiation or bargaining. She didn't have many cards left to play.

She lost track of her second counting around the forty-minute mark. It seemed as though she had been separated from Will – she felt alone.

Just a standard interrogation technique, designed to soften her up. Leave the prisoner for a while to stew. Well, Freya had developed a hard counter to that kind of gameplay.

After almost twenty-four hours on the run and zero rest, she settled her thoughts, embraced the silence, and went to sleep.

Freya woke up when they pulled the bag off.

She blinked, and discovered she was in what looked disturbingly like a medieval dungeon. Most of the walls were jagged stone, much of it mossy or full of weeds. The floor was no better, though, incongruously, the ceiling consisted of a pane of glass that showed the grey, open sky beyond, and the far side of the cell was likewise glass – including a doorway. Both of those, however, were opaque.

Freya was cuffed to a metal chair in the room's centre. Two other figures were present, one male, one female, both in black fatigues and combat rigs devoid of unit insignia or patches. They both wore black buffs around the lower halves of their faces.

Freya looked around, trying to work out where she was. The air smelled musky and damp. This wasn't entirely what she had been expecting, and it took a moment to collect her thoughts.

Admit nothing. Remember, it will only get worse if you do.

The glass door opened, and a third figure strode in before it closed and locked behind him. This one wore the same black kit as the other two, but his face was bare. He was in his fifties, square jawed and blunt-featured, like a block of stone hewn to resemble a man, then weathered by the cares of time's passage. Broad-shouldered and firmly built, he walked in with that swagger that marked a man accustomed to power. He looked at Freya with a smile as cold and hard as the rock face to her back.

"Freya Bauer," he said. "It's been a long time."

Harriet Parks was going back to university.

Her first stint, a few years before, hadn't lasted very long. After six weeks at Manchester, she had decided that droning lectures and overfilled tutorial classes weren't for her. Why go through that when she could easily just falsify a degree or two?

Academia might not appeal, but she was confident she could pretend it did. Before catching the morning train from London to Bristol she hacked into the university's systems and printed off everything she'd need to make it look convincing. Timetables and course notes for the linguistics class she was supposedly enrolled on, plus a convincing array of notebooks – complete with all sorts of stickers, Post-its, and pens.

On the train she took a much-needed nap before catching a bus from Bristol's station to the location of her first class at the uni's Priory Road complex. She knew she probably looked tired, but that was pretty in keeping with the whole student vibe. She was running off excitement. She hadn't done anything like this for a while.

The only downside was that if she messed up, a teenager would likely end up dead.

No pressure then. Her first priority was identifying Andrew. Once that was done, she could start watching for people that were watching him.

She reached the Priory Road lecture building and called Helen.

"Excited for your first day at uni?" Helen asked her.

"Buzzing," Harriet said. "Will you come visit me?"

"Not if you're living in student digs. I had enough of those while I was at studying engineering at Imperial."

"What about a hotel?"

"I could be persuaded. Stay in touch?"

"I'll message you when I make contact."

She had assessed the main Priory Road building before arrival, so she could look like she knew where she was going. She arrived fifteen minutes before Andrew's first class was due to start, and did a surreptitious scan. There was no sign of anything untoward, no figures that drew her attention hanging about outside the lecture theatre or in the adjoining café.

It wasn't long before she spotted Andrew. He was taller than she had imagined, and a little stooped over. Shy-looking, just her type.

"Hello, boyfriend," she murmured to herself, and set off towards him.

"I've never met you before," Freya said to the man. She knew his face though, from Wellend's briefing. Erik Gerhardt, VERT supremo. No reason to admit as much.

"You have, but you were young at the time. It is unsurprising that you don't remember. I was paying a visit to your father."

"I doubt that. Where is my friend, Simon?" Freya asked, using Will's false name.

"William Fraser is being held nearby," Erik said, his confident use of Will's true identity enough to alarm Freya. It seemed VERT were well informed. That didn't mean she was suddenly about to crumble though.

"He's your ex-husband, isn't he?" the man went on. "I was married too, once. An insufferable woman. She would say the same about me, and worse. The only difference was, she was right."

"I have no idea what you're talking about," Freya said. "My name is Amanda Carter, and I want to speak to a lawyer."

The man laughed, then nodded to the woman standing off to one side. She punched Freya. It hurt, but the sudden pain helped kickstart her defiance.

"Who the hell do you think you are?" she snarled, doing her best to maintain the pretence of her false identity. "I'm a British citizen! You can't do this!"

"Actually I can, regardless of whatever foreign nationality you're claiming as your own today," the man said. "New laws allow me to detain a select group of wanted criminals, yourself included, for a period of seventy-two hours without recourse to anything, lawyers included. Of course, international and EU law will have something to say about that, but the wheels of bureaucracy turn so slowly?

"Now perhaps we can cease these games, and you can begin answering a few questions. William has already provided some valuable information, but I'd like to cross-reference it."

"What have you done to him?"

"Kept him awake with some friendly encouragement. My

colleagues have been working on him since you arrived here. Nearly five hours now. Several of them wanted to do the same to you, but I ordered them to let you rest. It looked like you needed it."

He was playing with her. She forced herself to keep her emotions in check. There was no point in worrying about Will until she had done something to change the dynamic between her and Erik.

"You said you had questions, so ask them," she said. Erik walked around her, looking her up and down as he did so, letting the silence stretch. More games.

Eventually, he spoke.

"What are DedSec planning in Berlin?"

"I don't know what–"

Erik's other henchman punched her. She spat on his boots, and he raised his fist to strike again, but Erik checked him.

"Playtime is over, Freya," he said. "If we're going to make any progress here, you're going to drop this half-baked charade. I know exactly who you are. I suspect you know very little about me though. Perhaps we can change that."

That there was a proper hit, well struck and landing hard. The bag over the head, the cuffs, the grim-looking cell, the waiting, the casual interrogation style, the punches – Freya had seen it all before. That didn't mean it held no fear for her, it didn't mean she could resist it forever, but she had never responded positively to brute force. Erik, however, could use something more potent. Her curiosity.

"How did you know my father?"

"You don't ask questions here, Miss Bauer. Answer mine, and maybe we can have a civilised discussion."

Freya pretended to think about it. Then she told Erik to go to hell.

His expression hardened.

"I hope, for your sake, that you hate your ex-husband," he said. "I'm going to see how much more amenable William is to these questions."

"I thought you said he'd already answered them," Freya said with a smile. "That you just wanted to cross-reference?"

Erik said nothing more, but turned and left. Freya expected his two VERT henchmen to start weighing in on her, but they went with him.

Once more, she was left to the silence.

Will twitched as the bag was pulled away. He hadn't remembered dozing off – his stress levels had been too high, but at some point he must have. He grimaced in the light, looking around at the strange space he found himself in.

It only took him a few moments to work it out. He looked at the person who had pulled off his hood, a man seemingly built using the definition of "grizzled brute".

"A zoo," Will said, trying to banish fear with the observation. The man looked unimpressed. He was accompanied by two other figures, all in the same grey and black fatigues, but the duo stood back while the man hit him.

"You're a smart one, which bodes well for both of us," the man snarled, snatching Will by the jaw and turning his head back to face him. "My name is Erik Gerhardt. Yours is William Fraser, and you're going to confirm for me what your accomplice in the other cell has already told us."

Will was so terrified, he found himself speechless. Erik – the head of VERT, Will realised – let go of him and took a step back, seeming to compose himself.

"And yes, it was intended to be a zoo. I believe you are essentially the equivalent of an intelligence officer in your organisation? So, I take it you know the location of the Vertidiger's headquarters? Where are we right now?"

"DedSec isn't an organisation, it's a movement," Will found himself saying with a courage he didn't feel.

Erik looked at him darkly, then snapped a finger at one of his henchmen. The man pulled free a combat knife with a hooked tip and approached, roughly snatching hold of Will's hair.

"Hold still, if you want to keep your eye," the man grunted as Will protested, before pain flared in front of his ear. He cried out, but the grip remained firm, keeping him in place.

After a few seconds, the man stepped back. Will groaned, instinctively wanting to clutch at the wound but unable to with his hands still bound. He felt blood run hot down his neck. Only when the man passed something to Erik did he realise that he had been excising his Optik implant.

Or at least, that's what he thought he had been doing.

Erik held up the bloody little chip and snapped it between forefinger and thumb.

"You're a hacker, but you'll struggle without your interface," he said. "Now you're really on your own, William Fraser. So how about you start answering my questions, and stop trying to be smart? Maybe describe to me where we are right now. Prove that you have the potential to be useful."

Will tried to fight down the tide of fear and panic threatening to overwhelm him. His ear and cheek throbbed, but in a way it was a relief – Erik had made a mistake. Will's Optik implant, at least the one visible where most Optik implants were, was fake. The dud had been installed just for situations like these. The real one was completely subdermal, in front of the other ear. His interface remained undetected. Perhaps VERT weren't so clever after all.

"Well?" Erik demanded dangerously. Will began to speak, homing in on the facts, using them to straighten out his thoughts.

"Since a series of large donations from several parties in the Bundestag, der Vertidiger have been headquartered at the former Flaktower 3, Humboldthain park, one of a number of large defensive structures built by the Nazis to defend Berlin from Allied air raids during World War Two."

He spoke the information by rote. Erik seemed unmoved.

"Why are you being held in a repurposed wildlife enclosure then?" he asked.

"There was a brief attempt to build an extension to Berlin Zoo in the grounds of Humboldthain park," Will said, using the recitation of knowledge to try and calm his nerves. "Flaktower 1 was actually built near the Berlin Zoo, but was demolished soon after the war. The attempted zoo expansion alongside the remains of Flaktower 3 was scrapped before the public opening."

Erik grunted. "So, you've done your reading. I suspect you know less than you think though. If you really were smart, you would have stayed in London, instead of trying to bring your brand of anarchy to Germany."

Will didn't reply. He was wondering where Freya was, and how long he could hold out on his own. Erik had claimed she had already given him information, but he couldn't believe that. She wouldn't break under interrogation, not unless they had something on her, something more subtle than brute force.

"Why is DedSec in Berlin?" Erik asked.

Will began to tell him he didn't know what he was talking about, but Erik punched him again, making his vision sway and his jaw ache.

"You don't seem to understand the situation here, so let me spell it out," the VERT commander snarled. "Nobody knows you're here. Nobody's coming to rescue you. No law is going to see you released. There are only two ways out of here. The first is in a body bag, the second is with my blessing. To earn that, you're going to have to give me what I want. Is that clear?"

Will tried to swallow his fear. He knew fine well they were trying to intimidate him, but understanding that didn't make it any easier. He tried to do what he always did when faced with a challenge – think it through logically.

"I have information you need," he said. "Information about the hacker organisations operating in this city."

Erik laughed humourlessly.

"You think you're in a position to negotiate? We'll soon beat that misconception out of you."

"Information gained under duress is rarely wholly reliable," Will said. "Someone suffering interrogation will typically only give out enough to reduce their punishment, or will be economical with the truth. But if you give me a reason to help you, I'm far more likely to put the effort in."

Will thought Erik was going to hit him again, but instead he crossed his arms, glaring down at him.

"What do you want then?" he asked eventually. "For your cooperation?"

"Freya goes free. You take her and you drop her off at Berlin airport, no questions asked."

"You think anything you can tell us is worth giving up a DedSec operative like her? I know the role you both played in the end of Albion. I will not allow that to happen here, to Vertidiger. You came here to destroy us, and the safer, more secure Germany we are trying to build."

"I came here to close my DedSec account," Will clarified, warming to his words now. "Clearly, I'm not in much of a position to be doing anything about VERT's influence with the German government anymore."

"Playing the disaffected card won't get you far," Erik said. "If you want me to release Freya, you had best be offering something tangible. Something actionable."

"I can give you that, and more," Will said. "If you let her go, I'll help you get the drop on the hacker groups here who've been evading you. M-Bahn, Reboot, Bulwark. I know how those sorts of outfits operate. I have what you need to shut them down for good."

"You'll betray DedSec?" Erik asked.

"Not DedSec. There's no DedSec presence in this city besides the two of us. We're no threat to you, unlike the local German groups. And DedSec aren't your problem right now. You've got more pressing matters."

"Then why are you here?"

"We were sent to provide assistance to one group in particular," Will said, trying to decide how much to give away. "But they weren't what we were expecting."

"Go on."

"Not until we come to some sort of agreement. Freya goes free."

"How noble, to offer yourself to us in exchange for the liberty of your ex. I wonder if she would do the same for you?"

Will had been wondering that too. Right now though, personal feelings didn't come into it. Freya was the one being targeted here. As long as she was in Berlin, her life was in the firing line. Besides, Andrew was in danger too, and if it came down to it Will had to admit Freya would be better at protecting him than he ever could be. She had tried to reassure him that Helen Dashwood would keep their son safe, but with the knowledge someone might be out to destroy the Bauer family it was still cold comfort. The sooner they got Freya back to the UK the better.

"If you do free her, I can show you the backdoor weaknesses on CTOS that we exploit, plus the one I used on whatever system your drones are running. And I'll give you locations and good fits for all the hacker groups operating in this country. Together, we could wipe them out in a day."

Erik looked at him intensely. Will felt sick with nerves, but he refused to show it.

Abruptly, Erik motioned at one of the guards. Will tensed, afraid he was coming back with the knife, but instead the man reached into one of his fatigue pockets and drew out an Optik hands-on device. It was Freya's, he realised. It had been seized when they had been captured.

"Open it," Erik told him, tossing it into his lap as the other guard moved behind him and took off his restraints. He hissed as his sprained wrist was twisted further.

"I don't know the passcode," he said. "It's not mine."

"If you lie to me one more time, I'm going to break your nose."

"Right, well then..." Will trailed off, rubbing tentatively at his wrist. He knew how to access the physical part of Freya's Optik and knew that doing so would allow VERT to get to the actual data that Freya still had logged on her own chip. They could try to force the chip remotely, but he doubted they had the hacker expertise for that. Going in via the device would be much faster.

He began to tap in a series of numbers into the Optik's screen. He did know her code but, more importantly, he knew she had a DedSec wipeout program installed. It would clean the device, rendering it useless and leaving Freya's information accessible only via her chip. It gave DedSec activists a chance to erase any links between themselves and the movement when they found themselves in a tight spot.

"It's got wiping failsafes inbuilt," he said, feeling a moment's relief as the screen unlocked to reveal a blank home display. "Must have required her fingerprints, or direct proximity to her implant. You won't get anything from it."

Will passed the device back to Erik, who looked through it briefly, unimpressed.

"You'll need to work harder in the future if you want to guarantee your own freedom," he said.

"I will," Will lied. "But let Freya go."

"Perhaps," Erik said. "I'm not in the habit of negotiating with my prisoners, especially when they're members of an international terrorist organisation like DedSec. Luckily for you, I already owe Freya Bauer."

That surprised Will, but he was too cautious to ask about it.

"Did she talk about her father, when you were married?" Erik went on.

"Not often, no."

"You know that he was murdered here, in Berlin?"

"Yes."

"Do you know who did it?"

"No."

"I do. I know why as well. I'm not sure Freya does."

"Now you're the one playing games," Will dared say. Erik's expression darkened, but he made no aggressive moves.

"I'm going to go and have another talk with your ex," he said. "And you're going to be moved to somewhere a little more salubrious. One of the bunk rooms. You'll be working for us now."

"Agreed," Will said, daring to hope they had arrived at some sort of understanding. "As long as Freya goes free."

"We'll see how our chat goes," Erik said. "I'm not sure she'll enjoy it."

"Thought you would leave me to stew for a little longer than that," Freya said as Erik and his underlings stepped back into the cell.

The head of the Vertidiger said nothing, but gestured. One of the subordinates moved towards Freya. She braced her gut for a punch, but to her surprise the woman stepped behind her. There was a click, and her cuffs slid off.

"William is more intelligent than you, Freya Bauer," Erik told her.

"I'm sure he'd absolutely love to hear that," Freya answered, bringing her sore wrists round and rubbing at them.

"He's giving us what we want, so we're giving him what he wants. Your freedom."

Freya experienced an unexpected bout of anger. What the hell was he doing? Did he not think she could handle this? Didn't he trust her to work a way out for both of them?

"What has he offered?" she asked sharply.

"A way into the groups undermining civil order in this country. Having someone familiar with the operations of organisations like Reboot will make for an excellent asset. We have been attempting to turn a senior member for a long time, and this is almost as good."

Freya realised the other VERT grunt carried her backpack. He unzipped it and dropped it at Erik's feet. Erik then leaned down and retrieved Freya's wallet from within.

"Ordinarily, I would not have negotiated with William," he said as he glanced through Freya's cards. A small smile passed across his face. "But I do believe in honouring debts, and I have owed one to your family for some time now. To your father, specifically."

The supposed connection had been plaguing Freya since Erik had first mentioned it, far more potent than the blows and threats she had been dealt. She managed to avoid reacting. It wouldn't do any good at this stage.

"These forgeries are barely passable," Erik carried on, glancing through the cards in Freya's wallet – Amanda Carter's cards. "Your father's work, now there was real talent. I've seen genuine documentation that was less convincing than some of the identities he created."

"Stop toying with me," Freya snarled, her anger continuing to build. Erik looked at her, and to her surprise his expression softened. There was no aggression or brute disdain. Freya realised he had come across the photo of her as a child.

"Not toying, not any longer," he said, his tone matter-of-fact now. "You don't know about Thomas's past, do you? You don't know why he died?"

"He fell foul of the wrong sort of people," Freya said, turning defensive. She didn't want this, she realised. She didn't want to discover that an authoritarian brute like Erik Gerhardt had known her father well enough to have information about the cause of his untimely end.

"That is true, but it was more specific than that," Erik said. "Thomas Bauer was an informer."

18
Second Impressions

The Ghost had to decide how he would do it.

That was all part of the fun. He sat, scrolling through Andrew Bauer's social media, ignored by everyone else in the busy campus café. It was an open plan space that made up part of Bristol University's Priory Road complex, alive with the chatter of classmates and the patter of keyboards. The Ghost was too old to pass without notice as a student, but he was not too old for the university estates department polo neck he had on. It was amazing what you could buy at thrift shops.

The Ghost disliked students. British, German, or anywhere else, they were united by their entitlement and their conviction that anyone should care about their youthful, malformed opinions. How quickly those around him would cease their inane chatter if they knew there was a wolf such as he among their flock.

It just so happened that their arrogant attitude also meant they wouldn't spare a glance at someone on the minimum wage, responsible for cleaning and tending to the environment they inhabited. That made his current disguise ideal. A groundskeeper on his lunch break, nothing more.

He ignored those around him as they ignored him, instead focusing on his Optik's retinal display. More specifically, his prey. Andrew Bauer. It was like looking at a younger version of Thomas, resurrected from the dead. It made his fingers itch. He needed to kill him. He could admit it was more than a job. It was an obsession.

Andrew hadn't been his first port of call in the UK. He had initially intended to track down and eliminate the mother of the family, Belinda. The location of her flat had been supplied to him by Kaiser's anonymous DedSec informant, but finding the old woman hadn't been as simple as he had hoped. A knock at her front door had gone unanswered, and two days spent remotely viewing the block via the wasp drone he had bought had shown no sign of Belinda coming or going. He had even asked her elderly next-door neighbour, who had claimed she had gone on holiday. The trail was cold.

In frustration, he had turned to finding out just who Kaiser's DedSec informant was, intending to ensure that he wasn't being double-crossed. Teuton had eventually agreed to give him intelligence that led to a prominent hacker named Wellend, though the Ghost had stopped short of contacting him directly. He knew his face, and that was enough, for now.

Thankfully, finding Andrew Bauer had been easier. It had been a simple thing to hack into Bristol's student database. The Ghost had found the courses Andrew was enrolled on. From those he had constructed his timetable, finding which lectures he was attending.

One was about to finish. The Ghost had placed himself strategically across from the theatre's doors. He nursed a coffee and scrolled through his online presence.

The girlfriend was a complication, but hardly so. He would kill her as well. From what he had seen on Andrew's social media, they certainly looked smitten.

The Ghost had never had a long-term partner. He struggled to keep them, it seemed. He had never allowed it to get him down, though. There were other passions in life.

The lecture theatre began to empty. The Ghost maintained the pretence he was eyeballing his Optik's readings, but his attention was now firmly on the crowd of chattering, oblivious youths spilling out into the foyer and the adjoining café.

Andrew was amongst them. It was the first time the Ghost had seen him in the flesh. It sent a thrill through him, and made his guts twist with equal parts loathing and excitement. He truly did look like his grandfather. His vitality, his smile – the Ghost hadn't anticipated just how much it would affect him. Killing Thomas Bauer had been a job, nothing more. Killing his family had become a quest, a personal crusade that was threatening to mark its third decade in the coming years. And now, at last, the freshest, greenest shoot of the Bauer tree stood before his shears.

His girlfriend, the person spattered across so much of Andrew's online presence, had been with him during the lecture, and now walked with him, laughing at something he had said. Her name was Sara, and she wore a black leather jacket over a mustard-coloured jumper, a tartan skirt and tights. According to the Ghost's online findings, they had met on this course, and had been together for almost a year.

The Ghost decided he would definitely kill her as well. Kaiser wouldn't care. He knew this was more than just an assignment. It was vengeance. It couldn't be more personal for either himself or for Kaiser.

The pair paused close to the main doors leading out onto the campus. They exchanged some more pleasantries, and then, to the Ghost's mild surprise, they parted. Andrew headed outside, while Sara came towards him.

The Ghost did nothing. There was no panic. Why would there be? He was a university employee on a work break, finishing the last of his crappy campus coffee.

As he had anticipated, Sara wasn't actually coming towards him. She moved past, and sat down at an unoccupied table, as oblivious to his presence as everyone else around him. The only issue was that the seat unintentionally put her in his only blind spot – he had chosen his own table carefully, and it was the best in the café for watching the lecture hall entrance without being observed in turn. Now though, he felt abruptly vulnerable.

He blink-opened the GBB news app and scrolled through it for a while, finishing the dregs of his coffee. It was time to go, but he made sure he gave it a few minutes. Contrary to his appearance, he was hyperaware of the girlfriend's presence. She had pulled out a laptop and was animatedly typing away, a sheaf of what he assumed were handwritten course notes on one side. After a while she got up and went to the counter to order.

Time to exit. The Ghost picked up his coffee cup and minimised his Optik HUD before standing and walking out. The cup was empty, but nobody knew that. He didn't want to leave a trail, even in a café bin.

He still hadn't decided how he was going to do it. But he knew one thing.

It was going to be soon.

Pretty sure our potential psycho murder-assassin man was sitting at a table in front of me, Harriet messaged Helen after sitting back down with her chai latte.

The grey-haired man had left. Harriet didn't follow him.

Doing so would run the risk of being made right away – it was dangerous enough that she had taken a seat so close to him. The fact that time had elapsed between his exit and Andrew's made her confident he didn't intend to swoop on him right away. She had managed to get a few pictures with the camera fitted into the logo of her laptop's back, but none of them had a good angle. Still, it was better than nothing.

Under six feet, grey hair, a little stubble? came Helen's reply.

Yep. He was passing himself off as staff. Pretending to be at the uni.

That makes two of you then.

That much was true. This first phase of the plan had gone without a hitch. She had walked into the lecture theatre like she belonged and sat down next to Andrew. In a class of over a hundred, nobody checked whether or not she was a student, or was supposed to be in the room.

Andrew hadn't interacted with her – he was clearly too shy to say hi first – but confidence had never been something Harriet lacked. They had exchanged pleasantries and she told him she had just transferred from an outside class in computing. He had said his dad was good with computers, to which Harriet – or Sara, as she was calling herself – had acted mildly interested.

I'm sending you the pics I got, but they're not great, she messaged Helen.

I'll get to work on the composition right now, then hopefully we can get a match, Helen responded. *Look after yourself, dearie.*

It's Andrew I'm worried about, Harriet wrote back. *He seems like a nice kid.*

That's a relief, since he's your boyfriend. You're going to have to teach him something about online security.

That made Harriet smile. Combining their abilities, she and Helen had really done one over on Andrew's online presence.

Thankfully, he didn't have a huge online footprint – probably partly due to the influence of his mother, according to Helen – so bolting his socials had been the only necessary step towards altering the oxymoron that was "online reality".

The phrase "bolting" involved locking someone out of their social media. There was more to the plan than just that though. Helen successfully manufactured fake messages to Andrew's email claiming there had been a security breach, and that his account had been suspended for forty-eight hours while the problem was rectified.

After this they had cloned his account, hidden the real one from the search function, and started to apply changes. Andrew was in a relationship with a girl named Sara Smith. Andrew had been with Sara for just under a year. Andrew had recently visited the Greek island of Paros with Sara.

Andrew had photos with Sara. An impromptu shoot with Harriet, and some Photoshop wizardry, and suddenly she – or more accurately, Sara – was a part of Andrew's life. There they were, in a Greek restaurant, and again eating ice creams on Brighton Pier, and again, on last month's Freshers Week pub crawl. There were retrospectively added birthday well-wishes, life milestones, photo tags, most of them uploaded mere hours before but date-tagged to pop up much earlier. Harriet was even still adding some, pretending to check the course book laid out next to her laptop every so often.

It was shallow, but it all added up. Harriet hoped it would be just enough to stop whoever had been sent to hunt down the Bauers from becoming suspicious about her presence around Andrew. She needed to be as close as possible to him to protect him, and to make direct contact with his hunter. There was no way they were going to be able to ID the assassin while keeping

Andrew safe remotely. Now, anyone following the real Andrew would still only be friends with his real, unchanged profile, but anyone searching for Andrew would only discover the lucky, hitched Andrew going out with Sara Smith. And that included their hitman.

I'm going to go check outside Andrew's flat, make sure he's not been tailed then get some surveillance set up, Harriet sent to Helen, finishing her chai. *Let me know if you get an ID.*

The message went unread for a few minutes. That was unusual for Helen. Harriet already had a sneaking suspicion the news, when it reached her, wouldn't be good. It sounded as though Freya had gotten herself and her family snagged up in something real bad.

Harriet shrugged off the sense of foreboding and headed out.

19
The Haunting

Teuton expected herself, Luther, and Revolver to meet Kaiser in his office, but instead they were directed by the doorman to the east wing of the Jägerhalle.

She was nervous. Despite the whole setup being in place, everything had gone wrong. She felt like it was her fault, even though she knew it wasn't.

She should have been allowed to kill Freya when she had first set eyes on her.

The east wing of the Jägerhalle was a wide, open space, with a black-and-white tiled floor and plenty of light pouring in through a series of tall windows.

Old game trophies proliferated throughout the villa, but this room was their epicentre. There were head and pelts, elephant tusks and tortoise shells and the jaws of crocodiles. Nor were the animals relegated to the wall. There were half-a-dozen full, stuffed predators arrayed on plinths, two lions, a cheetah, a hyena, a leopard, and a crocodile.

To anyone with a sense of humanity it was a macabre display, and even Teuton, who didn't really find opposition to animal cruelty high on her list of personal convictions, always felt uncomfortable beneath the blank, dead stare of the legion of exterminated wildlife. She suspected that was why Kaiser was seeing his three M-Bahn heads in that room in particular.

The crime lord was standing at a table at the far end of the room, dressed in his usual white suit and trousers and sorting through what looked like a pile of old junk. Besides the usual vices of a man of his occupation, Emil Kaiser was fascinated by African big game hunting. He had inherited it from his grandfather, another Emil Kaiser, who had once been a colonial official in Germany's fledgling empire, before the outbreak of the First World War. Grandpapa Emil had spent two decades living in Tanzania. After the outbreak of the Great War, he had become an officer in the German colonial forces there, fighting a war against the British Empire in Africa that was far removed from the well-known blood-and-mud of Western Europe's trenches.

The current Emil Kaiser's father had lived a far less exotic life, and so as a child he had cleaved to his grandfather – or rather, the idea of his grandfather – and fallen down a rabbit hole that appeared to border on morbid obsession. The Jägerhalle was like a macabre museum to hells of late nineteenth and early twentieth-century European colonialism in Africa, though Kaiser seemed oblivious to it. Occasionally he would take Teuton from one severed and stuffed head to another, describing in great detail how his grandfather had killed each one. As far as Teuton was aware, he himself had never been to Africa.

"Don't dawdle," he snapped as Teuton, Revolver, and Luther hesitated at the far end of the room. They approached and stopped before the table, a long, low piece that Teuton realised was covered in old relics of the Kaiser family's Africa odyssey.

There were trinkets and fetishes, yellowing maps and journals, a set of binoculars, even an old cork pith helmet.

Kaiser looked up at them. There was no friendly pretence. His eyes burned with anger. Teuton realised in that moment why they had been summoned to the Trophy Room. It wasn't because it was intimidating. It was because it didn't have a carpet.

"What the hell have you three idiots been doing out there?" he demanded, his voice low. Nobody said anything until he continued.

"I gave you a simple job. The simplest job of your lives! My hard work gift-wrapped Freya Bauer and placed her into your hands. All you had to do was deliver her here. Instead, you dropped her!"

"There were complications," Revolver dared suggest.

"Reboot?" Kaiser snapped. "I founded M-Bahn to subsume Reboot, and all those other hacktivist organisations. My show is going to be the only one in town. If you couldn't stop a bunch of social justice teens from snatching Bauer, what hope do you have of beating them at their own game? How do you plan on subverting their movement?"

"VERT have her now," Luther said, as though that news was any better.

"Which is just as bad," Kaiser snarled. "I've worked hard with the proper parties in the Bundestag to make sure my empire isn't in the Vertidiger's sights, but it's election time, and those bastards need results. They could start hitting us, and then it's war. It also means they've now got an ace in Thomas Bauer's daughter. They can parade her to the public, or they can use her to try to infiltrate other groups. None of which is what we need. Bauer's head, that's what I require!"

He was ranting, and Teuton knew that was never a good sign.

"Now I'm going to have to make serious plays," he was saying. "Call in favours. I'll have to tell the Gespenst to delay his own hit as well, at least until I've tried to get Freya back."

"We're going to try and get her from VERT?" Revolver asked, his incredulity overcoming his fear. "But they have her at Humboldthain. It's locked down tight."

"Then perhaps you begin to understand the magnitude of your failure, given that I am now having to contemplate an operation against it," Kaiser said. "You've left me with no choice. My authority has been slowly undermined for years. You have just accelerated the process. I act quickly, within the next forty-eight hours, and reestablish myself as the most powerful man in this city, or..."

He trailed off, looking hard at all of them. None met his gaze.

After a brief silence he reached in amongst the detritus on the table and drew something from its sheath. It was a long knife, sixteen inches or more. Its head was curiously rounded, the blade flat, the handle simple wood, chipped and worn. It gleamed dully in the sunlight streaming in through the windows.

"Do you know what this is?" Kaiser demanded. The other two stayed resolutely silent, so eventually Teuton answered.

"It's a simi knife," she said.

"Correct," Kaiser replied. "A weapon used by the Maasai, a people native to Kenya and Tanzania. It belonged to an askari soldier in service to my grandfather during the Great War."

He placed the long knife on a cleared space in the centre of the table, in front of the trio, the handle facing towards them.

"There are four of us in this room," Kaiser said, his voice losing its fury, becoming cold and matter-of-fact. "Only three will be leaving it. Decide right now among yourselves who that will be."

While the other two both stared at the knife, Teuton did the intelligent thing. She stepped back.

Revolver and Luther reacted much more slowly, but it was Revolver who got to the simi knife first. Luther grabbed him before he could swing it though, and the near-blunt head didn't look much good for stabbing. They grappled with sudden, desperate fury, threatening to crash into the table before Luther's legs gave out and they both went down.

It was painful for Teuton to watch, and not because she felt any sympathy for either. Luther was old, and Revolver probably hadn't been in a fight in his life. They had been chosen to lead the sham that was M-Bahn because they were members of Kaiser's extended crime family and had some links to the hacker underworld, enough to get the group up and running. They had already proved, however, that they were inept at running operations themselves.

Revolver got a punch in, cracking Luther's glasses. While his erstwhile comrade recoiled he managed to snatch the knife and slash wildly with it.

The clumsy blow nicked Luther's forearm. Rather than injure him though, it just seemed to make him realise this really was a life-or-death situation.

"Will you two hurry up," Kaiser complained loudly.

Luther went for Revolver with a snarl, pinning him to the tiled floor by his throat and bashing the hand holding the knife off one of the table's legs repeatedly, until Revolver let go with a yelp.

Luther snapped up the knife. Revolver raised his hands to ward away the expected blow, babbling desperately for Luther to stop.

He didn't. Instead, he started to hack. It took a while for his clumsy blows with the near-blunt, old weapon to get past the arms, even longer for Revolver's screams to stop. Teuton had seen plenty of bad things down the years, but she found herself looking away a long time before it was over.

Eventually Luther stumbled back to his feet, shaking and wild-eyed.

"Compose yourself," Kaiser ordered him dispassionately. Briefly Teuton thought he was so worked up that he was actually going to have a go at Kaiser as well, but he managed to regain a semblance of control.

"I have new orders for you. Listen very carefully," Kaiser told him, speaking slowly. "Assemble M-Bahn. Arm them and bring them here. We need to act, and quickly. No more incompetence. No more failure. Do you understand?"

Luther, still panting, nodded.

"I said do you understand?" Kaiser snapped.

"Yes, I understand," Luther replied.

"Then go."

The bloody figure turned to leave, but Kaiser checked him. "The knife."

Luther froze, seemingly having forgotten he was still carrying the dripping simi. After what looked like a hard internal struggle, he turned and slowly, carefully, placed the weapon back down onto the table. Then, without looking at Revolver's corpse or the blood that was now forming a dark, glossy sheen across the flagstones, he hurried out. Teuton made to join him, but Kaiser checked her.

"We have more to discuss," he told her before calling for a team of house staff to come and clean up the mess via his Optik. As they did so, he spoke to her.

"What happened out there?" he asked. He was no longer angry, nor agitated – he seemed genuinely curious.

"Other forces intervened," Teuton said. "Repeatedly."

"We have a leak," Kaiser admitted, a fact that didn't surprise Teuton. "My contact in DedSec is denying it. They claim it's impossible. Clearly they are mistaken. The funds I was in the process of so generously providing have been frozen."

"Someone told Reboot how to make first contact, and we've been playing catchup ever since," Teuton pointed out.

"Exactly, and now we're on the cusp of either victory or defeat," Kaiser said. "It should not have been this difficult."

"You should have let me kill Freya the moment I met her," Teuton said, not disguising her bitterness.

"I know, my daughter, but her death was supposed to serve a higher purpose."

"Avenging Mother would have been enough."

"Perhaps," Kaiser said, looking thoughtful. "I will admit, I wished to do it myself."

Teuton understood the imperative. She was Kaiser's only offspring, a fact that they had both succeeded in concealing from the world, at least thus far. When Teuton had still been a child the police had struck, right here at the Jägerhalle. Led by a brute of a detective named Gerhardt, there had been a struggle. During it Teuton's mother, Bella, had been accidentally killed.

Teuton had been taken away and adopted. That had almost been a blessing. It had cut ties with Kaiser and allowed her to raise hell. Three different sets of adoptive parents later and she had been on her own, eighteen years old, running her first big crimes and, at the age of twenty, making her first kill.

She had worked her way back into her father's presence, and he had welcomed her with open arms. She became his enforcer, but always the desire for revenge had guided her. She had personally tracked down Gerhardt, and only Kaiser's insistence that she spare him had stayed her hand. His time would come, Kaiser had insisted. He wasn't in a position to go to war with the police or Gerhardt's fledgling new organisation, the Defenders. There were other targets.

Kaiser had explained how they had been betrayed. A simple forger named Thomas Bauer, who Kaiser had long employed and who he had permitted into the heart of his council, had been informing on Kaiser's operations. The police raid on the Jägerhalle had been his fault. And that made him responsible for the death of Teuton's mother.

Kaiser had already been avenged on Thomas before Teuton had been reunited with him, but that was not the end. Thomas had a family. Teuton had begged her father to exterminate them. He had agreed.

Unfortunately, it had been easier said than done. The forger had hidden his family well, in England it seemed, and they had only recently picked up a lead. A member of DedSec, an American-spawned hacker group, had admitted that Thomas Bauer's daughter was an enforcer in the movement, and had agreed to lure her to Germany in exchange for a considerable donation from Kaiser.

Teuton had then messed it up. She felt responsible. It enraged her. Freya Bauer owed her a childhood. The fact that she was still alive and in Berlin was bringing shame to the memory of her own mother.

"I have failed our family," Teuton found herself saying. Kaiser looked sorrowful. He came around the table, avoiding the house staff carrying out Revolver's corpse, and hugged her firmly.

"It's been a difficult time," he told her. "For all of us. But we'll be OK. Things have worked out."

"Maybe you should have sent me to England instead of that

idiot Gespenst," Teuton said unhappily. "Maybe I'm better suited to hunting down a teenager and an old woman."

"Hush now," Kaiser said, breaking the hug and patting her forearm. "I am about to order the Gespenst to capture the boy, so all is set when we have Freya. Things aren't as bad as they seem. In fact, we've been fortunate."

"Why?" Teuton asked, confused.

"VERT have taken Freya," Kaiser said. "Which means, for the first time, we have Thomas Bauer's daughter and former Inspector Erik Gerhardt in the same place."

"In Humboldthain," Teuton pointed out. "Bristling with defences."

"They can't stay there forever," Kaiser said. "That's why I'm assembling M-Bahn here, along with every hired gun in the city. We're going to lay an ambush, and I will show everyone in this place, from the Bundestag to the scummiest hostel, that nobody crosses our family and lives."

The Ghost pursed his lips, fingers darting across his laptop's keyboard.

The call had come through. Take the boy. Apparently, Kaiser was facing complications, and didn't fancy letting him make the kill out in the wild. He wanted Andrew Bauer seized, so that his execution could be performed with on-demand ease.

That wasn't what the Ghost had anticipated. It almost ruined things. But on the other hand, it would be a pleasure to be able to toy with his prey before making the kill. It had been a long time since he had done that.

Now the question became "how?" The Ghost had not expected a hostage situation, though he always made sure there were contingencies. He had with him the basic tools of the trade – tie cables, a hood, chloroform. He anticipated he could hold the boy in the hotel room he was staying in for two days at least, by which time Kaiser had assured him he would have taken Freya. Knock Andrew unconscious tonight, bundle him into the back of the car he was renting, lug him to the hotel – he would tell anyone who asked any questions it was his son's eighteenth birthday and that he was just worse for wear.

The only thing that remained was gaining access to Andrew's flat. The Ghost had located it in a row of houses next to a park. He knew the number, on the third floor. It would be easy enough to enter the building itself, but he anticipated that Andrew had flatmates, and that would complicate things.

The laptop screen showed a screed of information, before a picture pinged up, a video. The Ghost smiled, his aging features underlit by the screen's glow as he realised what he was looking at.

It was a video of a living room, messy and unkempt. Two boys were sitting on a couch facing the camera, neither speaking. One was Andrew. The Ghost watched them from the webcam mounted on their TV.

"The haunting begins," he murmured to himself.

20
Hard Truths

"Unbelievable," Harry exclaimed, making Andrew glance over from the TV.

"Unbelievably good, or unbelievably bad?" he asked his flatmate. Wordlessly, Harry turned his Optik so Andrew could see the screen.

Arsenal had scored, leaving Liverpool two goals adrift. Harry was watching it via his Optik's HUD, but the score still displayed on the hands-on device. Andrew shrugged.

"I quite like Arsenal."

"Shut up. You're only saying that because they're top of the EPL. You don't even like football!"

"I'm from London though."

"So am I!"

"Then why do you support Liverpool?"

Harry huffed and sank back into the grimy old couch, glaring as his eyes darted back and forth, following the match playing out along his retinas. Andrew went back to his own display, trying to find something to occupy his attention. Ever since his social media accounts had been locked he'd been going spare. He was sure someone had broken into his Optik. When Mum got back, he was going to make sure she spoke to any hacker types she knew, get one of them on the case.

A part of him wondered if the blocking had something to do with what his mum was doing in Germany. He hoped not. That wasn't a part of her life that he wanted to be involved in. It was what had driven Will away from them, he was sure. And despite her assurances before she had left, he was worried about her. Worried she was falling back into old ways.

"You want pizza tonight?" he asked Harry, realising it was getting late and he didn't feel like cooking. For his own part, Harry never felt like cooking, and while their third flatmate, Toby, was good in the kitchen, he was currently away visiting his parents. That meant takeaway pizza.

"Whatever," Harry said, not taking his eyes off the game.

"What do you want?"

"The usual."

That meant pepperoni thin crust from Mr Scaletti's, a favourite among Bristol's student cohort. Andrew went with the margherita – it was cheaper after all.

He placed the order.

"Checking in," Harriet said via her Optik.

"Received," Helen replied, scrolling through the image cache she had open on her laptop. She was sitting in her flat's back room, everything booted up, Marmaduke curled in her lap.

"I was just about to call you," she told Harriet.

"Am I not on time?" she responded. They had a system of checking in every half-hour, to make sure Harriet, and by default Andrew, was OK.

"You're bang on," Helen said, glancing at the time. "But I've got some information I need to share."

"Go ahead."

Helen took a breath, checking what she had found one more time. She had run a facial reconstruction AI through half-a-dozen different programs, first recreating the man she had seen at her door, the same man, she had no doubt, that Harriet had spotted in Bristol, and trying to get a match for them along with the half-snaps Harriet had been able to get via her own laptop.

There had been nothing. In this day and age, that was unheard of. Everyone was profiled. It wasn't just the authorities. Many Optik systems and commercial apps operated on facial recognition. For someone who could access most databases at will, everyone was tagged. Everyone had an ID that couldn't be avoided, short of living in a cave, or employing some high-end face-scrambling software, the sort Helen herself had been developing for years.

But the face she had constructed, a face she was certain was 95% accurate to the man she had encountered, had come up with no matches. Not even partials, at least not any decent ones.

The strangest thing was, it was such an unremarkable face. There were no defining features, no characteristics that leapt out. He could be anyone, an ordinary man with an ordinary life. That, ironically, was what had made Helen take note.

There were few hitmen or underworld Fixers in Europe that DedSec was unaware of. Helen had called in a few favours earlier in the afternoon, put the face around a bit, but nobody had been able to help. That in itself suggested that, whoever they were dealing with, it was someone who kept a very low profile. Extraordinarily low. He was the sort of operator whose presence was most clearly felt, conversely, when there was a notable lack of evidence. That made him one of half-a-dozen individuals Helen knew to be working in various places in Europe, people whose defining feature was the lack of information about them. They were known by their crimes. And only one of them was German.

"I think the man after Andrew is the Gespenst. The Ghost."

Saying the identification out loud gave her a moment's pause. She was too old to be worried for herself, but there was still fear for the kids. This wasn't the sort of person even a slick operator like Harriet wanted to be up against.

"The assassin?" Harriet asked, sounding unusually concerned. She had clearly heard the stories too.

"Yes. If he isn't *the* Ghost then he's certainly *a* ghost. I've got nothing on him. And that implies that he's an extremely effective, dangerous, long-term operative."

"The Ghost was thought to work for the German crime families, wasn't he?" Harriet asked. "He was active in the 90s. Surely he isn't still accepting hits? He must be..."

"About the age of the man we both saw," Helen said. "You need to be careful, Harriet. This likely isn't just some underworld thug. He's a killer. A mass killer. He's been doing it for decades. He's likely a psychopath."

"And it looks like he's currently walking towards Andrew's front door," came the terse reply.

Harriet had taken up position on the edge of the park bordering on Andrew's street. She had installed a spider drone with a camera, which had scuttled up the tree nearest the building's front door. Everything had been dull and uneventful, and Harriet intended to head into the café at the end of the street for dinner, when the drone had pinged her Optik.

Movement. A man heading up the short path to the flat's front door. The man she had seen in Priory Road, only this time he was carrying what looked like two pizza boxes.

"Be careful," Harriet heard Helen calling from her Optik.

She wasn't really listening. She was already up and running across the road towards the flat.

At this time of night, with orders pouring in, it took forty minutes for Mr Scaletti's to get a pizza out on delivery. By that time, the Ghost had driven to the street outside Andrew's flat and was able to leash the package drone as it arrived using a scrambler override on his Optik.

He loved technology like this. When it worked, it gave him a sense of power and control almost as absolute as when he was about to take someone's life.

He relieved the deactivated drone of its pizza satchel and carried it to the front door of the flat. He had continued to monitor the interior via the hacked webcam using his Optik. It seemed only the target and one other were present. That gave him a fifty percent chance of getting him at the door. And if it was the other one, it would be easy enough to remove him and carry on upstairs.

Apartment number six. Trying to suppress his excitement, the Ghost rang the doorbell.

21
Q and A

"You're lying," Freya told Erik, her voice riven with anger. "My father wasn't an informer."

"He was," Erik said, smiling without any humour as he drove the accusation home. "Did you never wonder why he was murdered?"

"We had no way of finding out why," Freya snarled. "I was a child when it happened. We were just trying to survive!"

"And you never tried to discover who did it?"

Freya did her best not to stand up and hit Erik. She had tried to prepare herself for interrogation, but she hadn't foreseen this. She felt nothing but anger and shock. She wanted to stop Erik from speaking, from saying anything more, but she knew she couldn't.

"I'm only telling you the truth, Freya," he said, his smile spreading as he realised that he had found her weak point. "You were young when he died. You didn't know him well. I did. I was his handler, while I worked with the police."

Freya forced herself to sit still and take breaths, no longer looking up at Erik. This was all happening on purpose. She had lost control, and now she had to regain it.

"You shouldn't be so upset," Erik carried on. "Thomas Bauer was a good man. He helped us a great deal before the end."

"Not you," Freya said, her voice tight with controlled anger as she looked back up at Erik. "Not VERT. He would never have assisted an organisation like yours."

"Perhaps not," Erik allowed, somewhat to Freya's surprise. "It was some time ago. Things were different. But if we had the laws back then that we now have in place, he wouldn't have died."

"Don't use him to justify what you and your kind are doing out there now," Freya said. "Even if he helped the police once, he would never throw himself in with your barbarism. VERT are worse than most of the people you call criminals."

A part of her still didn't believe Erik. Her father could have been killed for any number of reasons. There was no evidence he was an informer. But Erik had been his handler… no, he was trying to get into her head.

"He was doing the right thing, which is what we're doing now," Erik said, anger creeping into his voice. Freya realised he had buttons of his own, ones that she could push.

"I don't think you really believe that," she said. "I think you're a man the world has made bitter, or maybe you were always that way. Cold, hard, unfeeling. And self-righteous to boot. Maybe my father did help you. But that was when the authorities meant something. They stood for justice, peace, and democracy. I was old enough to remember him. He was warm and kind, and he wouldn't have supported what you've created here. He wouldn't have helped an organisation like VERT."

Erik smiled again. He knew what she was doing, just as she had sensed his own efforts.

"We're the same sort of person, Freya," he said.

"I doubt that."

"We respond more strongly to anger than fear. I respect that."

"I don't want your respect," Freya said, still trying to negotiate. "Free me, and Will."

"I can meet you halfway on that."

"No, I want Will too. Release us, and we'll go straight back home. To London. Scout's honour."

"You're not very good at negotiating. You know that, right?"

"What do you want from us then?"

"I already have what I want. A DedSec intelligence officer."

"Then why are we having this conversation?"

Erik looked down at the Polaroid of Freya as a child. She wanted nothing more than to lash out and snatch it from him, but she managed to overcome the urge. That wouldn't end well.

Erik held the photo up to inspect, looking almost thoughtful.

"I wanted to talk to Thomas's daughter," he said, looking at her, as though comparing her current state, bruised and bloodied, to the grinning, youthful innocence of the picture. "You may not believe it, but I regret what happened to your father. I met your mother too, and I saw you once, though you won't remember me. You had a good family. We should have protected you all. Still, this is what happens to those who consort with criminal scum."

Freya stood up. It wasn't an abrupt motion, but she maintained an icy eye contact with Erik, and his guards bristled. He didn't react, other than to lower the Polaroid.

"Who killed him?" Freya asked.

"Now you want to know?"

"Don't mock me. Was it Kaiser?"

"Yes. Indirectly. He used one of his hitmen. We aren't sure

who. Their identity remains elusive. All the more reason that organisations like VERT need more authority. This country has gone to the dogs."

"If only," Freya said. "Exactly why did he kill my father?"

"The help he was providing us with was discovered."

"How? Was he betrayed?"

"No. Kaiser grew suspicious and began tailing him. We helped advise Thomas. Helped him relocate to England."

"And why did he come back?"

Erik was silent.

"Tell me," Freya demanded, all but shouting.

"He was assisting us with one more case," Erik admitted. There was no more taunting, no more mockery. No games. His expression was defiant, as though daring Freya to strike him.

"He was trying to provide the evidence we needed to bring in Kaiser," he went on. "But Kaiser got to him first. I begged to be allowed to arrest him, but my section chief refused. I left the Bundeskriminalamt soon after. Kaiser was the one who got away. I promised I wouldn't allow myself to fall into that position again. I was a man with all the power, but constrained from using it, and it led to many failures, the greatest getting my informer killed. I founded der Vertidiger so I would never know that feeling again. Justice can bear no restraints, or it isn't true justice."

Freya snatched Erik's wrist. The guards lunged forward and grabbed her, dragging her off, but not before she had taken her photo back.

"I told you already," she snarled. "Don't use my father as an excuse for what you're doing here."

"I'm only telling you what happened," Erik responded with equal vehemence. "You're fortunate that I'm willing to honour the sacrifice your family has made. Go, before I change my mind."

Freya stood undecided, wrestling with her conscience. She couldn't leave Will here, in the clutches of an organisation like VERT. Equally, there was nothing she could do right now to help gain his freedom. She had no cards to play, unless she made a counteroffer.

"Keep me, and free Will," she suggested. Erik scoffed, a reaction that made Freya want to go for him again.

"VERT has a file on you, Freya, and with all due respect, you're not as valuable an asset right now as William Fraser. You're muscle. He's brains. VERT has a lot of muscle. It could use more brains, especially one wired to the hacker underclass you both belong to. He's a valuable piece of the puzzle. You, not so much."

The accusation stung, but Freya could see Erik's logic. VERT could deal with riots and physical unrest, but a hacker war was a different proposition entirely. If they could harness Will's abilities, it might give them the edge.

"We aren't going to hurt him," Erik went on, again sensing her weakness. "Quite the opposite in fact. If he cooperates – and I think he's the type of man who will – then he could even find himself in our employment. We can wipe his criminal record too, at least here in Germany. That's the sort of power we now possess."

"Which is exactly why you don't need more of it," Freya said darkly.

Erik shrugged. "I told you, I'm releasing you, so don't push your luck. You may find you've used it all up. I suspect not all the advice that led you here came from people who wish you well."

Freya's eyes narrowed. "What more do you know?" she demanded.

"I've heard that Kaiser's looking for you," Erik said. "By taking you in, I've probably saved your life. He doesn't just want you for who your father was. You've ruined his operations in the past."

"When?" Freya asked. "I've been in England since I was a child!"

"DeLock," Erik said. "We had intel we were sharing with SIRS over in London about Kaiser's connections to that arms manufacturer. DedSec helped bust them open. You were involved, weren't you? You and William?"

"Kaiser was behind DeLock?"

"And you gave him another reason to hunt you down. So I'd leave now, while you can. Before any of them get to you. You'll be driven to the airport, and once there you'll purchase a one-way ticket back home. Back to London."

"What if this is my home?" Freya asked. "Berlin."

"Is it?"

"Perhaps," Freya said – defiance was all she had left right now.

"Then I suggest you look for a new home," Erik said. "If you ever try to come back to Germany, we won't be as forgiving."

Erik bent and picked up Freya's backpack, pulling out her Mister Scruff mask. He grunted in vague amusement.

"You hackers and your silly disguises. Do you think they really work?"

"They're good enough to block your facial recognition tech," Freya pointed out.

"Perhaps. But we have so much more in our arsenal. We aren't just Albion. That little English fool Nigel Cass never had a clear enough vision. I'm building so much more here."

He returned the mask to the bag, then handed Freya her wallet.

"Everything's there," Erik said. "Except your Optik. That had a little accident. Now, get out of my country."

Freya returned her photo to the wallet.

"It's not your country," she told him. "Not yet."

The guards led her out.

Alexander was waiting for Erik after he left the cell, once Freya had been taken away.

"Should we be releasing her?" he asked. He was VERT's second-in-command, ex-military like Erik, still young but showing promise. He had plenty of ambition, which Erik always looked for in his subordinates.

"We've got what we want," he replied, dismissing the concern. "Her ex-partner is a valuable asset, and one captured DedSec operative is sufficient for our purposes. Meyer and our allies in the Bundestag can use this to show that VERT is working, and can whip up fears that DedSec are now spreading to Germany from America, via London. It's everything we could have hoped for."

"Very good, sir," Alex said, following Erik out of the cell block and towards the main body of the flak tower and its central control room. "What about tonight?"

"Have the gatherings started?"

"Yes, sir. As we anticipated, the largest concentration of protesters is at the Platz der Republik. The police are reporting unrest elsewhere though."

"Drones up?"

"Yes, sir. We're tracking it all."

"Good. Issue a stand-to. I want the Defenders fully mobilised within the hour. Riot gear on."

"Yes, sir."

A part of Erik had worried about letting Freya go. Ultimately, he expected it would make William easier to control. Someone as obviously stubborn as Freya wasn't going to be useful, but Erik had shown that he could be reasonable, and without her around Erik suspected Will would prove more malleable.

He had made his choice, and the news that there were going to be protests tonight helped lighten his mood. It was going to be another chance to display the strength and efficiency that VERT prided itself on. Tonight was going to be a good night.

"Let's go break some skulls," he said, smacking Alex on the shoulder.

22
Delivery Date

"About time," Harry grumbled, looking up. "Over an hour!"

"I'll get it," Andrew said, pulling himself from the couch. The game had finished two-nil to Arsenal, and Harry was in a foul mood. Andrew was considering eating his pizza in his room.

He threw on his shoes, unlocked the flat door, and headed downstairs to the front entrance. Like a lot of the accommodation in this part of town, the stairwell was well-built stone Victorian architecture fallen on hard times, the paint flaking, the banister scarred, and everything smelling vaguely of piss. Still, the extra space and cheaper rent made it feel like an upgrade on the student halls they had all endured during their first year.

He reached the front door, a heavy, graffiti-scrawled thing, and unlocked it before hefting it open.

Darkness was settling in outside. A man stood on the doorstep, carrying a pizza satchel. He smelled of cigarettes. Will didn't recognise him, and he wasn't wearing a Mr Scaletti's branded jacket, but the main surprise was that the store's app had told him it was going to be a drone delivery.

"Thanks," he said as the man opened his satchel and slid two pizza boxes out. "I thought this one was flying in?"

"Bloody drone broke, didn't it?" the man, an east Londoner by his accent, complained. "Third time this week!"

He held out his hands-on Optik component with the payment app open. Andrew accepted the pizzas, their delicious, warm aroma making his stomach grumble. He held his own Optik over the delivery man's, sending a digital payment.

"Andrew!"

The voice made him look up just as the payment went through. To his surprise, he saw the girl he had been chatting to in his lecture earlier that day hurrying up to the front door. She was new to the course. What was her name again? Sara?

She was smiling, but the look in her eyes was off. She approached sharply, almost pushing aside the pizza man.

"I'm just in time then," she said, glancing down at the pizzas. Then, to Andrew's utter astonishment, she went on her tiptoes and kissed him.

The second felt like an eternity as he stayed frozen in shock. She broke and began to head in through the front door, which Andrew had kept open with his foot, tugging on his elbow to pull him in as well.

"Date night is well overdue, mister," she said. Then they were inside in the stairwell, the door banging shut in the delivery man's face and the lock engaging.

The girl shoved Andrew back against one scabby wall, almost upending the pizzas in his arms, and pressed a finger to her own lips.

Silence. Andrew realised his heart was racing. Something was very, very wrong.

The strange girl looked down at the base of the door. The

delivery man's shadow was still visible, but after a moment, it disappeared. Andrew eased out a breath he realised he had been holding.

He could only think of one explanation as to what had just happened that made any sort of sense.

"Did my mum send you?" he asked.

The girl stayed silent for a while longer, still looking at the door, as though she was expecting it to explode in afterwards. Nothing happened, and eventually she spoke.

"Yes."

"To… protect me?"

"No. Parents hire me to give their nerdy uni sons a quick kiss in front of other people, to help them with their self-confidence."

She looked back at Andrew, and while her expression was amused, there was still a hard look in her eyes – fear and tension.

"My name is Harriet," she carried on. "Harriet Parks, but I guess you can keep calling me Sara if it's easier."

"What's happening?" Andrew asked, feeling utterly lost and foolish.

"I'm saving your life," Harriet said.

"From what?"

"The delivery man. Now, I need you to deactivate your Optik."

"Why?"

"Do you always ask strange girls who just randomly kissed you this many questions? Just do it."

Frowning, Andrew called up his Optik HUD and shut it down. The device's standard settings only permitted it to be turned off for an hour at a time during the day, but his dad had showed him how to bypass that particular default when he'd gotten his first implant, when he was fourteen. The display went dead.

"Now hold still," Harriet said before, to Andrew's surprise, she reached up and used her nails to snag the Optik's post-dermal component, linked to the ear implant via the neodymium magnet. She tweaked it free, making Andrew yelp and clutch his ear.

"What the hell?" he demanded, the chip still buried in his skin aching.

"I've seen a hitman remotely fry people by overloading their implant," Harriet said, removing her own processor. "Doesn't take long but looks like it hurts a lot. I'd rather that didn't happen to either of us. Now let's go."

She started up the stairs, waving him after her urgently. He began to follow.

"Flat six, right?"

"Yeah. How did you know?"

"I know lots of things. I take it you have flatmates? Are they in?"

"Just one right now. Who was the delivery man?"

"A German serial killer known only as the Ghost. Long story, really."

She turned abruptly on the first landing, Andrew almost bumping into her, her expression now fierce.

"I know it might seem like it, but this isn't a joke. That man outside has been sent to kill you by people in Germany who want your mother dead. She's dealing with them over there, but here and now, our job is to get you to safety. So I'm going to need you to do exactly what we say, no questions asked."

"'We,'" Andrew said.

"I hope you're just saying 'yes' in French right now, Andrew."

"You said 'we'. Who else are you with?"

"A seriously badass hacktivist and digital Robin Hood whose name I won't be sharing until I know she's cool with it."

"Are you… criminals?"

"We're DedSec, handsome. Let's go."

She carried on, up to Andrew's flat. He followed her, trying to digest it all. Everyone had heard of DedSec – heroes to some, the worst sorts of rabble-rousing anarchists to others. Did that mean his mum was involved with them too?

"Act like you know me," Harriet told him.

"Like you did downstairs?" Andrew asked.

"Not quite to that level."

Harry opened the door to flat six, angry expression turning to confusion as he found himself facing not just Andrew and two pizzas but a girl in a tartan skirt, leather jacket, and cosmetic cat ears.

"Hey, I'm Alice, from upstairs," Harriet said, looking at once apologetic and concerned. "I just bumped into Andrew in the stairwell. Really sorry about this, but we think we've got a gas leak in our flat. The carbon monoxide thingy is going crazy, and there's a seriously bad smell. I've called the fire brigade, but I thought I better tell everyone and get everyone out. Not sure I'd be able to land a flat for the next year if my previous block blew up with everyone in it!"

"Seriously?" Harry asked, looking from Harriet to Andrew, who shrugged.

"Yeah," he said, feeling incredibly awkward. "Can't you smell it?"

Harry frowned and shrugged.

"To be honest I was going to go over to Abby's place after the pizza tonight anyway," he said.

"I guess I'll hit the library, the study spaces where they allow food will still be open," Andrew said. Harry scoffed and headed back inside.

"Let me get my laptop?" Andrew asked Harriet quietly.

"Be quick about it," she said, glancing back down the stairwell.

Both Andrew and Harry, the latter now carrying his pizza box, reappeared at the door moments later, each with a laptop satchel.

"You think it'll take all night to fix?" Harry asked Harriet, who shrugged.

"Probably. We had this happen before, last semester. We had to spend the night in a hotel. The uni paid for it at least."

Harry merely grunted and traipsed off down the stairwell. Andrew and Harriet followed but hung back.

"What now?" Andrew muttered. He was still trying to come to terms with what was happening.

"Now, we hope the delivery man isn't still outside," Harriet said. "And if he's not, we get you on a train back to London right away. That's the only place we can keep you safe."

They reached the front door. Harry was holding it for them. Thankfully, there was no sign of the delivery man. Nevertheless, Andrew could feel his dire presence hanging over him. In an instant, he had been thrust into the murky world he knew his mother inhabited, the place she had spent her life shielding him from. It was as though someone had suddenly turned off the lights. Andrew didn't know where he was or what he was doing anymore. All he could do was trust Harriet, and hope his mum was doing better than he was.

Harriet got them both on the last train from Bristol to London. She made sure he was seated at the back of the rear carriage before reactivating her Optik, hoping as she did so that they were out of range of any potential chip-frying. She called Helen.

"I've got him," she told her. "But it was close."

"Shots fired?" Helen asked.

"Thankfully not. I think he's trying to kidnap Andrew. I think if it was a straight hit, he would just have taken us both out. Like I said, it was close."

"The important thing is you got away."

"For now. We're on our way."

"I've got the safe house where Belinda is all set up. And I've got a plan for banishing our ghost. Permanently."

"I'm glad you do, because I don't," Harriet said. She was trying to seem clear and confident for Andrew, but in truth her nerves were fried. The encounter at the front door had been far too close.

"We'll discuss it more when you arrive. I'll meet you at the station."

"Gotcha."

She gave Helen the ETA, then hung up. Andrew was in the process of getting his own Optik device reinstalled and had pulled out his hands-on device. The sight of it gave Harriet sudden, gut-wrenching concern.

"Did you use that to pay for those pizzas?" she demanded, pointing at the device. She remembered what he had been doing when she had thrown herself between him and the so-called delivery man.

"Yeah..." Andrew said, trailing off as he realised the import of the question.

Harriet snatched the Optik's hands-on interface and immediately turned it off, desyncing it from Andrew's HUD. She considered throwing it out of a window too, but it was probably too late for that.

"What do you think he did to it?" Andrew asked.

"He could have done anything," Harriet said, her mind racing through the possibilities. He was still on their trail, she was sure.

"Is he following us?" Andrew said. Harriet looked at him,

trying to decide how much to tell him. He was a quiet kid, a world away from what she knew about his mother. Clearly he was still reeling from what was happening. DedSec wasn't for everybody. She wondered how much he knew about his mum's involvement.

"Probably, yes. But unless he appears dressed as a train conductor asking for tickets, we're safe for now."

"What… if he does?"

"Then don't use your bloody Optik to pay him."

Andrew was silent, then spoke up again, his tone urgent. "What's happening to my mum? All she told me was that she was going to Germany, and to look out for Gran."

"I don't know much," Harriet admitted. "But your gran is safe. The friend we're going to meet is looking after her."

Andrew nodded. "So my mum's in DedSec?"

"Yeah. I didn't know you didn't know."

"Honestly, it's a relief. I thought she was like… a gangster or something."

"She's way cooler than a gangster."

"When I was a kid, I wanted to join DedSec. I've always been good with tech, thanks to my dad."

"Pretty sure neither of them would appreciate me encouraging you to become part of the movement, kiddo. I don't think they'd be too thrilled to get back from Germany to discover I've given you your own hacktivist mask and callsign."

She could tell immediately from Andrew's expression that she had said something wrong.

"Dad's over in Germany too?" he asked.

Harriet cursed silently. She hadn't signed up to get involved in Bauer family drama.

"Mum just said she was going over with someone. Didn't say it was Dad."

"Well, I suspect it's a good thing they're both out there together."

"You think it's dangerous."

"I think your mum is a total badass, and your dad's way smarter than I am. They're probably kicking ass as we speak."

The rest of the journey passed without incident. Helen was as good as her word. She met them off the train at Paddington before they headed together for the taxi rank.

"We're about to join your gran," Helen told Andrew with a reassuring smile. "But as far as public interactions go, you're my grandchildren."

"Guess that means no more kissing," Andrew said, surprising Harriet with the dash of humour.

"You're a bit young for me anyway," she told him.

"Why, how old are you?"

"Twenty-three."

"I'm nineteen!"

"And when you're twenty-three, you'll realise just how vast a gulf those four years are."

"Barely a day back at uni and you're already getting out of hand, Miss Harmon," Helen teased as they left the station, both DedSec activists instinctively keeping their eyes down to avoid the worst of the surveillance installations.

"You said you had a plan, Grandma?" Harriet asked Helen. "Because right now I feel like a sitting duck. A plan would definitely help with that."

"Funny you should mention ducks," Helen said. "Because it involves killing two birds with one stone."

23
Sliding Doors

They didn't bag Freya again when they took her from Humboldthain to the airport. That was VERT's first mistake.

Her anger had cooled and hardened into something razor-sharp and unyielding. There was no more dismay at what Erik had told her. It made sense that her father had worked with the police. He had been a good man, a man who had tried to help others and see that justice was done – it was just a shame the law and justice no longer appeared to be in tandem.

The news about his killer was more difficult to stomach. For so long they had been abstract, nameless and faceless. Wolves, stalking her, never giving her rest. In a sense they still were – she still didn't know who had pulled the trigger – but she did know who had ordered it. Emil Kaiser, a name she had heard before, always in association with the worst of Berlin's crime families. She had long suspected him, but it still left her with an icy feeling of anger.

The exit from the cell she had been held in by VERT led up a short flight of dilapidated steps and out onto level ground directly beneath the graffiti-marred bulk of the flak tower, whose immediate entrance was a mesh wire gateway. The guards took Freya to the left, to a motor pool where ranks of grey VERT vehicles stood, row after row of armed carriers, jeeps, and what Freya took to be drone units, shrouded by tarpaulins and linked up to electrical charging stations.

Freya was taken to one of the jeeps and sat in the back with another surly-looking VERT guard. She wondered if Erik was trying to show off, send out a message of strength for the DedSec enforcer to take back to London with her.

How much could she trust what he had actually told her? She didn't know for sure Kaiser had been behind her father's death; she only had his word, and the crime lord's brutal reputation. For that matter, what would she do if Erik was lying about Will?

The jeep set off, along the drive leading to the flak tower's entrance and down the slope of the hill that comprised Humboldthain park. They reached a high wire fence that looked electrified. She saw mounds of earth along the slope to the left and the right, lower down than the fence itself. She realised they were drones, employed as static defence and surveillance, their rotors removed. The area in front of them, previously wooded, had been cut back to provide an open field of fire down the slope.

Freya noted it all, her mind unable to stop processing possibilities. Erik was making a mistake, and she was happy to let him continue.

She could do so much more from outside than in.

They reached the base of the hill that marked the edge of the park, where there was one more gate. Beyond it lay Berlin, and a ride to Brandenburg Airport. It was getting late, but the streets seemed busy. Through the tinted windows, she noted people glaring in disgust at the VERT transport. She almost expected someone to throw something, but had little doubt that there were armed drones escorting them from above, deterring any violence.

The city seemed uneasy, but Freya wasn't entirely sure who that boded ill for.

They arrived outside the airport's main terminal, and Freya disembarked. Two VERT troopers did likewise, one holding up a tablet with a camera. He said nothing. After a moment, a pixelated vision of Will appeared on the screen. She hadn't anticipated the surge of relief she experienced at the sight of him.

"I told them I wanted evidence that they'd released you, so I guess this is it," he said, Freya having to lean in to hear him properly over the sounds of the airport. "They've really let you go?"

"Looks like it," she said warily, glancing at the stony-faced guard holding the screen. "Apparently I'm flying back to London."

"Good. Go and get Andrew. Give him a hug from me."

Previously a suggestion like that would have left Freya flying off the handle. Now, though, it didn't seem unreasonable that the man who had once abandoned them was asking her to hug their son.

In that moment, Freya made up her mind.

"Are they treating you all right?" she asked him, trying to sound casual. "Is that a black eye?"

"If it hasn't come up as a black eye yet it will by tomorrow morning. But no, I'm fine. Seriously. Get out of here and get home. You've got a family to take care of. And Wellend."

Freya felt a spike of anger at the mention of the traitor. Will was right, that was a loose end that deserved to be tied up and thrown in the Thames on a black night. But she couldn't think about that right now. She could only afford one reckoning at a time.

"I won't let him get away with what he did," she said. "DedSec won't let him get away with it."

"I'm sorry about Andrew," Will said after a moment's pause. "I was… a coward. There's something more you should know as well, something before you go."

"What is it?" Freya asked, genuinely perplexed. She hadn't been looking for a confession, much less expecting one.

"I've been in touch with Andrew," Will said. "I don't mean recently, since we came to Berlin, and I don't mean back-and-forth between us. He didn't know. I've… been monitoring him."

"Are you saying you've been stalking our son?" Freya asked incredulously.

"That's not a term a hacker likes to hear levelled at them," Will said. "But I've been keeping an eye on him remotely, and helping him with his finances."

"What do you mean?"

"Well, the student loan he was set to get wasn't exactly as high as the one he's now receiving. And he isn't even going to have to pay it back, or at least I was going to make sure it showed that he had. Not sure I'll be able to do that from VERT's flak tower but hey, it's a couple of years before he graduates…"

"You hacked the university's loan system?" Freya asked.

"Yes."

"And what else?" Freya went on. "His grades?" She felt angry, deceived. Even if Andrew hadn't known, it felt as though she had been kept out of the loop, like her ex-husband and son had conspired on something without her.

"Not his grades," Will said hastily. "It's all his own work. Just the money side of things. And I made sure he got into good student housing in his first year."

"We had the money covered," Freya said sharply. "Why would

you interfere like that? If you wanted to support us, you could have gotten in touch. You could have reached out. To me or to him directly."

"I know, and I'm sorry. Like I said, I was a coward. But I didn't abandon him, at least not as fully as you think I did."

"Time's up," the VERT guard holding the screen said, clearly beyond bored with the meaningless exchange.

"I know you'll look after him," Will said. "Don't mention anything I've told you."

"I won't," Freya said. "Goodbye, Will."

The VERT troopers departed, leaving Freya alone. She simply stood looking at the entrance to the airport's main terminal, lost in thought.

In the panic of the past day she had wanted nothing more than to escape the jaws of this trap, get back to London and make sure her family was safe. Suddenly, she had that option. And suddenly, it didn't feel like the right thing to do.

She would be abandoning Will. A month ago such a suggestion would probably have simply led to her saying "good". Yes, Will did still deserve some comeuppance for how he had abandoned her and, more importantly, Andrew. But should it involve being locked in a cell by authoritarian brutes and seemingly forced to betray other activist groups? Freya knew from her experiences of Albion just how utterly untrustworthy organisations like VERT were. Erik may have honoured an old promise by releasing her, but it was pretty clear he was a cruel bastard of a man, and she had little doubt that as soon as he stopped being useful, Will would be discarded in the worst way possible.

She couldn't abandon him. The realisation that he had been looking out for Andrew had shocked her too. He had gone about it in an underhanded way – a cowardly way, as he had said – but it was still there. He wasn't as rotten as she had thought.

And there were other considerations too. The wolves. She had been running from this all her life. She had believed what Belinda had told her, that her father had simply ended up with the wrong people, that there was nothing they could do about his death, nothing except avoid ever going back to Berlin. But that was untrue. Thomas Bauer had a very real, tangible killer – Kaiser, and his underlings – and that same brute was now trying to murder her and those she cared about. Now she was in a position to do something about it, to stop acting defensively and do what she loved. Go on the attack.

For the first time, vengeance was no longer an abstract fantasy. The hunter would become the hunted.

It was like her mother had said. A reckoning.

"Hello, miss?" said a voice, dragging her from her thoughts. She realised an airport security guard was standing in front of her, concerned.

"Are you all right?" he asked.

"Yes, fine," Freya said, nodding. She realised abruptly how cold she was, standing outside like she had lost her mind. She wasn't entirely sure yet where she was going to go, but she did know it wouldn't be into the airport.

She went and found the nearest bus back to town.

Freya formulated her response on the bus. She knew she had to move quickly. Erik would hear soon enough that she hadn't boarded a flight, and she had no real idea what Kaiser was planning. Now that the attempts to lure her into being picked up by M-Bahn had failed, she assumed he would step up a level. Knowing the sort of organisations men like Kaiser ran, she had to assume all sorts of undesirables were currently being paid to track her down.

She had to go to ground, even briefly. In her current state she doubted there was much she could hope to achieve. She was starving hungry, exhausted, injured, and friendless.

Solving those problems involved getting off the bus in the city centre. To do so she donned Mister Scruff and triggered its facial scrambling program. Helen had developed it and had installed linkup systems in the mask that allowed Freya's Optik to interface with it. Once triggered it would change the appearance of the mask to mimic AI-generated faces on any electronic device that was attempting to get a match. The Optik would likewise project matching fake credentials to any system running a deep profile on her. It was the perfect digital disguise. The only downside was it had no effect on the naked eye, so she had to keep her wits about her. Any police or VERT ground-pounders had to be avoided.

It seemed that tonight they were all preoccupied. She had barely gotten off the bus when she noticed people hurrying by, buttoned up, with hoods up, or masks on. Groups of figures gathered on street corners and at the entrances to alleyways. Freya made sure she didn't catch any eyes. In the distance, there was the wail of a police siren.

Berlin was having a sleepless night. She had read about the planned protests before her arrival. Pushback against the government, against the new laws, against VERT's increasing authoritarianism had been happening for months, and with the elections in just a few weeks it was all building to a head. It reminded Freya of London during the rise of Albion.

Freya bought two new hands-on Optik sets, both blank and ready to be synced with implant data, before booking into a hotel. The receptionist seemed disturbed at her bedraggled appearance, but all that really mattered was that her debit card worked.

If her plan was going to pay off, Will's Optik would need to be active. She knew he had a covert installation, and she suspected VERT had yet to locate it, but she couldn't call him, or link up their HUDs to confirm it. VERT's headquarters would detect that.

She headed straight back out again to a grimy-looking takeaway shop opposite the hotel, and returned with kebab and fries. Consuming them wasn't pretty, but it brought welcome relief to her aching stomach.

Sated, she went back down to reception and managed to procure a few large plasters and a roll of bandages and cotton buds. She showered, tending to her injuries. The cuts to her head and hand were fairly superfluous, once cleaned. The thigh injury stung as she washed off the dirt and excess clotting, but it didn't seem deep. She bandaged it up.

Her new Optik hands-on had finished syncing to her implant. She downloaded the security systems DedSec employed, then sat on the edge of the bed and called Helen.

To her immense relief, she picked up.

"It's good to hear you, dearie," she told Freya. "Is this secure?"

"I hope so," Freya replied, trying to keep her voice level.

"And you're safe?"

"Yes. Will isn't though. VERT have captured him."

Helen was silent for a moment. "That's bad news."

"It is. I'm going to get him out."

"You won't manage that on your own."

"I'm hoping I won't be alone. Is Andrew there?"

"He is, and your mother."

After a moment, Andrew's voice came in over the Optik. "Hey, Mum."

Freya closed her eyes, fighting back tears. "Hey kid. How's it going?"

"Pretty crazy. I'm in London. Are you OK?"

"Yeah, I'm OK. Just missing you. I'll be back soon."

"Is Dad with you?"

The question was the one she had feared the most. She made herself tell the prepared half-truth. "Not just now, but he will be soon."

"Is someone really trying to kill us?"

"Yes, but I won't let them, and neither will Helen. I'm sorting things out over here, and Helen will keep you safe where you are. Just do what she says, and you'll be fine. And remember to tell her you have an egg allergy."

"When will you be back?"

"I don't know exactly. Soon. Much sooner than I expected."

"That's good. I can't wait to see you."

Freya told Andrew she loved him, voice cracking. Helen came back on.

"You're sure you're safe?" Freya asked.

"Yes. My friend Harriet and I are hunting for whoever was sent here for your son and mother. We've got a few leads, but no definite ID. We do, however, have a plan."

"Just make sure you're in one piece when we get back," Freya urged. "You're as precious to me as any family, Helen."

"Don't you worry yourself, dearie. Focus on getting yourself and William home."

"I will."

She ended the Optik connection and closed her eyes, struggling through the crashing despair.

Then her determination resurfaced, defiant, angry.

She set an alarm for four hours.

Her sleep was dreamless. She woke and got dressed, rocking the grungy look, bloodstained black jeans and all. Luckily that would help her fit in where she was going.

She was going to make sure something like this never happened to her or her family ever again.

And to do that, she needed to go clubbing.

24
The Lion's Den

Wellend was exhausted, but he couldn't sleep.

He sat back in his chair, laptop screen burning into his tired retinas, trying to decide what to do next. Outside the old stationmaster's room the hackerspace was quiet, everyone asleep or gone home.

It was all going to hell, and they were trying to blame him. Over the past day Wellend had received a screed of increasingly furious messages from Askari. Freya Bauer was still on the loose. They had failed to capture her.

None of which was Wellend's fault. He had supplied her, practically giftwrapped. He had no idea how Askari had managed to botch the capture, but it didn't surprise him. Freya was nothing if not determined and resourceful. He had warned Askari multiple times.

Perhaps he shouldn't have done this. Perhaps this was his comeuppance. It was a betrayal, there was no denying it.

He sighed and rubbed his eyes, taking another draught of coffee from his mug. No time for remorse. What was done was done. DedSec needed the money. *He* needed the money. With the recent crackdowns, other financial avenues were rapidly disappearing, and the authorities were becoming ever more capable when it came to tracking down and closing rogue accounts and laundering operations. The movement was on the brink, and when all the idealism had run its course, it needed finance and investment. All for the cause.

His Optik buzzed, coinciding with a ping from his implant. He frowned, wondering who would be contacting him at this time.

The answer, apparently, was Harriet Parks. He read her message.

Getting some strange reports from Germany. Apparently, Freya Bauer and Will Fraser are in Berlin? Did you know?

Wellend felt a cold chill. Had Freya reached out? He hadn't realised she and Harriet knew each other well enough for that. Or maybe it was just rumours? But where were they coming from? Wellend had been monitoring things online and had seen nothing go public as yet. By now Freya must know that Wellend had sent her to her death. What if she had spoken to Harriet directly?

What have you heard, he responded to Harriet.

Quite a bit. I think Freya's in trouble. We should meet ASAP.

It didn't seem like she had spoken with Freya yet. That was something at least. He couldn't let his involvement become public knowledge. If other senior DedSec members found out he had betrayed two of their own, the fact that he had brought in the necessary funds to keep the movement going for years to come wouldn't spare him. Most of the others were idealists. Their bouts of morality, in Wellend's opinion, were what was keeping DedSec from realising its true potential.

That was a problem for the future. Right now, he had to make sure there wasn't a leak. He had to find out what Harriet Parks knew and, if necessary, silence her.

He messaged her back.

Let's meet.

The bouncer named Sven recognised Freya.

"Wait here," he said, marshalling her off to the side of Berghain's queue. After a while the Reboot activist who'd first brought her to the Berghain, Tex, appeared out the main door.

"What are you doing here?" he demanded.

"Taking Reboot up on its offer," Freya answered.

"Where's your friend?"

"He's been detained."

Tex patted her down and took her inside.

"You go first," he said over the rising music. "You know the way."

Up Freya climbed, past the packed dance floor, until she came to the final floor and the door stamped with Reboot's morbid logo.

"Go in," Tex said.

The room beyond was different from her first encounter. The place was busy with Reboot members, who seemed to be stripping out the contents and boxing them up. Freya stood unnoticed until Tex whistled and waved over the tall brutish man.

"Look who someone abandoned on our doorstep," Tex said humourlessly.

"Have you checked her?" the man demanded.

"Yeah."

"And nobody's followed her? Nobody's running surveillance?"

"If they were, they will have lost her. She came to us dark. Wasn't showing up on any of the systems we monitor."

"Where's her friend with the exploding suitcase?"

"Wouldn't say."

"I'm here to speak to Leona," Freya cut in, her slender patience worn out. "Urgently."

"You had your chance," the man pointed out. "We wanted to work with you. Instead, you caused this–" He gestured to encompass the room and its hectic-looking activity. "You drew a lot of heat down on us with your antics. We're having to pull out. Find a new home."

"Something for your non-techno members to get excited about," Freya said. Their expressions implied they didn't enjoy the quip.

"I'm sorry I brought heat down on you," she said. "That wasn't my intention. Think about it from my perspective. I had arrived and fallen in with a group who weren't who they said they were, at least initially. The only sane course of action was to get out and reassess. I would have done the same thing again, until I could be sure who I was dealing with could be trusted."

"And you can be sure of that now?" Tex asked.

"Let's say I've gotten a better lay of the land in the last twenty-four hours."

"So, what, you're here to take us up on our offer?"

"Nearly. Where's Leona?"

Reboot's undeclared leader looked as unhappy to see Freya as her companions. Leona ushered Freya into a corner of the wide room, perching on a stack of boxes.

"You're brave, coming back here," she said.

"Or desperate," Freya replied with a cold smile. "It's a big city, and I need a friend."

"Where's the friend you had? Will?"

"Taken. By VERT. That's the main reason why I'm here."

"I'm sorry if they have him, I really am," Leona said. "But if that's the case there's not much we can do. We've lost activists to them before. I have yet to see any of them again. I fear the worst for some of them."

"They had me too, and yet here I am," Freya said.

Leona looked at her sharply. "You escaped?"

"No, I was released, and I saw a good deal of where they're based. It isn't as impregnable as it seems."

"Why did they release you?" Leona demanded. "Are you leading them back here?"

"No. No tails. No debts or bargains either, on my part. It was Will who got me out. He promised to help VERT's leader crack open the hacker groups in this city. Groups including yours. You're right to up stakes and move, but that will only be a temporary solution. I want to get Will out before he's forced to come good on his promise and betray any of us."

"You two have really messed everything up, you know that?" Leona said.

"I know, and for that I apologise," Freya said. "I should never have taken this job. We were betrayed, by someone back in London."

Back in London. Not back home. She kept talking.

"I need to make it all right and stop something like Albion from happening again, but I can't do it on my own."

"Spell out what you want," Leona said, calling over a trio of what Freya assumed were Reboot's most senior members, including Tex.

"I need about a dozen or so of your best fighters, a few more spotters, and your three fastest vehicles. We're going to break Will out of the Humboldthain flak tower. And after that, things are going to get really interesting."

"I don't like it," Leona's tall lieutenant, Max, said when Freya had finished explaining her plan.

"It's minimal risk from your perspective," Freya said. "A bit over a dozen activists, a few cars, a few guns, and you could turn everything on its head."

"Even if I were profligate with the lives of my friends, you speak as though Reboot can afford to lose a dozen dedicated members," Leona said. "We're not DedSec. We don't have a legion of underground contacts or a web of runners and informers. We're a close-knit group. We don't undertake big operations like this."

"But you'll need to at some point, if you want to make a difference," Freya pointed out. "You think you've done well so far, and you probably have. Hacking bankers' accounts and redistributing the money to homeless charities and food banks. Plastering propaganda up on government websites. Spray painting your logo on walls. It's all fine, but it doesn't raise you above the status of minor annoyance. If you're anything like DedSec, you're going to have to aim higher."

"Who said we want to be anything like DedSec?" Tex pointed out.

"You want to make a difference, don't you?" Freya asked. "A real, lasting difference. You don't want to make ripples. You don't want to make moves on a board, or even upend it. You want to change the whole rigged, rotten game for one with fair rules that people stick to, and that doesn't use dice that one side can load. That's what DedSec's doing, slowly but surely. And you can do the same here."

Even a week ago saying anything like that about DedSec would have been the last thing Freya would have done. But it wasn't just for show. Amidst the chaos of coming home, the struggles of being hunted, interrogated, and seeing the people out on the streets, Freya had connected again with the feelings she had experienced in the early days of DedSec. The years had dulled her to the importance of the organisation, giving a voice to the voiceless, hope to the hopeless, but the hard experiences of the past day had sharpened that edge once again. DedSec wasn't Wellend, a fanatic who would betray his own people to further his distorted view of the cause, and it wasn't M-Bahn, a shallow front for criminals, to subvert and taint good deeds. DedSec was like Reboot, a shared, common quest to make common decency for everyone.

"You don't seem like the ideological type," Max said.

"Ideology's why I'm here." Freya said. "You've seen the specifics of what I'm proposing. Don't you think it can be done?"

"We'll need more than a dozen plus a few extras," Leona said. "At least double that number again watching the roads. VERT will put pressure on the regular police. They'll have blocks set up all the way."

"But you can intercept them?"

"Probably. Or at least disrupt them, help make sure the transport from Humboldthain gets through."

"That's vital, or this will all be for nothing," Freya said. "We can't fight VERT alone. We're going to need Kaiser's help."

"It's clever," Max allowed. "And incredibly risky."

"It's only clever if it works," Leona said, still sounding unsure. "Even best-case scenario, we're going to suffer tonight. There'll be casualties."

"It will work," Freya insisted. "Because it has to. If not, they'll prey on Will at their leisure. He's a good guy, but he's not a fighter, not tough like you or I. He'll break, and then they'll bend him to help them hunt you down. All of you. Wherever you're planning to shift this hackerspace to, it won't stay hidden for long."

"I tend to respond better to encouragement rather than threats," Leona said.

"Then how's this for encouragement – I've just given you a blueprint for beating VERT and M-Bahn in one night."

Leona looked thoughtful, her fair features set. Then, abruptly, she smacked her palm down on top of the crate they had been leaning over and gestured to Max.

"Stop the evacuation."

Max looked for a moment like he was about to argue, then thought better of it. He barked a few words, and the frantic movement around them stilled.

"Everybody listen up," Leona called, her voice taking on a strong, authoritative tone. Freya realised immediately why, regardless of whether or not Reboot had a proper command structure, she was in charge here.

"We're not leaving, not yet," she carried on, looking fiercely at those around her. "It's good to live to fight another day. Sometimes though, fighting is all you can do. And we haven't done enough of that."

By now everyone had stopped what they were doing. Some looked curious, others excited. So many of them were so young, Freya realised. She felt a pang of regret at what she was doing. Some of them looked just the way she probably had, getting caught up for the first time in a big operation. And look how that had turned out for her.

But she needed help. Hell, she needed an army. Men like Wellend or Erik or Kaiser wouldn't have hesitated. And tonight, neither would she. There was no use trying to hunt wolves alone.

"Most of you know this woman, Freya Bauer," Leona said, pointing at her. "She's a fellow Berliner, though she might not sound like it. You know that when she came here, we tried to get her on our side. It didn't work at first. She had reservations.

Well, she's on our side now. And what's more, she's going to help us turn the tide."

"How do we know we can trust her?" one of the older Rebooters asked, his arms folded, expression fierce.

"You trust me, and I trust her," Leona began to say, but Freya cut in.

"I could have gone home tonight," she said. "I have a family back home. Right now, to the best of my knowledge, they're being hunted by men sent by Emil Kaiser. He ordered the death of my father, over twenty years ago. Until tonight, I wanted nothing more than to get home and make sure my son and my mother were safe. Now, however, I understand I can't protect them there if I don't act here. I'm sure a lot of you can appreciate that. The safety of our loved ones, of our families, may well depend on what we do tonight. Germany is being pushed down a dark road, and we're going to drag her back into the light."

"How?" another of the activists asked. Leona smiled.

"Gather round, and we'll show you."

PART THREE

RECKONING

25
An Ugly Night

Once the briefing was completed, Reboot geared up. Crates were unpacked once more, exposing the extent of Reboot's armoury. Freya had seen far more impressive. There was a collection of G36s and MP5s which, according to Leona, were old German military surplus which VERT had bought and which Reboot had intercepted.

"We weren't planning on using them," she said. "Just keeping them out of VERT's hands."

"Full irony marks if you do now though," Freya pointed out.

Besides those there was a collection of AK47s, M1911 pistols, and most interestingly, a trio of Goblin assault rifles, one of which belonged to Leona herself. Ammunition wasn't in huge supply, and there wasn't enough webbing or pouches to go around either.

"Next time, make sure you intercept the tactical gear too," Freya pointed out.

"We're not paramilitaries," Leona said unhappily.

"We're revolutionaries," Max clarified.

"The crossovers might surprise you," Freya said. She selected one of the G36s, checking that it was clear and glancing through the dual combat sight. It had a carry handle in front of the sights, and the stock was foldable. She liked it.

"Not many of us have combat experience," Leona pointed out. While she had done well to rally the others earlier, it was easy to sense her nerves now. For her own part, Freya was too busy to feel worried about what ifs. The plan was bold, but it might yet work, and she knew she could improvise. There was no point in getting worried at this stage.

"We're not going to be live on this one for long," she tried to reassure Leona. "In and out. I'll prep the insertion team before we leave. Just tell everyone to follow my lead and, when the time comes, don't hesitate. Let the adrenaline do its job."

She called the team they had assembled shortly afterwards. They were divided into three groups. The smallest consisted of Tex and the other guy who had picked them up when she and Will had first arrived, Termite. They were staying remote. Then there were the road monitors, six teams of two, who would drive along the 100 and 115 motorways and, with the assistance of Tex and Termite hacking into the road camera systems, keep an eye out for police roadblocks.

The remaining dozen, including Leona and Max, were Freya's strike team. Most of them were a bit older and more physically capable than the other Reboot activists Freya had seen. Max and one other were even ex-military. Freya had her reservations about even this picked group, but she kept them to herself. She believed she could get them in and out again. She had to, or none of this would work.

"On paper, this should be simple," she told them. "Everybody knows their task?"

There were nods. They were nervous, she could tell, but she also sensed a streak of cold, hard determination. A lot of them had probably imagined stuff like this. Going on the offensive. Taking it up a level from online activism or distributing leaflets. They looked like the protesters Freya had seen out on the streets earlier. Ready for it.

"Everyone got their Optiks?" Freya added, checking they were all equipped and fully interfaced. Unsurprisingly, they had a much better set of tech gear than combat kit.

"Nothing left to do but get out there and do it," she said, snapping a magazine into her G36. "Let's saddle up."

It looked like it was turning into an ugly night, and it wasn't just Berlin's mood. A cold rain came and went, turning briefly to sleet. According to Freya's Optik it was three degrees Celsius, with the possibility of snow.

She wasn't sure if that would help them in the long run, but short-term it would probably be good to keep visibility down and surveillance operators confined to their heated booths. Nobody wanted to be out on a night like this. Only hunters.

They piled into a van out the back of the Berghain, masked up. Freya had retrieved Mister Scruff, while Max had an armoured faceplate, featureless apart from the eyes and a glowing reboot symbol on its forehead. Leona's was the most impressive, a multicoloured lion with kaleidoscopic eyes and a bushy, neon rainbow mane. They exchanged a nod as they took the final seats in the back of the transport.

The vehicle lurched into motion. Now Freya's nerves came into play. This was the quiet time, the gnawing time when all had been set in motion, but the moment of action had not yet been reached. She knew better than to try to run through the possibilities and the unknowns that lay ahead, and likewise banished thoughts of home, of Belinda or Andrew, from her mind. None of that would do any good. She began to count the seconds.

It was only a fifteen-minute drive to the street Freya had earmarked as their disembarkation point.

"Looks quiet," the van's driver called back to them.

"Everybody set?" Freya asked, feeling her heartbeat picking up. There were general affirmatives. She looked across at Leona, face inscrutable behind her snarling, multi-hued visage.

She nodded.

Freya lifted her rifle and opened the back door of the van.

M-Bahn gathered beneath the taxidermied elephant, under the landing outside Emil Kaiser's office in the Jägerhalle. Kaiser himself addressed them from the upstairs, leaning against the balustrade, his tone harsh.

"Tonight, we show everyone else, who runs this city," he said. "Not DedSec, or Reboot, or any other group of agitators. Not VERT, or their political shills, or the rest of the mob in the Bundestag. It's us. The power behind Berlin's throne. We decide who lives and who dies, when there's peace and when there's war. And right now, it's war."

There were thirty-six foot soldiers of Kaiser's empire below, gazing up at him. About half were M-Bahn; the rest were his enforcers and members of subsidiary crime groups, added to give some backbone to the fledgling hacker group. It wasn't the finest force he had ever assembled, but the time had come to act, and all of them were masked up and armed to the teeth.

"You are all aware of the target's identity," Kaiser carried on. "She should already be in our hands. Tonight is your opportunity to rectify that. We go in, we find Freya Bauer, and we kill anyone who tries to stop us. Is that clear?"

Apparently it was.

"Final weapons checks, and we assemble on the driveway outside," Kaiser said. He dismissed the motley assembly, all bar Teuton, who climbed upstairs to speak with him.

"You're sure about this, Father?" she asked quietly. "Once we make a play this big, there'll be no going back."

"If we don't, there will be no going back regardless," Kaiser said, brushing aside her concerns. "I have staked too much on capturing and killing the Bauers now. Everyone knows this is my work at play. If I don't succeed, my reputation will have been destroyed. Our reputation. A lifetime's work establishing myself, rebuilding the Kaiser name, all undone. And besides, there is more to it than mere vanity. Your mother cries out for vengeance."

Teuton's expression hardened, as Kaiser had known it would. Thomas Bauer, that treacherous police informant, had led the authorities to Kaiser's home one fateful night, almost thirty years before. The death of Teuton's mother, Bella, in the chaos and confusion of the raid, had been a hammer blow, one that had simultaneously broken Kaiser's heart and hardened his resolve. All the other problems down the years, even the DeLock debacle, paled in comparison to that particular injury.

"We tried to be too clever before," Teuton said. "Luring her in. Let me kill her on sight."

"No, or it was all for nothing," Kaiser said sharply. "It has to be a spectacle."

"What about the others? Has the Ghost tracked her family in England down yet?"

"Yes, he has the son in his sights. He's ready to strike. He awaits only word that I have Freya."

There were footsteps on the stairs. Kaiser looked past Teuton, annoyed, to find Luther approaching nervously.

"What do you want?" Kaiser demanded.

"Forgive the interruption," Luther said, not meeting Kaiser's gaze. "But I've just been tipped off by a contact. It seems a specific set of VERT CTOS servers are suffering a DDoS attack, right now. They're the ones responsible for the headquarters at the Humboldthain flak tower."

Kaiser frowned.

"Humboldthain?" he wondered aloud. Unlike their black sites, the location of VERT's headquarters was known, a mark of the organisation's pride and arrogance. "Who's attacking VERT in their own backyard, tonight of all nights?"

"Maybe it's something to do with the unrest," Teuton suggested. "Word is the riots are heating up."

"No," Kaiser replied, feeling a sudden, unwelcome certainty. "It's her. It's Freya Bauer."

26
Denial-of-Service

Freya and her team piled out the back of the van and split off into two groups of six that ghosted quickly and quietly down either side of the street they had emerged onto. At the far end, across the road running parallel with it, was the dark, rising mass of Humboldthain park, the wooded hill with the infamous flak tower at its crest.

Freya felt her Optik ping, and moments later the message she had received scrolled up on her lens.

The DDoS attack was underway. She relayed as much to Leona and the others.

Termite and Tex had been left back in the Berghain to run the remote part of the plan. They had identified the servers running the CTOS program responsible for much of the electronic security protecting Humboldthain. A DDoS attack – distributed denial-of-service –was as crude as it came with regards to hacking, but it would give them about a minute before Humboldthain's systems were back online. Nowhere near long enough to storm the flak tower itself, but enough to get past the perimeter fence.

"Move," Freya ordered, waving Leona across before rising and sprinting in a low crouch over the parallel street. It was deserted, so only the ugly glow of the streetlamps bore witness to Reboot as they bolted across the open ground and reached the wire fence that ran around the foot of the park.

It was an electrified mesh, or would have been but for the DDoS interruption. There was only one way to find out, and certainly no time to hesitate.

The G36 slung across her back, Freya snatched at the wiring with both hands. There was no jolt of pain, no terrible shock. She planted her feet on a lower section of the fence and began to climb rapidly, the wire rattling as she hauled herself up. Her wounded leg twinged, but she ignored it.

It didn't bear thinking about what would happen if the barrier became electrified again before she was over.

She crested the top, descended a little way down, then risked a jump on the remaining distance. A large drift of autumn leaves from the park's trees had built up on the other side, and they cushioned her to a degree, but she felt it again in her thigh.

There was a flurry of similar thuds as the rest of the team dropped down as well. Freya remained crouched, unslinging the G36 from her shoulder, probing the darkness beneath the trees around her through Mister Scruff's eye slits.

There was no movement. She glanced briefly left and right, seeing that all the others were over and waiting on her signal.

A dull hum filled the air. She realised that the fence had just gone live again.

That window of opportunity was shut, but hopefully another was already open. She dialled up Tex on her Optik's retinal display.

"How we looking?" she asked.

"Well, we're underway," came Tex's response. "Their systems have gone to the backup program. Not CTOS."

That was good news. Freya clenched a fist and punched it up the slope, signalling for the others to advance. They began to climb, into the branches and the undergrowth and the darkness, into what Freya had no doubt would be the most desperate fight of their lives.

"Word from surveillance, sir," Alex called to Erik, having to shout over the sound of the riot engulfing the VERT line. "CTOS is down!"

"What?" Erik barked incredulously as around him bodies crashed against shields and improvised weapons against helmets, while batons cracked and shuddered, bruising flesh and fracturing bone. Erik was containing the rioters moving up from the university, but he abruptly wished he wasn't. A few minutes ago Alex had informed him that intel from the airport claimed Freya hadn't boarded a flight. She was still in Berlin, and worse, seemingly now the CTOS servers used by VERT for surveillance and security were being hacked.

"There was a DDoS attack initiated over two minutes ago, sir," Alex was saying, looking at the reinforced Optik screen secured to the back of his riot gauntlet. "The system has gone to its backup, but the Humboldthain garrison believe the perimeter fence might have been breached."

"It's DedSec," Erik said with grim certainty. "It's Freya, and that bookworm we left in our cells."

A piece of brick cracked off the helmet of the VERT trooper directly in front of Erik, causing him to stumble back and almost break the line. Erik snarled, taking only a split-second to reassess the situation.

He'd been misled, and there was nothing he hated more. Suddenly, the riots tonight seemed meaningless. Perhaps they were even all part of Freya's plan. Cause chaos and draw VERT's manpower out onto the streets, leaving Humboldthain only lightly guarded.

Well, she could only fool him for so long. He had shown mercy before. He wouldn't again.

"Issue a general order to all units to withdraw immediately towards the flak tower," he snapped at Alex. Behind the visor of his riot helm, the lieutenant looked shocked.

"All units? Even the ones engaged? What about the rioters? What do we tell the regular police?"

"Tell them to cancel all leave and do their damned job," Erik shouted. "I want every single man and woman in the employ of the Vertidiger converging on Humboldthain *immediately*!"

"Yes, sir!"

Erik stalked away from the buckling cordon, headed towards one of the VERT armoured vehicles parked up behind the line. He was angry, and looking for something to channel that anger into.

There was going to be a reckoning, and it was going to be tonight.

Freya's team pushed up the slope. She had a compass on her Optik's display as well as schematics Tex had been able to hack from a freedom of information database, but for a short while she was still worried they weren't going in the right direction. The darkness beneath the park's trees was almost impenetrable.

Then, after a few minutes, she felt concrete beneath her feet. They passed over the roadway that led to the flak tower's main gate, which in turn meant they were on course.

She called the others to a halt beyond it, and blink-checked her Optik. This was the most uncertain part of the plan. For it to work, Will's own Optik implant had to still be functioning and online. She was afraid that VERT would have removed it, in which case their only hope was to cut their way back out through the fence with the rubber-sheathed shears Max had brought.

She searched for Will's implant with her own Optik, hoping they were in range and that the flak tower's makeshift cells wouldn't block it. She had to refresh three times, pensive and stressed, but finally Will's Optik popped up, or rather the implant that still carried the data from Will's device.

She found the specific app she needed and began to download.

Get ready, she texted him, knowing he would see it via his own lens but couldn't reply. *We're busting you out.*

The app finished downloading. Freya opened it and ran through it, checking it worked the way she assumed it would. Hacking was far from her personal comfort zone. She was the one who protected the one doing the hacking, and made sure they got out in one piece when they were done, but doing it now gave her an unexpected exhilaration.

If it worked, VERT were going to be, briefly, totally defenceless.

She moved with the others further up the slope, until they reached the tree line. Ahead were only stumps and low undergrowth, a killing field felled in front of the flak tower itself. It stood above them, a squat, blocky shape silhouetted against the city's light pollution beyond it. There was another fence and, more importantly, a series of squat shapes in front of it. Freya had seen them on the way out.

They were CT drones modified to be used as static defences. With their rotors removed and their underslung weaponry placed on top, they had been half buried into the slope of

Humboldthain park and partially covered in foliage. Armed with general purpose machine guns, the automated point defences would be able to mow down any unidentified individual who set foot beyond the tree line.

The Reboot team didn't have the firepower to knock out even one of the turrets, let alone enough to get beyond them. Hopefully though, they wouldn't need guns.

The DDoS attack had knocked the CTOS 3.0 servers running the flak tower's defences out of the game completely for about a minute, only long enough for them to get over the perimeter wall. At least, that was the plan.

"The defence systems are back online," Leona warned quietly. "But it doesn't look like they're using CTOS. Take a look."

Freya opened the NetHack view on her Optik, turning her world a fuzzy grey. By focusing and blinking on specific spots in her field of vision, she was able to highlight the defensive systems ahead of them, namely the line of embedded CT drones turned defence turrets, demarcated in red. They were still fully functional, and a quick scan failed to identify the program running them.

"We don't know what it is," Leona admitted. "Erik Gerhardt himself ordered it to be developed, because he doesn't trust CTOS. We're still working on cracking it."

Freya had suspected as much. She remembered Erik's dislike of CTOS from Wellend's briefing. She was hoping that a privately developed, new system would still have plenty of backdoors that could be exploited, namely friend/foe recognition. They had in effect gained ten minutes where VERT's headquarters weren't running off CTOS, and that meant she had access, via Will's Optik implant, to the same techniques he had used during their last encounter with a VERT-controlled CT drone.

She shared the app with the rest of the team. While it downloaded, Leona dropped in beside her.

"They must know we're here by now," she murmured.

As though on cue there was a rattling sound. Freya had heard CT drones back in London make that noise before, and it was never a good sign. Their weapons systems were cycling up.

"Down," she barked, snatching Leona and throwing them both into the undergrowth.

At the same time, the drones opened fire.

Hard rounds ripped through the foliage overhead, cracking through branches and sending leaves and splinters raining down on them. The rest of the team dropped, mercifully just before they were cut to pieces.

"Back down the slope," Freya yelled over the thudding discharge of the trio of drones in front of them and to their immediate left and right. "Move back and stay low!"

She dragged Leona a few paces, until she was confident the Reboot leader hadn't frozen. Then she let her make her own way down.

Freya suspected the drones were programmed only to open fire when someone passed into the kill zone, but she also suspected that somebody was watching them, either through the drones' optics or through cameras installed in the trees around them. Realising that the Reboot team were too wise to walk directly into the kill zone, they had overridden the automatic system and opened fire manually.

Which was smarter than Freya had given VERT credit for.

Nevertheless, there was a reason for the presence of the kill zone. The parkland's slope meant that past the trees the embedded drones didn't have an angle. After no more than a few seconds of scrambling desperately downhill through leaf mulch and over roots, it was clear that the GPMG rounds being directed their way were ripping through the bark much higher up.

"Here is good," Freya shouted, trying to marshal the Rebooters. They had likely been rattled by the sudden salvo, and with good reason. Freya ordered them to check for anyone missing in the near-total darkness beneath the boughs; then, when she had ascertained that everyone was present and unharmed, she ordered them to check that they all had the app she had sent downloaded.

They did. That meant they were heading straight back up.

The CT drones ceased fire. Freya made sure everyone had their Optiks out – she was fairly certain Will had only done that for effect when they had been on the rooftop of the art gallery, but she didn't entirely understand any of this stuff, and she didn't want to take any chances. Taking the lead, she led them back to the edge of the trees.

The drones didn't fire again. Moonlight picked out their barrels, smoking faintly. Freya had slung her G36, and had her hands-on burner Optik raised. This went against every ounce of instinct in her body, even more so given she was supposed to be the one used to facing these sorts of situations. A defensive perimeter she could work through. Relying on a hack to do so, however, was way outside her comfort zone.

She stepped out into the open, holding the Optik up. If she had downloaded everything correctly, the device was showing itself as another VERT drone.

Nothing happened. In a moment of surreal silence, Freya began to walk forward.

Slowly, their own Optik hardware clutched in their hands, the others followed.

The distance closed. Freya expected with every pace to see

the barrel of the drone's weapon flare, for a sudden hail of bullets to rip her to ragged ruin and gut Reboot's best and brightest. But there was nothing. The drone remained stubbornly inert. No doubt in the flak tower's control centre its operator was having a screaming match with their supervisor as they tried to override the emplacement's targeting protocols. Opening fire on unknowns was one thing, but the systems were hardwired not to be able to shoot anything they identified as belonging to VERT.

That didn't mean they wouldn't be back in control soon. Freya began to run.

She raced past the drone, and found herself presented with another electric fence.

"Cutters," she hissed urgently to Max as the others joined her.

He had barely started to chop his way through the fence when there was the crack of a gunshot. There was someone on the other side, and they had just opened fire.

More shots sounded as Freya dropped to her knee and returned fire. She could see almost nothing in the darkness. Sparks sprayed fitfully from the electric fencing as bullets cut through it. She heard a grunt and realised Max had been hit in the shoulder.

"Cover him," she barked at the rest of Reboot, who seemed to have frozen, stunned. Leona began to shoot first, blindly into the dark beyond the fence, as Freya threw herself to Max's side and pulled him back.

"Put pressure on it," she told him, directing one hand to the wound, the blood glistening and black in the erratic light of the muzzle flashes. "I've got to finish the fence."

Freya retrieved the fallen rubber-sheathed cutters and got to work where Max had left off, doing her best to ignore the whizzing sound of bullets passing close by, or how the fence shuddered every time a round sliced through it. At this rate both sides would have shot it up so thoroughly the cutters wouldn't even be necessary.

She chopped away the last wires and used the cutters to snag the centre of the section she had removed, dragging it back and leaving a sparking, fizzing gap. Knowing there was no time to widen it, she scrambled through, expecting at any moment to feel either the unwelcome jolt of electrocution, or the brute agony of a bullet. She had been shot before, twice. It wasn't something she ever wanted to experience again.

She dragged herself through more leaf mulch and rolled, feeling several rounds smack into the ground around her, throwing up debris. She hauled the G36 round off her shoulder and began to shoot again, trying to pick out anything ahead. The flak tower loomed directly above them now, a brutalist crown for Humboldthain's hilltop, a callback to the last war that had ripped this country apart.

Leona was through the fence, the multicoloured fangs of her feline mask bared. She added her firepower to Freya's. She detected muzzle flashes from what she thought was a low wall at the base of the flak tower building, and directed her shots in that direction. The return heat became gradually less intense, while that of the attackers grew as more Rebooters made it through and spread out to the left and right. One helped drag Max past the fence.

"Cease fire," Freya said, having to repeat the order before it got through to the adrenaline-charged hackers.

"Anybody hit?" she asked. Besides Max one other, Console, had been clipped. Both could go on. Both would have to, unless they wanted to end up in a VERT cell.

"We have to keep moving," Freya urged, getting to her feet. "We're close now."

They headed for the wall. As they went, a message from Tex flashed up via Freya's lens.

All VERT forces disengaging from rioters. You're about to have a lot of company.

That was bad news. Freya had expected a slower response. Their window of opportunity was minutes from slamming shut.

But they were so close. Freya found the stairs alongside the wall and took them up to the flak tower's open base level. She spotted blood there, but no bodies – VERT's meagre garrison had pulled back inside, leaving the outer defences open. That included the reconfigured zoo block.

She reviewed the stolen schematics of the place via her implant, squinting slightly as she zoomed in on her exact location. The old 90s animal enclosures, a short-lived attempt at expanding Berlin Zoo, weren't fully part of the flak tower complex. They lay in its shadow, in a depression in the park's southern slope that had been hollowed out and turned into what was supposed to be an animal sanctuary, but which was now used to pen VERT's prisoners.

More gunfire rang out, a series of bullets cracking off the stone wall at Freya's back. VERT troops had manned the flak tower's twin roofs looming over them, and now had a good angle down onto where they were standing.

"Get to the base of the wall," Freya shouted, pushing the closest Rebooters to the foot of the tower, where the VERT grunts wouldn't be able to hit them. "Wait for me there!"

Without waiting for a reply, she threw herself towards the wide set of stairs that led down into the enclosure, more shots ricocheting off the concrete around her.

This was where she had been led out from before. She descended, momentarily thankful for the cover the depression provided. The crumbling walls on either side of her were marred with old graffiti. Ahead lay a corridor leading off to the different enclosure blocks. There was no sign of any resistance. There was a metal gate, but it lay half open.

Probably a bad sign.

Rifle raised, Freya eased past the door, checking her corners. Still nothing. The dark cell where she had been held was directly to her left. The next four cells were deserted, abandoned. No Will.

This was what she had feared most. They had moved him. Into the flak tower, or to another location? She remembered she could still track the implant and blinked up the finder settings on her Optik. Sure enough, it triangulated Will, or at least his implant, inside the main flak tower building, directly above.

Not ideal. Freya hadn't anticipated breaking into the tower itself. The plan had been to snatch Will from the enclosure, steal one of the VERT combat vehicles from the neighbouring motor pool, and use it to ramraid their way back out again. They surely only had a few minutes before the full CTOS umbrella enveloped Humboldthain, reactivating all the automated defences.

But they had to try. She charged back up the steps from the enclosure, another flurry of shots from above cracking wide, and hit the wall where the Reboot team were sheltering, next to Leona.

"They've moved him inside the tower," she panted, smacking the cracked concrete beside her. "I'm going in to get him. Take the others and grab one of the armoured carriers. If I'm not with you within the next five minutes, get the hell out. The whole of the Vertidiger is currently converging on us."

"I'm coming with you," Leona said. "Don't argue, there's no time. Max will get the others out."

Leona was right, there was no time. Freya led her round the base of the wall to where she remembered seeing the tower's main entrance, a mesh gate. Her only remaining hope was that it was deactivated, because she doubted she would be able to shoot it open.

They rounded the corner and found the gate intact and locked.

End of the road.

27
Hunters Hunted

Teuton rarely observed uncertainty in her father, but she was seeing it now. It quickly led to frustration, an emotion she shared. None of them had expected this.

It appeared the Vertidiger's headquarters in the flak tower at Humboldthain was under attack. Not just a cyberattack, but a physical assault. Those at the Jägerhalle were trying to piece together what was happening through a mix of personal contacts and online chatter. M-Bahn had been allowed to use the villa's control centre to try to hack into Humboldthain directly or patch through to the VERT channels to find out more, but thus far they were having little luck. It was more apparent than ever to Teuton that the organisation she was supposedly a member of really had just been set up as a cover for luring out Freya Bauer. In terms of doing hacking of its own, the likes of Luther and the others weren't up to much.

"It must be Reboot," Teuton said as she stood with Kaiser, near the back of the control centre, watching the frantic work going on across multiple desktops and monitors. "No one else has the capacity to take action like this. In fact, I didn't think even Reboot could do it. They're just a bunch of script kiddies."

"I've seen plenty of people beaten by kids down the years," Kaiser said darkly. "Why would Reboot be trying to break Freya out though? You saw her trying to escape from them, at Berghain. Are they trying to do what we were planning? Get her and kill her?"

"Luther claims Reboot were trying to warn Freya about M-Bahn," Teuton said. "I don't think she trusts anybody."

"Unfortunately not."

"We should move now, before this plays out any further. If they're trying to rescue her, she could disappear with them."

Kaiser didn't respond. It was strange to see him acting indecisively, but she could understand his desire for more information. Right now it was like being blindfolded in the middle of a gunfight. It was obvious a lot was going down, but exactly what was happening was impossible to tell.

"Do we know for certain Freya Bauer is imprisoned at Humboldthain?" Luther asked abruptly from where he was sitting in front of one of the screen banks.

"What do you mean?" Kaiser asked. "Teuton had a positive ID on her capture by VERT, and I have other contacts who said they saw the transport carrying her arriving at the park."

"I think she may have left since though," Luther said. "And now she's going back."

"What are you talking about?" Kaiser snapped, striding over to where the hacker was working. Teuton joined him as Luther pointed up at one section of his monitor.

"I've managed to gain entry to Humboldthain's CTOS-run surveillance cameras. This one here shows the main gate."

Teuton realised immediately what she was looking at, or rather who. There were two figures, armed with assault rifles, poised outside the gate to VERT's flak tower. The one in front had a cat mask on, the exact same one Teuton had seen in her briefings, and had spotted in person at the Berghain. It was Freya Bauer, and like Luther had said, it looked more like she was breaking into VERT's headquarters than breaking out.

"Her partner," she said abruptly, making the connection quicker than the others. She had seen them both together, Freya and William. According to the intel Kaiser had gleaned from their DedSec contact, he was her ex-partner, but from what Teuton had seen they still worked well together.

"She must have gotten out, or been released," she went on. "And now she's going back for him."

"Then she's an even bigger fool than I took her for," Kaiser said. He smacked Luther on the shoulder, looking at Teuton.

"We're going to miss the party if we don't act now. Luther will keep the pressure up from here. Teuton, you arm the others. We're going after Freya before VERT kills her."

Will had been sure it was Freya as soon as his implant alerted him to the fact that one of his apps was being remotely downloaded.

He didn't know whether to be angry or relieved. He'd driven a desperate bargain to get her out, to get her back to London and Andrew, but here she was, risking her life presumably in an effort to free him.

Maybe she just wanted the satisfaction of killing him herself.

Either way, he doubted she would get the chance unless he did something. Even if she had found allies in Berlin – Reboot, he presumed – it would be almost impossible for her to reach him in the bowels of the flak tower. His hidden implant was still viable, but if he tried to use it to reach out to her directly, he was certain VERT would trace the Optik's usage. The cell he was being held in was old school, just a regular lock. He'd need to fall back on something besides hacking to get out and lend a hand.

He heard the rattle of gunfire, reaching him through the old firing slit that occupied the upper wall of the bunk room. They were really in trouble.

There was nothing he could do but try. He went and banged on the door, calling for the guard. After a moment the slat was drawn back, exposing a worried-looking VERT trooper.

"They're coming to kill me," Will told him urgently. "It's M-Bahn. They know I'm going to give their identities and location to you."

"You'll be safe here," the guard said, trying to appear more stoic than he looked.

"I doubt it," Will said, taking the fear he felt for Freya and turning it into supposed concern for his own safety. "They've already hacked your outer defences. I can get them back up and running again though. I know how they operate. Take me to the base commander and tell him I can help."

The trooper looked conflicted. The slat banged shut again, and Will overheard him talking briefly on his radio. He held his breath, knowing that this was the only play he could make. It seemed unlikely to work, but he had long ago learned that a great deal of confidence twinned with a high-stress situation could yield unexpected, positive results.

After another pause during which the sound of gunfire from outside only increased, there was a thud of locks and the door swung open.

"I'm to take you to the control centre," the guard said, waving him out of the bunk room. He had a baton drawn. "Don't try anything."

"The only thing I'm trying is not to get killed," Will said, holding his hands up as he stepped out.

The control room lay at the flak tower's heart, and was rammed with monitors and communications systems. It seemed badly undermanned, only two VERT operators and what Will took to be the acting base commander present. They all looked far too young for the role. He could only assume that Freya had deliberately hit the place while something else was keeping Erik Gerhardt and the rest of his grunts occupied elsewhere.

"They've knocked CTOS out, haven't they?" Will asked the commander, going off his assumption that Freya had used the app she had pulled from his implant to get past Humboldthain's automated and electronic defences. The young officer pursed his lips, looking just as uncertain as the guard still hovering at Will's shoulder.

"They're not your friends?" he asked Will.

"My only friend abandoned me here," Will said, laying on the bitterness. "You don't know how DedSec operate, do you?"

The commander offered only a shrug. He seemed totally unsure.

"I promise you, they don't take kindly to snitches, to rats," Will pressed on. "They get liquidated, immediately. It's how the organisation maintains its secrecy and its internal integrity. Your leader presumably told my former friend that I agreed to help VERT in exchange for her freedom. That means, whether she wants it or not, a hit will have been put out on me. They want to silence me before I can break them wide open for der Vertidiger."

"My orders are simply to keep you contained until Colonel Gerhardt gets back, which should be soon," the base commander said.

"It better be very soon, or I'll be dead, and likely you too," Will said, raising his voice. "I can get your defences back up and running. I know the hacks they've been using to drop CTOS. Let me access your systems, before it's too late!"

The commander looked on the brink of panicking. The other VERT troopers in the room stared at him, desperate for directives, for leadership. It was clear only those not yet trusted in external operations had been left behind in Humboldthain.

"How many men do you currently have at your disposal?" Will pressed the officer.

"Not many," he admitted. "It's only a skeleton force. The colonel wanted to make a show of strength against the protesters. The automated defences were supposed to be enough."

"Well, they're no use right now. I know what the attackers are using. They'll be in here in no time if you don't let me fix things."

"Fine." The commander waved at one of the two operators to make way for Will at one of the consoles. "This is the main security interface. They're using a jamming device, and we don't know how to override the automation. Get it up and running again."

"With pleasure." Will hardly dared to believe his luck as he sat down and quickly familiarised himself with the displays.

He had to work fast, before they realised what was happening. Hopefully Freya would be in a position to take advantage. If not, he had no doubt he'd be locked back up in a matter of minutes, or worse.

He cycled through a set of security camera angles, seeing Freya in her cat mask and one other with a lion head moving towards the main gate into the flak tower.

Humboldthain's backup system had actually been locked out, and Will doubted Freya would have anything to get through it, but then that was exactly why Will had tried so hard to get to the controls.

He located the main gate on the digital switch panel, and unlocked it.

It took a second for any of the VERT onlookers to realise what he had just done. The commander shouted, and the guard launched at him, snatching him by the shoulder and hauling him up off his chair. Will went with him, throwing the guard off balance and landing a decent punch for what felt like the first time in his life. The man stumbled back, and for a brief instant Will stood defiant, blocking them from getting to the controls and resealing the door.

The two VERT operators rushed him. He doubted he could have taken even one of them, but with his sprained wrist still aching there was nothing he could do but grapple for a few precious seconds before his arms were pinned painfully behind his back and he was rammed down over the desk.

"The door, get the door," the commander was shouting. Will looked up as one scrambled to lock the gateway, fixing his eyes on the camera monitor, praying Freya had realised what he had just done.

She had. She and her lion friend were through and were progressing down a corridor. He saw the muzzle of Freya's rifle flare on the camera, and a second later heard the thundering report of the gun's discharge ringing through the block. She was close. Will presumed she had worked out she could track his implant's location. That was his only remaining hope.

"Bar the door and keep him restrained," the commander shouted, snatching up his radio to report the ingress, presumably to Erik. Will felt brief despair as he saw the door to the control centre slammed shut and barred with a manual set of locks. It was heavy and steel-plated. No amount of guile was getting through that one.

At least, no amount of tech guile. There was silence for a while from the corridor outside, and then a voice he recognised as Freya's shouted, muffled, from the other side.

"You've left two of your men out here, Mister Defender. Open the door, or I'll kill them both."

Will looked at the acting commander. He was pale-faced and looked close to a breakdown. Right now, Will wasn't sure whether that was a good thing or not.

"How do I know you have prisoners?" the man demanded, speaking to the door. "Tell them to identify themselves!"

There was a short, indecipherable conversation before a different voice called out.

"Trooper Kauf, number six-seven-eight-two-one."

Another joined it.

"Trooper Lindz, number six-three-one-one-nine. I'm sorry, sir!"

"Lindz has been shot in the thigh," Freya's voice added. "I'd recommend getting him medical attention, soon. Alternatively, I can make sure neither of them ever need medical attention ever again."

"Don't test her," Will told the commander, hissing through the pain in his wrist as the man pinning him tightened his hold. "She doesn't like to be messed around with. I speak from experience."

"I just want the prisoner," Freya shouted. "You don't even have to open up completely. Just toss him out."

"So considerate," Will muttered.

"You won't get away with this," the commander shouted back. "Reinforcements are converging on here as we speak!"

There was an echoing bang, startlingly loud even from the other side of the door. Will's eyes widened as he contemplated what Freya had just done, before her voice called out.

"That bullet went down the corridor. The next one goes in Kauf! Give me the damned prisoner!"

"Move him to the door," the commander snapped at the one holding Will. The other control room operator began to protest, but the officer snatched him and marched him to the entrance.

"You can have him," he shouted. "You'll all be back in the cells soon enough anyway!"

The door was unbolted, and before Will could collect himself, he found himself being shoved out almost on top of Freya, nearly getting a face full of rifle muzzle. She aimed at the opening while the lion covered the two VERT prisoners on their knees.

"Back inside," Freya snarled at the commander before he could step out after Will, menacing him with the rifle barrel. "And lock the door again. If I hear it unlocking while we're still in the corridor, your two friends are toast. That's English for dead. Understood?"

The door slammed shut again, leaving Will on the outside. Despite himself, he realised he was grinning. This was just like the good old days. Freya manhandled him down the corridor before he could even offer his thanks.

"No time," she said. The lion – Leona, Will now realised – walked backwards keeping the two VERT prisoners covered until they'd made it past the corridor.

"Pretty sure it's going to be a warm night out there, so usual rules apply," Freya said as they reached the main gate, able to unlock it manually from the inside. "Do exactly what I tell you."

"Understood," Will said, not even considering a witty retort. He could hear the gunfire even before the wire gate rolled open.

28
Exit Wound

Freya led the charge out from the gateway and along the side of the wall towards the adjoining motor pool. From the amount of shooting going on, the rest of the team were in serious trouble, and VERT reinforcements were starting to arrive.

Even worse, a warning flashed up on Freya's Optik HUD. Its DedSec-installed defensive systems were reading a deep profile attempt, and worse. Was it VERT? Whoever was doing it, they were now trying to hit them remotely. She took a moment to punch back, scrambling her data signature to delay their efforts.

Max and the rest of the gang had at least succeeded in getting their hands on some hardware. A VERT armoured troop transport was rolling up to the entrance, one Reboot activist manning the 30-cal. in the turret. She shot down towards the roadway leading to the base of the flak tower, rather than up at the tower itself. Fresh VERT troops marched up from the street.

Freya urged Leona and Will to sprint ahead towards the dubious cover of the transport, even as return fire struck sparks off its reinforced metal chassis.

The rear hatch was open, and the transport compartment

was packed. Freya got Will and Leona onboard, covering them with a burst of fire up at the flak tower's parapet while the 30-cal. continued to hit the approach road. Then, when they were in, she threw herself after them.

"Everybody on?" she shouted, checking that none of the team were absent. "Then drive!"

She swung the rear hatch shut as the transport lurched off, before pushing her way forwards towards the drive compartment. It was only partly separated from the troop section, and she was able to shout through at Max who, with his shoulder bound up, was directing the vehicle.

"Don't take the road, go down the slope," she urged. "The main entrance will be rammed with VERT!"

"What about the drones? And the trees?"

"Stop when you get to the trees. Shoot the bloody drones."

The instructions were simple enough. She saw the secondary wire fence loom through the armoured transport's vision slit, followed by a clattering impact as it simply rammed the obstruction, sparks flying and electrical charge flaring as they powered through with the momentum of the slope and the power of the vehicle's engine.

"Drive over that drone," Freya shouted as Max revved them through the remains of the fence. The CT drones manning the perimeter only had a one-hundred-and-eighty-degree arc of fire, so couldn't hit them when they were coming from the direction of the flak tower, but they would be fair game once they passed them towards the trees.

Max slammed over the top of the nearest, crushing it into the dirt. Seconds later the rattle of machine guns added to the cacophony as the other embedded systems along the line opened fire on the transport's rear. A constant deluge of impacts came from the outside of the hull. The vehicle made a terrifying sound and began to slow. It wouldn't make it through the next gate.

"Turn us around before the trees," she told Max. He did a hard U-turn, and Freya was afraid that, combined with the angle of the slope, they were about to roll over. She clutched the empty weapons rack on the transport's side as they yawed, before rocking back in the opposite direction.

They now faced towards the slope, taking fire head on. Max grabbed the belt of the plucky Reboot activist manning the pintle GPMG and dragged her down before the hail of fire from the drones could cut her to pieces. Then he threw the vehicle into reverse, almost ramming into a tree. The engine smoked alarmingly.

"Out," Freya shouted, riven with adrenaline. They were minutes from safety.

She threw open the rear hatch and dropped down in amongst the trees, dragging Will out and urging the others to follow. Bullets came at them from all directions, blasting away splinters, shredding bark, and spanking off the battered frame of the armoured carrier whose bulk was still protecting them from the worst of the fire. The drones to the left and the right almost had an angle on them though, and only the slope kept them from being annihilated.

"Head for the fence," Freya shouted, helping Max and their impromptu gunner out.

"Do you still have the cutters?" she asked Max.

"Yes!"

"Then let's move!"

She had just started downhill again when she felt a searing pain along her right shoulder. She had been hit, and the shock of it made her stagger.

Will grabbed her by the arm and pulled her behind the nearest tree. Unlike the rest, he had hung back until she had left the transport's cover.

"Hold still," he told her as he checked her over, in between twitching every time a bullet hit the far side of the trunk they were sheltering behind. "Well, even I've had worse, so you'll live."

"How can you tell? It's dark!"

"All right, fine, you're dying then. Either way, can we go now?"

Will's attitude helped sting her out of her shock, which was probably the idea. The wound hurt, but she suspected it was just a bad graze. The life-and-death rush she was in the middle of quickly eclipsed it.

She got up and ran with Will, downhill, stumbling over roots and undergrowth in the dark. Gunfire continued to rain down around them.

Freya caught sight of the last perimeter fence ahead. The rest of the team clustered around Max, who worked desperately with the rubber cutters.

"There's trouble in the street on the other side," Leona said to Freya. VERT vehicles rolled up the far side of where they were about to emerge, onto Gustav-Meyer-Allee. They were seconds away from being cut off again.

"We're through," Max shouted, shoving the shorn fencing out of the way. Freya urged the others into the gap and across the road to where the van they had arrived in was parked up. The mounted gunner on the lead VERT transport began to open fire, the booming report of his weapon echoing up the street.

The Reboot team charged across in front of the oncoming traffic, trying to escape VERT's jaws as they threatened to snap shut around them. Another Rebooter was clipped by a bullet, but Leona helped her to the van. Its driver revved the engine.

They piled in the back, the thunder of the oncoming column of VERT hardware deafening. Freya saw holes appear in the open rear door as she leapt inside, dull popping noises ringing out as bullets punched through.

"Drive," she screamed before the doors were even shut. The van sped off with a screech of tires.

Freya looked down at the Reboot team, hunched over in fear. Somehow, they were still alive.

Freya worried that wouldn't be the case by the end of the night.

"Thank you," Will said as the sound of gunfire was gradually eclipsed by the engine noise. "To all of you. I honestly didn't imagine you'd come for me."

"DedSec wouldn't be too chuffed if I left a knowledgeable asset like you in the hands of a group like VERT," Freya said, as casually as possible. In truth she was flooded with relief.

"Whatever the reason, I'm glad to be out," Will said.

"Don't be too happy just yet," Freya told him. "That was the easy part."

"I'm sorry, what?"

"That was the easy part," she repeated. "Or did you think we were just going to head for the airport?"

"I had rather flattered myself with that expectation, yes," Will said tartly. "Where the hell are we going now?"

"To the fancy end of town," Freya said. "You and I are going to have a reckoning with my wolves."

Erik was in the front seat of his command jeep when he received word from Humboldthain.

"What do you mean the prisoner's gone?" he snarled, fury the likes of which he had never before experienced gripping him. "Which direction are they headed?"

The answer was, seemingly, to the edge of town. The transport the terrorists were using – it had to be Freya leading them – had evaded capture and was just about to hit the 115 roadway.

"Get the police out there and intercept them," Erik ordered the useless subordinate he had left in charge of Humboldthain. "Close off all the exits as well. If those criminals aren't in one of my cells by tomorrow morning, you'll be taking their place."

"Orders, sir?" the driver sitting next to him asked cautiously.

"Pursue them, with everything we have," Erik snapped. "Get me to the 115."

While Freya and the rest of her picked team drove southwest, the rest of Reboot swung into action. The pairs picked to patrol the 115 hit the inevitable police blockades before they could get set up, hurling paint bombs and flares that lit the highway up with a hellish red glow.

The van came storming through the smoke, swerving to avoid half-deployed tire-poppers and simply driving through barriers and cones.

All the while Freya tried to get her team's head back in the game. There was exhilaration that they had struck a blow against VERT and lived to tell the tale, but they were coming down off the high of combat, and Freya knew only too well that could be a dangerous time, especially for people inexperienced with the jagged peaks and troughs that came with armed violence. She noticed even Will's hands were shaking, and he had barely stopped complaining about the second half of the plan, a half that promised to be even more dangerous than launching a surprise assault on the headquarters of the Defenders.

She tried to occupy his mind by getting him to check her shoulder wound. As she had suspected, it was shallow, but it still stung when he sprayed it with the antiseptic they had brought. The van had, wisely, been stocked with bandages, patches, and other rudimentary medical supplies in anticipation of returning casualties. Will bound up Freya's shoulder while she made sure the others attended to their wounded friends, keeping them all occupied. Thankfully none of the wounds seemed bad, though Max looked pale with pain and blood loss. She convinced him to swap out for the getaway driver during what was about to happen.

"Everybody set?" she asked. It seemed like they were, but the fear was back now, the nerves. Freya felt it herself, though she refused to acknowledge it.

She felt a brief pang of regret for dragging them into this. Most of them weren't natural fighters, though they had acquitted themselves well at Humboldthain. They were idealists mostly, wannabe revolutionaries who, tonight, had just become the real thing. Freya reminded herself that this wasn't just a personal vendetta, though revenge was at the heart of it. Tonight was an opportunity to strike a fatal blow not just against VERT, but also against the criminal forces that threatened to drag down German society in the midst of social unrest.

Tonight they were going to beat VERT, and the sham that was Kaiser's M-Bahn. And they were going to do it by setting them against each other.

29
Script Rewrites

Kaiser was marching from the entrance to the Jägerhalle towards the line of vehicles parked up on the long driveway when Luther accosted him. M-Bahn members were busy pouring outside around them and mounting up, checking weapons and kit as they went.

"They're coming this way," he said, bouncing the tracker he had set up directly to Kaiser's own Optik implant. Teuton, who had been striding alongside him, patched in as well. She understood immediately what Luther meant.

Using VERT's communications, he had triangulated the direction of most of the Defenders' units. They were currently surging down the 115 highway, presumably in pursuit of the team that Kaiser and Teuton had watched break the prisoner out of Humboldthain on VERT's own cameras.

That meant they were heading towards the Grunewald. Towards the Jägerhalle.

Teuton could sense Kaiser's thoughts. Coincidence? The 115 road was a good way to get away from Humboldthain quickly, but it led out of the city, and that didn't seem like a sensible option.

Easier to go to ground in Berlin than in the adjacent countryside, though the nearby Grunewald forest would offer some shelter.

The alternative was equally surprising but would have fit well with everything Teuton had seen so far of Freya Bauer.

"They're coming for us," Kaiser said. He sounded certain. Teuton felt a sudden rush of anticipation. Freya must know. She was as eager for a showdown as they were.

"Stop them," Kaiser ordered Luther bluntly. "Derail them. The last thing we want is a battle drawing VERT down on top of us."

As Luther began to speak to his Fixers via his Optik, Kaiser turned to Teuton. His expression was murderous.

"What if VERT comes for us as well as her?" Teuton asked.

"Then we'll destroy them as well. The Bundestag won't back them when half of their number are liquidated while they attack the property of a private citizen."

It didn't seem that simple to Teuton, but she could feel herself being caught up in her father's lust for havoc. This was what she had yearned for. Vengeance was coming.

She heard Luther's voice as he reached the villa's control room, and realised their Optiks were still linked as he barked orders to his M-Bahn fixers.

"Eyes on your screens! I've pinged you the tracking number you'll need. All we have to do is stop it getting any closer. Let's show these script kiddies how a real hacker gang works."

The van lurched brutally to the left, almost throwing Freya against Will.

It had been more than a bumpy ride so far. The driver, Lagomorph, was doing her best to dodge around the police blockades while the other Reboot teams kept them occupied. This, however, seemed even more serious.

Freya made her way to the front of the van, looking through into the drive compartment just as another lurch rocked the vehicle.

"I'm losing control of the steering," Lago shouted, knuckles white on the wheel. "Something's trying to take control!"

Freya didn't get a chance to respond before warnings superimposed themselves on her vision, more numerous and urgent than the last hack attempt. Multiple attacks, across all spectrums. She responded quickly, hearing as she did so an exclamation of pain.

She twisted to find the Rebooters in the back clutching at their heads and necks, clearly in distress. Only herself and Will seemed unaffected. He made eye contact with her, undoubtedly receiving the same warnings she was getting.

"We're under attack," he said. "Someone's overloading their implants. Our DedSec downloads are keeping them out, but only for now.

"M-Bahn," Leona snarled through gritted teeth, clutching her ear where her Optik was implanted.

"Doesn't the van have a scrambler?" Will demanded.

"No!"

"We need to hit them back," Freya said urgently as the vehicle swerved again. Lago had slowed down in an effort not to crash while she fought with the override orders being rammed into the van's onboard computer.

"Trying," Will said, eyes blinking and swivelling furiously. "This is a big one. I need more."

"Tex and Termite," Leona managed, her voice riven with pain. Freya was already calling them.

"We're seeing it," said Tex's voice in her ear. "This is massive. They're hitting everything!"

"Link me to them, for God's sake," Will barked. Freya patched him through to Tex's Optik. She was deleting warning messages on her own HUD as quickly as they came up, but she was sure even DedSec's advance defensive systems were moments from overloading.

"The lights," Lagomorph shouted. Freya looked back to the front, and realised what she meant. The lamps illuminating the highway had started to go out ahead of them, one by one, plunging the roadway into complete darkness.

"I can't get the headlights working either," Lago said as everything in front of the windscreen turned black.

"Not happening," Will growled, banging a fist against the side of the van. Several of the Rebooters had dropped onto their knees in the footwell, in agony. Freya desperately linked her HUD to Will's, twinning their defences as she tried to join in their effort to fight back, locating the van's systems and beginning to download a DedSec security patch to them.

"We're better than this," she said to Will, Tex, and Termite as they worked. "We're better than Kaiser's goons. Come on!"

The van had practically come to a halt. There were flashing blue lights in the darkness outside – police cars, undoubtedly surging towards them. Freya could do nothing but send a second patch and pray.

"Well?" Kaiser demanded as he reentered the Jägerhalle's control room. Luther was bent over a keyboard, sweating profusely, the other M-Bahn members looking no better as they worked.

Kaiser had never had much time for the work of hackers, but the opportunity to hit out remotely was a powerful advantage, and it was time he used it in full.

"They've almost stopped," Luther said, not looking away from the screen. "Still on the highway."

"Almost?" Kaiser demanded. "I'm paying you well, why is this band of amateurs getting the better of you."

"They're not getting the better of me," Luther said tersely. "And they're not amateurs. Two of them are DedSec. They're fighting back."

Kaiser growled with frustration and called Teuton on his Optik.

"I can't trust these idiots here," he said, loudly enough for all the M-Bahn fixers to hear him. "Get everyone else back inside and get this place prepped for defence. We'll finish this here."

"I'm through," Tex said. Will had routed him the ID address he had identified as being behind the deluge of cyberattacks they were currently experiencing. He worked furiously, hands dancing across the keyboard as he called up attack scripts and directed them to the source. Next to him, Termite was labouring to get the lights along the highway back up and running.

"They don't like that," Tex said, grinning through the pressure as he saw a screed of garbled text pop up from the location he had hit – Kaiser's villa, he realised.

"They know you're coming," he said to Will via the Optik link.

"Not surprising," came the response. "Just keep hitting them. I've found the script they're using to overload our Optiks."

Tex had panicked at first when he had seen the scale of the M-Bahn attack, but they were bringing it under control, each of them working to fix a different issue while giving the M-Bahn hackers something to think about. He sent a second hit, then a third, glancing occasionally at his Optik display, checking on Will's progress. He was simultaneously trying to shield the Optiks of the Reboot team with him while getting the van's systems operating again. Tex was almost jealous of his abilities.

“That should be the lights back up,” Termite said. “The number of hostile hits is dropping rapidly.”

“Keep it up,” Tex said. “We’re beating them.”

“Everybody okay?” Will called, taking his focus off his Optik’s display for the first time since the attack had begun. The Reboot team around him still looked in some discomfort, but the attacks on their Optiks had now ceased. He glanced at Freya, who stood at the front of the van, working with the driver.

“How’s that new update I sent you?” he called.

“Working,” Freya responded. “We think.”

“Steering’s back under control,” the driver called. “Headlights are still busted, but the highway lamps are back up.”

“Then I suggest you put your foot down,” Will said, slipping back into the embrace of his Optik data and noting the presence of police drones and vehicles bearing down on them. “We’re almost surrounded.”

There was a jolt as they rapidly sped up again. Will helped Tex remotely launch another flurry of hits on their attackers, feeling a moment’s exhilaration as he did so. Nobody initiated a hacker war with him and won it.

“We need to pull out before they penetrate our systems,” Luther said urgently, daring to look away from his screen towards Kaiser.

“Stop speaking gibberish,” Kaiser snapped back.

“The security of the villa may be compromised if they get inside,” Luther replied.

As though to emphasise his words, a skull-and-circle logo abruptly interposed itself across his monitor, the ghastly apparition laughing in his face. Luther realised it was Reboot’s logo. He swore, trying to wipe it away, but his systems were now wholly unresponsive. He hit the keyboard in frustration, then simply pulled the plug.

"We've done all we can to slow them," he told Kaiser.

"You were meant to stop them, not just slow them!"

"Then with all due respect, I suggest you come up with an alternative plan. They're about to pull up outside."

"Father," said Teuton's voice over Kaiser's Optik, before he could unleash his fury on Luther. "We've got company at the front. Der Vertidiger."

30
Collision Course

Erik ordered the command jeep to pull up at the side of the street. He clambered out, holding the vehicle's radio to his ear.

"What's happening?" he demanded of Alexander. He had sent him to assume control in Humboldthain and coordinate movements while Erik was in the field. The former acting commander at Humboldthain had already been stripped of his rank.

"The police almost caught our fugitives, but they managed to evade all the blockades. Drones have tracked them to the edge of a property known as the Jägerhalle," Alex said. "It's one street over from where you've stopped. It looks as though they're attempting to gain access to the property right now. It belongs to–"

"I know who it belongs to," Erik interjected. Emil Kaiser, criminal overlord, a man too powerful even for VERT to touch, for now. Perhaps it was finally time to change that.

Kaiser represented unfinished business. He had expected that a reckoning with Kaiser wouldn't come until VERT had fully established itself, and he could bring down men whose dirty deeds were so numerous they had elevated them from a deserved prison cell to a luxury villa. They were the kind of men whose arrogance earned reprisal.

It looked like that wish would come sooner than Erik had anticipated.

"Freya's going after her father's killer," he mused. It didn't surprise him. Thomas Bauer's daughter was a woman with a score to settle. He almost respected her for it. She was relentless, and he regretted underestimating her drive. He wouldn't do so again. He should never have let her go in the first place.

He also suspected her former husband was with her. Erik wanted him too. A leading DedSec operative, one well-versed in their digital trickery, would be an invaluable asset to VERT. He could take them to the next level, if Erik pushed the right buttons.

He had moments to decide. Kaiser had powerful allies, but the opportunity to strike back against him after all these years was too good to pass up. Why not tonight? Freya had claimed that the hacker group known as M-Bahn ran with Kaiser's blessing. That made Kaiser, and the Jägerhalle, legitimate targets.

The bottom line was that he simply couldn't let Freya escape, especially not now. Not after she had led a successful break-in at Humboldthain. Not after Erik had mobilised the entirety of VERT in pursuit of her and her ex. Going off the police channels VERT had access to, the riots VERT troopers had been containing had gotten totally out of hand. Right now, though, they weren't Erik's concern. He was gambling on getting William back, and Freya with him. Two DedSec prisoners would placate questions in the Bundestag, and keep things on track. If he failed tonight, with the elections less than a month away, it could undermine everything. If Kaiser ended up killing her, the situation would be just as bad.

"We're going in after them," Erik told Alex on the radio.

"The drones are picking up a lot of heat signatures in the main building," Alex cautioned.

"All the more reason to hurry," Erik said. "If they know what's good for them, they'll surrender the fugitive."

"And what if they don't?"

"Then we kill everyone who resists. Relay that instruction to all units. I'm taking the first section in through the front."

"Understood, sir."

Erik waved the VERT troops stacked up in the trucks behind his jeep out onto the pavement. He felt an unexpected thrill, twinned with a fearsome determination.

Tonight, they would show Berlin what VERT could do. This city, and its future, belonged to them.

"You don't have to come with me," Freya said. They looked back at her in the harsh light of the streetlamps overlooking the spot where they had piled out of the van, in a quiet street to the rear of the Jägerhalle. She could sense their nervousness, but also fiery resolve. They had tasted the revolution. What was more, they had survived M-Bahn's attempt at breaking them. Now it was their turn.

"We knew what the plan was from the beginning," Leona said. She had removed her lion mask, her sharp features looking predatory and deadly. "We volunteered. If VERT is to fall tonight, we're going to play our part. If that brings down a brute like Kaiser too, then all the better."

"It's all of Berlin's fight tonight," Max added. He sat in the cab of the van, his wound tightly bound. It had taken a firm talking-to from Freya to convince him to remain behind, taking over the getaway driver role from Lagomorph.

"We need everyone to see what we're up against," Leona said. "VERT will stop at nothing to seize power, seize control. We can unmask them."

"Fine," Freya conceded. "Same as the flak tower then. We go in hard and fast. Pair off and work together. One covers, one moves. Neither unloaded at the same time. Keep an eye on your Optiks."

She unslung her G36. "And one more thing – Kaiser's mine."

They moved across the street and over the metal railings that demarcated the rear of the Jägerhalle. Freya motioned to Will.

"Stick close," she told him. "And try not to shoot me by accident."

"That was one time, and I missed," Will said. He was afraid, she could tell, but he no longer complained about the apparent insanity of their plan. Freya had given him one of the two blank slate Optik devices, syncing it to his Optik HUD in case he needed a screen to work with. He had asked for a weapon, and one of the Reboot crew had supplied a 9mm 1911. He looked awkward carrying it.

"So you know what this crime lord looks like?" he asked as they hopped the railings.

"I do. He's been hunting me, and I him, for years now, though I didn't truly appreciate it."

"He's the one who killed your dad?"

"I doubt he did it in person, but he ordered it."

"How do you know?"

"Erik told me."

Together they advanced through the expansive garden at the rear of the Jägerhalle, the Reboot activists around them armed, bent-double shadows that darted forward.

"The VERT thug-in-chief told you, and you believed him?" Will whispered incredulously as they paused behind an elm tree.

"He gave a good reason."

"Which was?"

"I'll tell you later."

Will sighed, but Freya ignored him. Now was categorically not the time to reveal her father had been an informant.

Freya covered Will with the rifle as he scurried through the darkness to a short, ornamental hedge. Freya followed once he was in place. She could see the villa ahead, a large, white structure with a steep tiled roof. It was dark, no lights showing at the windows. It was far too quiet.

What if VERT had decided to hold off? What if there was actually some sort of secret accord between them and Kaiser, or some understanding put in place to avoid contact? Regardless of the animosity Erik had claimed towards Kaiser, Freya knew well enough that organisations like VERT loved to bully groups like Reboot while avoiding the hard, dirty business of combating true, organised crime.

Too many doubts, too little time. Reboot still advanced – she spotted Leona, lion mask back on, breaking from cover to the right. Freya pulled Mister Scruff back down.

She was about to tell Will to move up again when she heard the rattle of an assault rifle, coming from the front of the house. Someone else, presumably VERT, was disturbing Emil Kaiser's night.

The M-Bahn attack on the van had delayed the Reboot side of things. Dawn wasn't far off. It was time they joined the party.

"Make for the fountain." Freya nodded towards a water feature beyond the hedge, not far from the back door to the Jägerhalle. Will seemed to gather his courage, then hurried forward while Freya trained her sights on the windows, looking for movement.

Just as Will dropped in behind the fountain's base, there was a loud thud, and brilliant illumination blazed from the Jägerhalle. Freya dropped back behind the hedge, momentarily blinded. Either Will, or someone else, had triggered the half-a-dozen floodlights rigged up below the house's guttering. They now shone down on the garden, picking out everyone and blinding them in turn to whatever was happening at the villa's windows.

Freya knew what was coming next.

"Everybody get down," she shouted.

31
Breaking and Entering

Kaiser's henchmen opened fire. The fury of at least four rifles eclipsed the sporadic firing from the front of the house, the chatter and thud of the small arms warring with the unwelcome whizz of near misses and the sharp cracking noises made as bullets struck trees or stone or ploughed up the close-cut grass.

This was a bad place to be. Quite apart from the fact that the hedge Freya was behind offered little in the way of solid cover, she couldn't see to shoot back. If she so much as raised her head, she was also certain she would immediately become the primary target.

She hugged the dirt, hearing bullets chew through the hedge just above her, and pinged a message to the displays of the rest of the team.

Shoot the lights.

That was easier said than done. They were small targets, and blindingly bright, and that was without considering the fact that Reboot – all of them inexperienced in actual combat – were badly pinned.

Will, got a solution? Freya asked, hoping he hadn't frozen beneath the barrage.

Already working on it.

Will had just managed to hit the dirt behind the fountain before the villa's defenders had opened fire. He kept low, heart racing, forcing himself to focus on his HUD. In moments like these the Optik was always mightier than the sword, or indeed, the assault rifle.

He located the villa's online systems via NetHack View, hitting them with a flurry of false requests to trigger its defensive programs. After that it was a case of hunting for the inevitable backdoor. He located it in a little over sixty seconds. The digital protection Kaiser had invested in was hardly top of the range.

As he had hoped, the lights were included in the villa's systems, and could all be accessed fully remotely. What he found he couldn't do, to his surprise, was turn them off. There was a failsafe built into the trigger that would take too long to bypass. Finally, a bit of competition.

Even as bullets cracked off the fountain next to him, he smiled. He might not be able to kill the lights completely, but whoever had programmed the failsafe had failed to account for the fact that they were on dimmers, and those dimmers remained fully, remotely adjustable.

He turned the brightness all the way down. Abruptly, the dazzling beams became little more than a dull glow.

Freya was ready as soon as the lights dimmed.

She vaulted the hedge and ran for the fountain. Will was still there, and she rolled in alongside him, making him yelp with surprise.

"Good job with the lights," Freya said. "You OK?"

"I've been better! This is why we broke up, Freya!"

"No, it's not! Coming to Berlin was your idea in the first place!"

"Does getting pinned down in the middle of a gunfight and having to hack my way out of it sound like something I would suggest?"

"It sounds like something you'd still manage get us into!"

"What about getting us out? Isn't that your job, bodyguard? I've done my bit."

"I'm working on it," Freya said.

At least the brightness was no longer as intense. She risked a glance over the edge of the fountain, noting a triangular window covered by a metal plate on the wall above them. She ducked back as buzzing rounds spat up water from the fountain's bowl and chipped at its stonework.

"We need to get in there quickly, before they lock it down even further," Freya said.

"You won't be going in through the back door," Will said. "I got a look at it before I started ducking. It's reinforced with some sort of lock code on it. I might be able to download something to crack it, but it will probably take more time than we've got. It looks pretty secure on NetHack."

Freya stared at him for a second.

"We're going in through the ground floor windows."

"That might work too," Will allowed, trying to mask embarrassment.

Freya sent another message via her Optik, knowing it would flash up via each Reboot activist's implant.

Hit the windows.

The dimming of the lights seemed to have caused the villa's defenders to hesitate. Reboot struck back, the air full of gunshots.

Now the defenders of the Jägerhalle – M-Bahn, Freya assumed – were blind to what was coming.

"Get ready to make a move," Freya told Will, her eyesight growing accustomed to the fire-shot shadows. "Is your safety off?"

"Yeah… I think so."

Flares, then hold fire on the windows opposite the fountain, she messaged the others. Then, she tapped Will's shoulder.

"Crawl."

"Crawl?"

"You want to stand up in this?"

Her words coincided with an eye-aching red glow that sparked up either side of them. Reboot had stockpiled flares, and all of the members, including Freya and Will, were carrying at least one.

Half-a-dozen of the emergency devices were thrown forward from cover, sparking and fizzing as their ends caught light. Soon, they spewed smoke, their bright red flames creating a hellish, churning wall between the villa and the garden. "Stay low," she told Will, starting to edge out into the bitter smoke. She kept her head down, elbows out, legs bent at the knee and flat against the ground. The fountain provided a sense of reassuring bulk, but she forced herself to go past it, into the billowing smog.

She was vaguely aware of Will's presence beside her. There had never been any doubt that he would follow her, despite his protests. In the past few days they had fallen back into the old way of doing things, the give-and-take that made them work well together, so well in fact that they'd managed to convince themselves for over a decade that they should be together permanently.

They were much better at this than they were at living with one another.

They cleared the worst of the smoke. The Jägerhalle was looming over them now, a dire shape that stood tall and unmoving despite the punishment it was taking, its façade lit red. The fire from its windows seemed to have ceased.

"Keep going," she urged Will. It was tough. Freya's wounds ached, and she expected at any second for a shape to loom in the window ahead and open fire on them. The space remained empty though, and Freya scrambled to her feet and dashed the last few yards.

They reached the back wall of the Jägerhalle, panting, hearts racing, Freya to the window's left and Will to its right. Bullets had already shattered its glass.

"Cover me," Freya told Will.

"OK."

Freya counted him off, and they both swept round into the window space, weapons raised. The darkness beyond was impenetrable, but there didn't seem to be anyone there.

Slinging her rifle, Freya used her sleeve to sweep broken glass off the windowsill while Will kept his pistol raised. Then she grabbed onto the edge and, with a grunt, hefted herself up, feeling like she was back at Chalmers's gym. Her shoulder twinged, but then she was over and dropping down into the room beyond.

She rolled and brought the rifle up. She could barely see anything, only vague shapes that could equally have been furniture or lurking M-Bahn. She swung the G36 from left to right, not daring to breathe.

A grunting noise disturbed Freya's concentration. Moments later Will appeared at the window, falling into the space beyond with a curse. Freya rolled her eyes.

"We need to find a light," she hissed. "I'm not using my flare."

"Finding a light *switch* would be even more useful." Will stood up and framing himself perfectly in the window space. "They're usually attached to walls."

"I really hope someone shoots you right now."

"After the past two days it's probably overdue."

No one fired. Freya rose and stalked through the room, eventually locating a switch.

The place was empty but for the furnishings that suggested a lounge, if said lounge had been owned by someone with a weird fetish for hunting. There were two doors, one to the right and another directly opposite the window, leading further into the villa. Freya moved towards that one.

She crouched down next to it and carefully turned the handle, listening for the telltale click of a booby trap arming itself. There was nothing. She held the door ajar just a fraction, listening intently.

The shooting from the rear of the Jägerhalle seemed to be dying down, presumably as M-Bahn withdrew deeper into the structure, but the same couldn't be said of what was happening in the rest of the villa. Gunfire echoed through the rooms, hinting at a full-on assault.

Freya felt huge relief. That was exactly what she had been hoping for. VERT and Kaiser were at each other's throats.

All she had to do now was actually find Kaiser and banish the shadow that had hung over her all these years.

32
Trophies

During the push through the garden, Freya had noticed one particularly large window that seemed to be protected by a steel shutter. It was an unusual shape, triangular, and shots from below had struck and sparked from the metal, but hadn't penetrated. It seemed likely it was some sort of safe room that had gone into lockdown when the attack had started. That felt like a good bet as to Kaiser's location, but it was far from certain. There were no blueprints of the Jägerhalle, nothing available online or even on the deep web. There could be a room in the building's core, or a basement, or tunnels acting as an escape route.

She checked the neighbouring room. As she had hoped, it led to the east corner of the house. There were two figures within, whom Freya immediately identified, though she pulled Will back into the doorway as she called out.

"Reboot," she said, as the pair brought their weapons up hastily. It was Leona and another member of the team, Hangover. They had just entered in through the window.

"Do you know if anyone was hit?" Freya asked her. The lion mask shook a negative.

"No idea. We just made a break for it."

"We need to move from room to room at the back and collect everyone who made it," Freya said. "But we also need to keep going deeper. VERT are going to storm this place, and Kaiser won't be around when they do. He might be gone already."

"We can collect the others," Leona said. "Where will we find you?"

"On this side, upstairs. I think that's where he'll be. Get yourself and the others out if you can't link with us."

"Understood."

While Freya had been speaking, Will had moved to the room's other door.

"Corridor," he said.

"Empty?"

"For now."

"Let's go then."

Freya took the lead. The corridor had white walls and a tiled floor, seemingly like much of the villa, with old black-and-white photos of moustachioed men posing with murdered animals, or pictures of white officers with ranks of African soldiers. Freya fixed her eyes on the far end of the long space, ready to open fire on anything that appeared there.

"There's another door on the left," Will muttered, pistol braced two-handed, the way she had taught him. He had always hated this sort of action, but found himself in the midst of it regardless – the dangers involved in being active, talented DedSec. It was why Freya had been paired with him in the first place. She was privately amazed she had kept them both alive this long. Now, however, there was an added incentive. They had to stay alive for Andrew.

Now wasn't the time to think about that. Will was right. A door on the left, black, set back from the corridor wall.

Take it, or carry on? The sounds of gunfire from the far end rose to a crescendo, making the walls and floor vibrate.

Left it was then. Rifle braced with the help of its strap, Freya opened the door with her other hand and swung inside.

Two bullets met her. They impacted into the wall less than a foot to her left, at head height, blowing out plaster.

She immediately reared back, swearing vehemently. Too damn close.

The brief moment had given her a snapshot of the space beyond, but not enough to pin down the shooter's location. It looked like some sort of trophy room, with all sorts of dead animal parts on the walls, and full taxidermied creatures occupying much of the floor. The Jägerhalle was an absolute freak show.

"Other door then?" Will asked, nodding back down the corridor.

"Do you want to stay here and make sure whoever's in there doesn't come out behind us?" Freya said. "We have to deal with them."

"After you then."

"Ever the gentleman."

Freya pulled out her flare.

"Is that the extent of your plan?" Will sounded about as incredulous as he always did whenever Freya attempted something. Rather than respond, she unscrewed the cap and sparked it off.

Vicious light blazed from the tip, followed a second later by smoke. Freya tossed it in through the open doorway, hearing it skitter across the black-and-white tiled floor.

The flare appeared to anger the shooter because they opened fire again. This time it wasn't just them either. Freya caught the sound of a second weapon barking at them.

"Get ready," she told Will.

The flare was in full flow now, filling the space with a crimson glare and broiling smoke. Agitated by the fact that their vision was being obscured, both shooters were blazing away, hoping to clip them when they made the break inside.

That was a basic mistake. Sure enough, silence fell as both shooters ran out of ammunition at the same time, and Freya heard the clatter of a magazine being dropped.

"Now."

She entered the room, mask on and rifle raised, sweeping through the crimson smoke and burning light. The shapes of beasts loomed around her, indistinct, long-dead predators, preserved only to now witness the violence of one human against another.

Freya found the first of Kaiser's henchmen behind the rearing remains of a lion – a man wearing a clown mask, caught in the process of trying to clip a fresh magazine into his AK47 while coughing heavily.

Freya put him down with a double tap. He slumped against the side of the lion, his blood marking its golden fur.

Freya moved past, looking for the second shooter. The flare rendered everything hellish and claustrophobic, even more so with the snarling, dead-eyed creatures surrounding her. She half expected one to leap at her.

There was indeed movement, though it wasn't one of the Kaiser family's long-dead victims. Someone broke from cover out of the smoke ahead, making a rush towards the far end of the room. Freya shot, but missed, her bullets blowing the stuffing out of a springing cheetah. The figure vanished, and Freya heard a door slam.

"Think that's all of them?" Will asked. He had moved in behind her and was watching her six, pistol raised, looking out for her the way they had done so many times before.

"Let's hope so," Freya said as they reached the end of the trophy room, finding the door the shooter had fled through. "We need to get upstairs."

"Do we really though?" Will asked. "You said the plan was to set Kaiser and VERT against each other. You've achieved that. There's still time for us to get out before this place becomes a proper warzone."

"I told you, and the others, that you don't need to stay," Freya said, refusing to let guilt take hold. "Kaiser is my father's killer. I want to look him in the eye before the end."

"A bit crazy, but then that's why I like you," Will shrugged. Freya didn't respond. She opened the door, and was once again greeted by the hammering of gunfire.

"Here we go again," Will said.

"Move in," Erik snarled into the radio.

VERT obeyed. Their commander watched from the edge of the driveway leading to the front of the Jägerhalle, one foot up on the tire arch of his command jeep, fired with angry determination. It had become obvious as soon as they had entered the villa's grounds that Emil Kaiser wasn't going to negotiate. Someone had opened fire from by the front door. That, as far as Erik was concerned, meant the gloves were coming off. He hadn't chased Freya Bauer and her ex halfway across Berlin just to lose her to some criminal scum like Kaiser. At the end of tonight, Erik would have Will, and the knowledge he needed to take the coming conflict to cyberspace.

On Erik's order VERT had brought up its heaviest kit, a trio of halftracks. They began to roll forward, supported overhead by a swarm of drones, their buzz filling the night air.

Gunshots soon answered them.

"Weapons live," Erik ordered through the radio. "Light them up."

The machine guns mounted on the assault vehicles began to batter away, the drones adding their firepower as they swept in on swarm protocols, monitored by the operators who were now back at Humboldthain. Erik observed the front of the Jägerhalle through a pair of binoculars, set to night vision, watching as windows broke and chunks were blown from the walls. The racket was incessant, furious.

It must have sounded as though another world war had broken out on the edge of Berlin's suburbia. That couldn't be helped now. The massive, overwhelming use of force would, by its very nature, be only brief. By the end of it, the positives would outweigh the negatives. They would have several high-value prisoners, and one of the most powerful criminals in the city would either be dead or facing life in jail. The raw power of VERT would have been demonstrated to all would-be agitators and revolutionaries. The riots they had abandoned would not flare up again.

Erik left his jeep, striding towards the action, no longer content to watch from afar. He wanted to be in there. After the mockery he had suffered, he wanted to recapture Freya and Will personally.

The front of the Jägerhalle had been suppressed – there was now no return fire. The drones circled the property, hunting for anyone trying to escape it, while VERT troopers stacked up outside the wrecked front doors. Erik joined them. He was flushed with adrenaline, in a way he hadn't felt since Afghanistan. It was intoxicating.

The entry into the villa was deserted, walls and doors peppered by rounds.

Gunfire rang out. The point man had engaged with someone

beyond. Erik drew his Austrian-made P-9mm and moved forward once more.

"Remember, I want the DedSec ones alive," he told the breach team firmly. "You all know what they look like. Kill everyone else."

"Sir, there's a call from the federal minister of justice coming through," came Alex's voice over the radio, disturbing Erik's rush. "Should I put him on?"

"No," Erik said without much hesitation. "This isn't a night for pen pushers and bureaucrats like Meyer. It's a night for men of action."

"What… should I tell him then?"

"That I'm indisposed!"

"Yes sir."

33
Lobbying for Success

This hadn't been part of the plan.

At Kaiser's insistence, Teuton stayed with him as he climbed up the staircase to the landing outside his office, overlooking the villa's heart. The lobby space below, dominated by the stuffed elephant, had become a rallying point for M-Bahn and Kaiser's other underlings as they were driven back from the front of the Jägerhalle by the military-grade firepower unleashed by VERT.

Teuton half expected her father to direct the defence from the landing space, but instead he carried on towards his office, only pausing on the threshold as someone shouted his name.

It was Luther. He stumbled up the stairs after them, gripping the banister, his spectacles gone and an empty pistol in his free hand.

"It's Freya," he panted as he reached them, looking frantic. "They came in through the back. She's in the trophy room."

"Then what are you doing here?" Kaiser snarled. "Get back down there and capture her."

"Let me go," Teuton said before Luther could muster a response.

"No, you'll kill her."

"Before she kills us! She's come here for you! We're surrounded!"

"We'll be fine. I just have to make a call. Luther, bring her here alive, or die trying. Those are your options."

"She isn't alone," Luther began, but Kaiser wasn't listening. He snatched Teuton's wrist and yanked her into the office, before slamming the door and stooping over the control box wired up to the wall next to it. He swiped his hands-on Optik component over it, and there was a whirring sound as, outside, a sheet of plate metal rolled down over the entrance.

"You're sealing us in?" Teuton demanded, noting that the triangular window overlooking the back of the office was already covered by its protective plating. "How are we supposed to get to her in here?"

"We need to stay secure until I can regain control of the situation," Kaiser said, pacing over to his desk.

"And how–"

"I told you, I'm going to make a call!"

Freya glanced beyond the door. She caught sight of a wide square room, stairs directly above her and along the wall opposite. In the centre was a stuffed elephant, locked in an eternity of silent trumpeting.

The dais on which it was mounted was being used as cover by four M-Bahn thugs. They were taking fire from the large double doors leading into the room from Freya's left. The angle she had gained on them left several of them exposed, but they noticed her almost immediately. One, wearing a leering oni mask, shifted and opened fire with a SMG-11, stitching bullets across the wall and doorway just after Freya threw herself back.

"I think this is the middle of the villa," she told Will. "VERT are attacking from the other side."

"That's well and good, but we're about to walk into the middle of a three-way battle," Will pointed out.

Freya heard movement from behind them. She spun, G36 up, but immediately recognised the lion-masked figure prowling through the last of the spent flare's smoke. Leona.

"Where are the others?" Freya asked.

"Spread through the back rooms, trying to keep our escape route open," Leona said. "M-Bahn keep popping up. This place is a maze."

"We're still looking for Kaiser," Will admitted.

"He must be upstairs," Freya said. "If VERT had already captured him, M-Bahn would have surrendered by now."

"There could be a level below us," Will pointed out. "A basement or panic room?"

"The window on the upper floor had blast shields," Freya pointed out. "I just need to get up those stairs."

There were no more rounds coming through the door leading out into the central lobby. Freya took another look. The M-Bahn gunmen were still pinned behind the elephant, and one appeared to be wounded. She saw rounds rip through the poor, stuffed animal's leathery hide, making the whole thing shudder and rock on its dais. VERT troopers in grey and black were the ones doing the shooting, from positions just beyond the double doors to the left.

The far staircase would require Freya to cross the entire room, but the bottom steps of the one on their side were almost immediately outside. With covering fire, maybe she could make them.

She was about to say as much when Leona shouted a warning

and opened up with her Goblin assault rifle. Freya went down on one knee, Will doing the same before she could drag him down – finally, he seemed to be learning.

Several M-Bahn gunmen had charged in through the other door into the trophy room. With the smoke from the flare gone, they took cover behind the nearest animals. Freya, Will and Leona did likewise at the opposite end of the room.

"Where the hell did they come from?" Will shouted.

"I told you, they're everywhere," Leona shouted back from behind one of the lions, the moment of irony not lost on Freya as their snarling visages crouched side-by-side.

Will snatched a few shots past the hyena he and Freya were behind. Freya told him to conserve his clip.

"Can you hold them here?" she asked Leona, who was busy reloading.

"For a while, I guess," she answered. "Maybe not if more arrive."

"I need to find Kaiser," Freya said. "Before he gets away."

"He may already be gone," Will pointed out unhelpfully. "I doubt a crime boss is going to let himself get caught up in the middle of something like this."

"Unless he wants me," Freya pointed out. "He knows I'm here."

"Go," Leona said. "We'll hold them here for as long as we can."

"I've got a trick or two that'll slow them down," Will added.

"Just watch your ammo," Freya reiterated.

They both let off a short burst of covering fire as Freya ran for the door.

The news had turned up. From Reboot's hackerspace, Tex tracked a video drone from the channel ZDF, moving into position over Kaiser's villa. More newscasters were on their way.

"Are we live?" he asked Termite.

"Just about," the other Rebooter responded, lips pursed as he alternated between his Optik and his laptop. "All the major stations are running a breaking story."

"They won't see a whole lot from up there," Tex said, smirking. "Let's give them some proper footage, shall we. Leona, you there?"

"Bit busy," came the terse reply over Tex's Optik.

"That's ideal then. Germany's watching. Are you ready to link up?"

"Looks like it. The nation can watch me getting gunned down in real time."

"Well, it is after the nine o'clock adult scheduling," Tex said, hunting down the necessary links on his laptop. What Leona was seeing appeared across the screen – it looked like she was involved in a gunfight in the middle of a macabre trophy room.

"No heroics," Tex warned as he watched Leona reload her Goblin assault rifle through her own eyes. "We don't want this feed interrupted."

"No promises," Leona retorted.

"We're live in three, two, one," Termite said, and tapped a key.

They both looked at where they had the ZDF news coverage rolling in the corner of their Optik HUDs. Abruptly, the aerial view of the Jägerhalle cut out, replaced with the live footage of Leona squeezing off a burst across the trophy room.

This was part of the reason Reboot had so enthusiastically risked itself to help Freya when she returned, why Tex's friends were at that very moment fighting and dying. This was going to make a difference. Not the fighting itself, but showing Germany, and the world, that it was happening. Proving that there was a rot at the heart of the country, and that it was spreading. When people saw gunfights happening in the capital, and when VERT were implicated alongside the use of extreme violence and a criminal overlord, even the most corrupt politicos in the parliament would have to answer some unwelcome questions.

Tex just hoped those currently in the Jägerhalle survived to see those questions being asked.

Freya began to fire as soon as she was through into the lobby, her abrupt reappearance causing the M-Bahn member who was supposed to be covering the doorway to duck down. She went left, keeping to the wall so she could use the stairs descending directly above her to stay out of sight of the entrance VERT were occupying, while still putting the bulk of the elephant and its platform between her and the M-Bahn gunmen.

She still felt exposed. It would be seconds before either VERT or M-Bahn got a killer angle. She kept going, throwing herself round onto the bottom of the stairs and racing up, momentarily exposed to every VERT shooter in the doorway.

She heard bullets crack into the wall alongside her, ripping through a rather poor oil painting of the African savannah. The room was shuddering and resounding with the fury of so many discharges, and it seemed impossible that she would avoid being hit, but M-Bahn were unintentionally providing covering fire, taking advantage of VERT's momentary distraction to open up on the main doors.

She reached the landing running around the back half of the room, throwing herself flat, bullets chopping into the space above. Pressed as far back as possible from the landing's edge, neither VERT nor M-Bahn had a clean shot. That didn't stop them blowing the banister railing to splinters.

There was a single door at the top of the landing, a little further along from where she was lying. It was covered by what looked like a high-grade blast shield, bulletproof metal, with an access box to one side. That had to be Kaiser's panic room.

She was about to start crawling towards the door, when she heard a voice bellowing over the incessant fury of the gunfire coming from below.

"Bauer! Stay where you are!"

Erik. The VERT troopers appeared to have ceased fire, and after a while the M-Bahn defenders did likewise. The sudden silence was shocking. It made Freya realise just how badly her ears were ringing.

"Give yourself up, Freya," Erik shouted from somewhere below. "It's over!"

"Not yet it isn't," she shouted back. "You'll know when it's done!"

There was a brief pause before Erik replied.

"I can still make a deal with you. You want Kaiser, don't you? Well, we can get to him. We can give him to you. Just give us William. We need his expertise, then we'll release him. All charges dropped. I promise."

"He won't betray DedSec," Freya called back, using the unofficial ceasefire to squirm closer to the armoured door.

"Maybe, maybe not. But I doubt he'd have the same qualms about breaking open the rabble-rousers we have here in Germany. We had already come to an accord before your uninvited return."

"He won't help you, Erik, and neither will I," Freya shouted, before firing a few shots from her G36 up at the skylight that constituted much of the lobby's ceiling. It shattered, glass raining down onto those below.

That kickstarted shooting once again. Freya needed that if she was going to have an uninterrupted chance at cracking the door.

Exactly how she was going to do that, she didn't yet know. Up close it was clear she wasn't going to be able to shoot her way through. The only sign of vulnerability was the lock on the wall, and even that looked impenetrable. It was a featureless metal cylinder, a smart lock that presumably required Kaiser's Optik to access.

She didn't know what to do, so, staying as low as she could, she blinked on Will's number.

"Sir, Meyer is calling again," Alex's voice said over the radio as Erik reloaded.

"I told you not to take calls from him," Erik snapped back.

"He's… he says that I'm in charge, sir."

"What?"

"He says that I'm acting colonel-in-chief, and that you're to be relieved of your duties. He… also says that I'm to order your arrest… sir."

"Put me through," Erik barked, his rage overcoming his desire to ignore everything happening outside the embattled villa. "Put that treacherous bastard on right now!"

Almost immediately, Meyer's insufferable voice crackled over the line's static.

"Gerhardt! What the hell is happening?"

"We're making a play," Erik growled. "It's now or never."

"It looks more like the start of World War Three," Meyer replied just as aggressively. "There's a live stream from the middle of that villa, from the middle of a goddamn gunfight! I've just had a phone call from the Stability Coalition's vice-president, Claud Schapps. He was contacted personally by Emil Kaiser just a couple of minutes ago. Why in God's name are you attacking Kaiser's home, much less with everything in your arsenal?

Schapps is going crazy, and I'm not surprised! I know you have history with Kaiser, but he's one of Schapps's major donors!"

"He's criminal scum, and his reckoning is well overdue. Besides, he's not the priority target."

"Dare I ask who is then?"

Erik hesitated. There had been a confrontation with Meyer coming for some time. He was too cautious, too worried about the optics presented by VERT when they were at their most forceful, their most powerful. That would have to change if VERT was to progress, but Erik had hoped to avoid it tonight.

What if he had overstepped?

"There are reports that Humboldthain was attacked earlier tonight," Meyer went on, his tone becoming colder and sharper. "Rumours of an escaped prisoner. I'm assuming the complete abandonment of riot control duties was also done on your order?"

"We have an opportunity tonight," Erik said, forcing himself to rally. "Two members of DedSec have been identified operating in Berlin, and I am minutes away from taking them."

"DedSec? Why was I not informed?"

"The intelligence was highly sensitive, and the situation is fluid. We–"

"You've gone too far this time, Erik! I'll be speaking with members of the party committee about all of this."

"The party wouldn't dare censor me at a time like this."

"Do you have any idea what's happening right now?" Meyer raged. "I'm only watching the morning news, and even without that live stream it's bad enough. There are riots spreading right across the city because your gang of thugs have abandoned their positions. The police are totally overrun. And that's before we take into account whatever's happening at Kaiser's right now.

Halftracks? Full combat gear? You're all over the TV, and that means you'll be all over the internet, worldwide! People across Europe are waking up to this as we speak!"

"I'll have the news drones shot down and kill whoever's streaming."

"Listen to yourself! Are you insane? If you want to stand even a chance of not spending the rest of your life in prison, you'll withdraw right now. Even if DedSec are operating in Berlin, you're doing more damage to us and our election chances in a few hours than any little hacker could manage with years of effort."

Erik cut the connection. His hands were shaking. That didn't happen often.

"Sir," the leader of the breaching team said uncertainly, his eyes visibly wide over the bottom of his mask.

Erik shoved him out of the way. Without thinking, he walked straight through the lobby's double doors, which had been chewed to splinters by the hail of back-and-forth gunfire, his P-9mm raised, firing it as he walked, towards where the villa's defenders were still cowering behind the shot-up remnants of a stuffed elephant.

One tried to rise and return fire and took a bullet to the forehead for his trouble. He collapsed back. Erik kept going. He felt nothing but fury, all-consuming, burning away every other thought and consideration, every hope and fear.

His weapon clicked empty. He had reached the nearest side of the dais. At the same time, one of Kaiser's gunmen stood, drawing a line of sight on him right between the elephant's bullet-scarred legs.

A hand snatched the back of his flak vest and dragged him off to one side.

It was the breach team leader. Another of the VERT troopers

put down the man who had begun to fire at Erik. The last of the defenders shouted, her hands up, her weapon discarded.

Erik pushed away the trooper who had saved his life and leaned heavily against the base of the dais. This wasn't how it was supposed to go. He had worked so hard for so long, just to get this far. How could it all have unravelled so fast?

He shouted, punched the ragged flank of the elephant, hearing his fury echo in the space that had been so recently riven with gunfire, empty and impotent now.

34
Hacker Wars

Will huddled low behind the stand the stuffed hyena was poised on, hearing it shudder as bullets thumped into it. Across from him, Leona finished reloading her Goblin assault rifle and eased off a burst that finally forced the shooter attempting to hit Will to duck back behind his own animal mannequin.

This wasn't what Will had signed up for, but there wasn't much he could do about it. The space between the trophy stands was too large for either side to rush, so unless one got in a lucky hit, nobody was going to make any headway. Right now all they could do was hope Freya had managed to track down Kaiser.

Her voice clicked in Will's ear, barely audible.

"I've reached the panic room!"

"Very nice," Will replied. "Does that mean we can go yet?"

"I'm still outside it. It's got a blast door, with a smart lock."

"Oh great."

"Can you open it?"

"What, from here?"

"Yes, from there! It's just a round metal box on the wall, no manual input, so it must use a remote connection. That means you can hack it."

"I love the confidence you have in me. Link me to your HUD."

After a few moments, what Freya was seeing popped up in the corner of his vision. He focused on it – hardly ideal while he was in the middle of a gunfight.

Freya was right, he knew the lock's manufacturer. He could possibly gain remote access, but the conditions for doing so were hardly ideal. Hacking under fire was just about the opposite of what he wanted to be doing right now.

"Can you open it?" Freya demanded.

"I can try," Will said. He was already hunting for the Jägerhalle's Wi-Fi connection. "But it's going to take at least a few minutes."

"Not sure I have that long. I'm upstairs, it's pretty hot up here!"

"Tell me about it," Will said, opening a series of apps and initiating a brute force attack on the villa's Wi-Fi.

"Is it working?" Freya asked in his ear.

"I'm trying," he responded tersely. "There's multiple stages to this. I'm Wi-Fi cracking."

As he did so, he used their shared HUD to find the OIN for Freya's Optik. It was a ten-digit number that a wireless carrier used to identify it as a specific device. He'd need it for this to work.

"You know I'm getting shot at right now?" Freya demanded.

"That makes two of us! Hold on!"

He located the OIN digits just as he managed to force the Wi-Fi password, using the connection to enter the smart lock's settings as stuffing and old fur rained down on him from the hyena, which had been all but demolished by gunfire. It was ironic, he thought, that Freya had come to Germany to do the shooting while he did the hacking, yet here he was dealing with both.

"Will," yelled Leona. "He's coming round your side!"

There was no time to even blink out of Freya's HUD. Instead, Will desperately hit the jamming app, locking it onto the approaching gunman's rifle just as he raised it to fire. There was a clicking noise, but no discharge. The man swore loudly, lowering the weapon, struggling to unlock it again.

Will used the moment's pause to refocus and snatch up his pistol with his good hand, squeezing off a wild shot at the figure. The M-Bahn gunman scrambled back, and Will immediately returned to Freya's display.

"You OK?" she asked.

"Yeah," Will replied tersely. "Just don't chat around with Kaiser when you see him, yeah? Kill him."

"Planning on it."

"Then we can get the hell out of here."

He quickly scanned through the smart lock's setting, locating the password – it required it to be reentered to change, so no easy fix there. Instead, he set about adding Freya's Optik to its list of recognised devices using the OIN number. No need for entering a password if the presence of the device itself should be enough.

"That might be it," he said into his earpiece. "Is the blast shutter up?"

"I'm about to find out," came the reply.

35
Dead Reckoning

The blast plate rattled up. Freya looked away and put two bullets through the lock of the regular door beyond, then kicked it open.

She entered what she guessed had to be Kaiser's office. There were more trophies, but it was dominated by a desk at the far end with a large monitor. The blast shutter that had previously covered the triangular window beyond was now raised, exposing the torn and battered garden beyond, illuminated by the rising sun.

Kaiser himself was waiting for her. He stood behind the desk, dressed in a white suit. She recognised him from photos she had seen online while laying out the plan with Reboot. She had tried to prepare for this, but even so, she nearly froze up with anger. His own expression was nothing short of maniacal.

"Welcome, Miss Bauer," he hissed.

Freya would have shot him there and then if something hadn't cracked into her G36, knocking the barrel down. She twisted just as a figure came slamming in from the side, from behind the door.

It was Teuton. The tall M-Bahn enforcer threw a punch that

connected with the side of her head, making Freya stagger and loosening her grip on the rifle enough for Teuton to tear it away. She kept advancing, throwing a second punch that Freya managed to block before swinging low herself, thumping a fist into Teuton's gut.

They grappled. Freya snarled, twisting Teuton's wrist and trying to throw her against the wall. Teuton kicked Freya viciously in the shin, trying to knock her legs out from under her and get on top. She managed to snatch Mister Scruff, wrenching it off, exposing Freya's wild, sweat-streaked features.

"I'm going to kill you, Freya Bauer," Teuton snarled, face inches from Freya's.

Freya snatched at Teuton's throat with her other hand and rammed her back against the wall.

"Why are you doing this?" she demanded as they strained at one another, sensing that the fury animating Teuton was just as potent as her own.

"You killed my mother," Teuton spat, ripping Freya's grip from her throat and headbutting her. She stumbled back, vision flashing. By the time she had recovered Teuton was on her again, using her greater height to her advantage, forcing her down onto her knees with a keening hiss of primal aggression.

"Enough," shouted Kaiser. He was brandishing a gold-plated Protocol Pistol from behind his desk.

"Release her," he ordered Teuton.

"Let me do it," Teuton snarled, looking feral as she tried to get a chokehold of her own on Freya. "Let me kill the bitch."

"Not yet! She has to see what's about to happen to her son first."

Freya had been trying to work out who Teuton's mother was, but the mention of Andrew immediately overrode everything else.

"What are you talking about?" she snapped, shoving Teuton

violently back as the woman finally let go of her. Kaiser had the Protocol Pistol levelled at her and was grinning. He motioned with his free hand, tapping the scratched old surface of his desk.

"Come here and see."

Freya glanced at her fallen rifle, but it was too far away. She had to know what Kaiser meant about Andrew. That was what Kaiser wanted though. She looked at Teuton instead, saw the hatred in her eyes.

"Who was your mother?" she asked her.

"You'll know before I kill you," Teuton promised, but Kaiser spoke up.

"Her name was Bella Kaiser, and she was my wife."

Freya looked between the two, realisation dawning as she recognised the resemblance. No wonder M-Bahn was just a play by Kaiser, when it was his daughter running it.

"How did she die?" Freya asked.

"We're not talking about her now," Kaiser shouted, turning red as he banged his palm off the desk and pointed the Protocol in Freya's face. "I said come here!"

Freya approached, tensing up further as she left Teuton in her blind spot. She expected a blow, but the crime lord's daughter restrained herself. Kaiser rotated the desk monitor so Freya could see it.

She knew what she was looking at immediately. It was the entrance to Snax, the greasy spoon café she and Will had visited so often. Icy dread gripped her.

"I wanted you to see this in person," Kaiser said, his flushed expression running counterpoint to his smart white suit and tie. "It's taken a lot more effort than I expected, but here you are. The daughter of Thomas Bauer. Now my wife will be avenged, and everyone will see that nobody crosses me, or my family."

"How was I responsible for her death?" Freya demanded, playing for time while she worked towards the more serious questions. Did they have Andrew? Why would he be at Snax? Helen had gotten him to safety. They had spoken on the phone!

"Your family is responsible," Kaiser said. "Your treacherous father went to the police. He helped organise a raid on this very house. They killed my wife, and likely would have killed me too if they could. Your father thought he could escape. But I am Emil Kaiser. I do not forgive, and I do not forget. I tracked him down, and he is dead, and now you will join him. You and your son. For what you've done to my operations in the past, and for the harm your family has wrought on mine."

During Kaiser's tirade spit had flecked the front of his suit. He was shaking, furious, wild with an anger that had been building, like pressure in a sealed cylinder, for decades.

"I don't know anything about your wife's death," Freya snarled, giving vent to her own fury. "I was still a child. I didn't kill her. Ending me and my son won't bring her back."

Kaiser looked momentarily startled by the suggestion, before hatred took hold once more.

"Do not speak to me of vengeance. Why else did you come here tonight, if not to take revenge on me?"

"You lured me to Berlin to murder me, much as you did my father," Freya exclaimed. "You expect me to simply go back to London and hope you don't follow me? Forget any of this ever happened? You've been there all my life, Kaiser. I didn't know it was you, but it was, stalking me, bringing fear to my mother, forcing us to change homes and always watch our backs."

"Good," Kaiser spat. "You deserve nothing less. Now watch your son die."

He blinked into his Optik's display and spoke.

"Gespenst. Kill the boy."

"Wait," Freya shouted.

"Watch the screen," Kaiser snarled, switching the heavy pistol to his other hand to keep it up and trained on her. "Watch it and feel as helpless as I felt with Bella dying in my arms!"

For once, Freya didn't know what to do. She stood rooted to the spot, frozen by fear and panic, unable to see a way forward that didn't result in her death or Andrew's, or both. All she could do was watch and hope. Hope for a miracle. Hope that Helen Dashwood was looking out for her son after all.

The camera moved, down towards the broad window that ran along most of the front of Snax. She realised that she was watching events playing out via a drone, presumably the same feed as the operator.

"Kill me if you have to, but leave him," Freya told Kaiser. "He hasn't done anything wrong. He's just a kid!"

"Yes," Kaiser hissed, not looking at the screen, but at Freya, grinning like one of his stuffed hyenas. "Plead. Beg me to spare his life. I want to hear it!"

The drone drew closer to the window front. The camera picked up figures beyond. Customers, seated at window tables, tucking into breakfasts of bacon rolls and coffee or croissants and tea. A targeting reticule appeared across the display, the drone's programming bouncing the little red circle from one profile to another until it found the one it sought. It was accompanied by a piece of text in the bottom left corner.

+Seeking Target: Andrew Bauer+

And there he was. Andrew Bauer, sitting with a steaming mug and a plate full of scrambled eggs. The window was grimy, and it took a second for the drone to properly lock on and ID the figure, but once it did, Freya experienced a moment of heart-stopping uncertainty. The words she had been speaking choked in her throat. In that moment she experienced something she hated more than anything else. She found her fate, and that of her son, in the hands of others. She was powerless.

+Target Acquired: Andrew Bauer+

"Say goodbye," Kaiser all but screamed at her from across the desk.

Whatever weapon the drone was equipped with, it fired. The glass immediately crazed around a tiny entry hole in the window, the cracks hiding what exactly had become of the figure, besides that they had slumped forward into their breakfast.

Freya said nothing, did nothing. Kaiser stared at her fiercely, and it briefly seemed as though he was going to shoot her.

It was Teuton who broke the terrible silence.

"How does it feel, to lose one you love?"

"I'm… still trying to decide," Freya responded. Kaiser's expression darkened. He finally looked at the monitor, and realised what Freya had already seen – the text in the bottom left of the monitor, text she had expected to change to "target neutralised", said something else instead.

+Seeking Target: Andrew Bauer+

It was the same message that had been running before the lock. The targeter was roaming about once more as the other people at the tables scrambled to their feet in panic, realising what was happening.

The drone was still looking for the person with the facial features that matched those of Freya's son.

"What's it doing?" Kaiser asked, clearly speaking into his earpiece. "Gespenst? Confirm the kill!"

He listened to the response, which Freya couldn't hear, then screamed.

"What do you mean you don't know? Get in there and find out! I want eyes on his body! Your eyes, not some damned machine!"

"It isn't him," Freya said, starting to laugh as she experienced a sense of relief more powerful than any she had known. "I don't know what poor bastard your assassin just killed, but it wasn't my son."

"It was, we all saw him," Kaiser snapped.

"We saw him through the eyes of a machine. Take it from me, I might not be any good at hacking, but I've worked for DedSec for long enough to know that those are easily fooled. *I* know that wasn't Andrew."

She looked hard at Kaiser, her body tensing once again, ready now, the panic and the indecision all gone.

"My son is allergic to eggs," she said.

She didn't give Kaiser the second or two he needed to understand. She moved.

To his credit, Kaiser reacted quickly. He shot her.

36
Scrambled

The Ghost strongly considered disobeying Kaiser's last order. In truth, he had been afraid of complications like this. After getting the ping from Andrew's hacked Optik payment app, he had set himself up on a park bench one street away from the café, rather than halfway across town, ready to intervene if the drone failed.

Apparently, it had. It wasn't recording Andrew as terminated. Perhaps it was a glitch, but it filled him with doubt.

Walking into a place where he had indirectly shot someone was always a terrible idea. Someone would be calling ambulances, the police. He knew about average response times. Building morning traffic would hamper the authorities, but he didn't have much more than five minutes.

In the end, it was his addiction that pushed him to act. He couldn't enjoy the rush unless he knew he really had killed Andrew Bauer. This uncertainty was turning the sweetest moment of his career bitter. He needed the satisfaction of seeing Freya's son dead.

He knew he should have done it in person.

With practiced efficiency, he packed away the laptop he had

been using to run the wasp drone and headed for the café, cursing the stiffness that the early morning London cold had seeded into his ageing limbs. The wasp itself he had already ordered onto a preset route that would lead it onto the tracks in front of a train just leaving King's Cross, and its obliteration as evidence. It had failed him. It deserved nothing less.

Two and a half minutes to the café. It was hard on his ruined lungs, making him wheeze. As predicted, the place was in chaos. People rushed out the front door, some in tears. The Ghost slipped a pair of spectacles from his pocket and put them on as pushed for the doorway.

"Clear the way, I'm a doctor," he shouted, his accent a perfect mimicry of English Received Pronunciation. "Make way!"

There were still people in the café, most of them clustered around one of the tables by the cracked window.

"Move aside, I'm a doctor," he repeated sternly, shoving his way in.

There was his latest victim, lying slumped over a table, blood drenching his scrambled eggs and spilled coffee.

The Ghost froze, disbelief warring with shock. The kill had been as clean as they came, a hole drilled in the right side of the man's head. But it wasn't Andrew Bauer. It was Kaiser's DedSec informant. Wellend.

"Well, aren't you going to do something?" the old lady demanded.

"What do you think I can do for something like that?" the Ghost hissed, realising even as he spoke that he recognised the woman. She was Belinda Bauer's neighbour.

His fury momentarily dissipated. Something was very wrong. He began to push past her, heading for the door.

"Off to try and find Andrew?" the old woman asked him,

standing firm. He stared at her. Just an old Londoner, a typical, grey Englishwoman, but she was smirking up at him, and her eyes were keen and deadly.

"We hacked your drone's facial recognition software," said a second voice. This one the Ghost knew too. It was the girl, Sara, Andrew's love interest. She moved forward next to the old woman, looking equally triumphant.

"It's the same trick we use to back-door CTOS or fool lock scanners. Poor, treacherous Wellend was here to tie up some loose ends, but in the end he was the one tied up."

"You can't protect him," the Ghost snarled. "I'll be far from here by the time the police arrive."

"That might have been true," the old woman said. "If I hadn't called them two minutes before you killed Wellend."

A heartbeat of horrified realisation, and the Ghost's instincts finally kicked in. He threw a punch at the old one, but to his surprise the younger one lashed out with catlike reflexes, knocking the blow to one side and twisting his wrist painfully in a clawing grasp. Before he could rip his hand free the old one cracked her walking stick into his shin.

He went down on one knee with a cry, and Sara struck him across the face.

For the first time in his life, the Ghost realised something truly horrifying. What he feared had been confirmed in the worst circumstances possible. He was no longer physically capable.

He tried to get up, but the stick delivered another cracking blow. That was when he made the second horrifying realisation.

He could hear police sirens.

Harriet turned on the waterworks for the police officers when they arrived. Helen stood close to her, a supportive arm around her shoulder, privately enjoying the performance as the authorities took their statements.

"She's already told you, this man tried to assault us," Helen said, getting in on the act. "Ask anyone else in the café!"

"And why were you in the café at the time of the assault?" the harried-looking Met officer taking their statements asked.

"I was taking my granddaughter out for breakfast," Helen snapped with faux indignity. "She's a student at Bristol, and she just got home last night to visit me. Is that a crime?"

"No ma'am, but we need to establish why you both remained in the café where someone had been fatally shot."

"We didn't know what it was at first," Helen said. "And unlike some, my family go into danger when others are running away. We thought we could help. We didn't realise… just how fatal it was. Then this man attacked us."

Harriet burst into fresh floods of tears, and Helen hugged her closer. Just a few yards away more policemen were cuffing the Ghost. His nose was bloody and broken, and his eyes were wild.

"They're DedSec," he snarled, pulling ferociously at his restraints as he tried to get at Helen and Harriet. "Both of them! They're hackers, criminals! They've set me up!"

"What on earth are you talking about, you lunatic?" Helen demanded shrilly. "You tried to attack us! My granddaughter is traumatised!"

"They're lying," the Ghost shouted back as he was hauled towards the waiting police van.

"Did you find the drone?" Harriet asked between sniffles. "I saw one, flying right outside the café window right before the bang."

"Yes, other witnesses reported the same." The officer jotted something down in his notebook. "We picked up a small delivery drone that had lost flight nearby."

It was good to know the police weren't totally incompetent then. Harriet had hacked it remotely after the Ghost had set it on what she assumed was a preset self-destruction course, overriding it and causing it to drop on the pavement nearby. The Met would need it as evidence.

More importantly, they had the laptop the Ghost had been carrying. Helen suspected it would take them a while to crack it, but once they did they would have all the evidence they needed. This would turn out to be the biggest arrest since the events of Zero Day.

"Can I take your details please," the policeman was asking. "I'll need them if you intend to press charges."

"Oh, we most certainly do," Helen said, providing false names, numbers and addresses for both of them. Neither were going to appear in court, but by then the so-called Ghost was going to have much bigger things to worry about.

As soon as the police departed, Harriet phoned Andrew.

"We got him," she said. Helen smiled as she heard his relief over the Optik.

"But what about Mum?" was his next thought. "And Dad?"

"Don't worry about them," Helen interjected. "If anyone can handle themselves over there, it'll be those two."

37
Sound of Silence

For one of the first times in his life, Erik didn't know what to do. He was keenly aware of the stares of the VERT troopers around him. Only their bravery in following him into the kill zone of the lobby had stopped him being shot down.

There was movement from a doorway off to the right, which drew an immediate flurry of shots from the closest VERT troopers. Erik looked up at the landing overhead. Up there. That was where Freya had gone. He had to follow her. He had to capture her, or else there'd be nothing left, nothing but the ignominy of a prison sentence.

"Cease fire," a voice shouted from behind Erik. He turned around and found Alex striding into the wrecked lobby, backed by a dozen fresh VERT troopers. The subordinate's expression was grim.

"What are you doing here?" Erik demanded, the anger he had vented in the wild charge starting to build again. "I didn't give you orders to join me. You're supposed to be coordinating from the flak tower."

"Not anymore," Alex said. "I told you, I've spoken with the

justice minister. He's made a few suggestions, and I'm here to implement them. It starts with removing you from command."

"Removing me... how dare you?" Erik barked. "I am VERT! You can't 'remove' me! You owe everything you have to me!"

"The police have a warrant for your arrest," Alex said stoically, not shying away from Erik. "And it would go some way towards rehabilitating VERT's image if we bring you in. If the Defenders project is to continue, it needs legitimacy in the eyes of the other authorities, and the support of men like Meyer."

"What did he offer you, you little traitor?" Erik demanded, stepping towards Alex. "How much is he paying you?"

"Nothing beyond the salary I'll receive when I'm in command," Alex said. "You lost control tonight, sir. You're on the cusp of ruining everything. Unfortunately for you, soldiers don't just follow orders anymore."

"I don't need orders, damn you," Erik spat, and raised his pistol. He pulled the trigger, but it merely clicked, empty. Alex didn't even blink.

"Take him," he said.

The VERT troopers accompanying him swept in from the left and right, snatching Erik. He fought them, bellowing with rage, wrestling himself free for a moment, until one punched him square in the face. He tasted blood, and felt the cold bite of cuffs as his arms were twisted behind his back, digging into his wrists.

"You won't get away with this," he said, spitting blood at Alex. "I still have allies. Meyer won't protect you when the time comes. He'll drop you, just like he's dropped me!"

"Gag him too," Alex said dispassionately to one of the troopers. "And prepare to withdraw. All units are to disengage immediately."

"We aren't going to finish clearing the house?" the leader of the breaching unit Erik had been accompanying queried. "What about the DedSec fugitives?"

"There's not much chance they're not either dead or gone," Alex said, looking around the bullet-riddled remains of the lobby. "And we should never have gone in heavy-handed like this. The world is watching. Pull out now, and we might still be able to salvage our reputation. Stay, and all of us will be up on criminal charges."

The breach leader nodded before barking a series of orders at his troopers.

"You heard the man. Jenz, Kratz, watch our six. Everybody up and out!"

It had suddenly all gone very quiet.

"Keep it raised," Will told Leona. A bullet had scythed though the leg of the stuffed lion she had been sheltering behind, and had in turn gone through Leona's leg. In getting the angle, the M-Bahn shooter had exposed himself to where Will was sheltering. He'd got him, hitting him with two bullets from his 1911. As soon as the man had dropped, Will had scrambled over to Leona, helping prop her up against the lion's flank.

"It's not the artery, so you'll be fine," he had said.

"It doesn't feel fine," Leona snarled, hauling her lion mask off. She was flushed and sweat-soaked underneath.

"It's probably lodged against the bone," Will had said. She had been hit just beneath the knee.

He ripped the bottom of his T-shirt off to bind the wound. About that time, he became aware of the silence.

It wasn't just in the trophy room. During the gunfight he had become accustomed to the constant, echoing report of shooting throughout the villa. But now, suddenly, it was gone. All of it. He found himself looking from the row after row of severed heads up on the wall, bestial eyes staring down at them blankly, to the body of the man he had shot earlier, blood slowly pooling out underneath him and around the base of the cheetah poised, frozen, above him.

"Sounds like it's all over," Leona said as Will raised her leg up, voice tight with pain.

"Sounds like it," Will agreed as his thoughts raced, trying to work out what had happened. Was this good news, or bad?

"Freya," Leona said.

She had gone silent on the headset just after Will had got the upstairs door open.

"I need to find her," Will told Leona.

"Go. I'll be fine."

"We can't be the last ones left," Will said, trying to rationalise what was happening. "You've got your Optik?"

"I do," Leona said, clearly putting on a brave face. "I'll contact the others. Rally them here."

Will picked up the Goblin rifle and put it in her bloody hands.

"I'll be back in a few minutes, as soon as I've found her," he said. "Don't run off!"

Leona chuckled, which was more than Will had hoped for. He got up and hurried for the nearest door.

Beyond lay a scene of devastation. Will edged out cautiously, discovering a high, square room, its glass ceiling partially shot in. It was dominated by a taxidermied elephant that looked like it had been through both World Wars. It was still standing, though, which was more than could be said of the four M-Bahn bodies slumped around one side of its base.

But where had they gone? Just moments ago the villa had resounded to so much gunfire that Will had thought it might come crashing down. Now though, there was nothing but a chilling, cold silence.

Or so Will had thought. As he stepped cautiously into the lobby, shoes crunching on broken glass, he caught the sounds of raised voices drifting from another room.

He looked up, taking in the stairs that led to the landing that encircled half of the room. Freya had been trying to get through a room upstairs. From where he was standing, he could half make out an open door.

That was when he heard the gunshot, ringing out from beyond it.

"Freya," he shouted, and raced for the stairs.

38
Big Game Hunted

The bullet meant to kill Freya skimmed her right shoulder as she threw herself to the left.

The Protocol Pistol's high-calibre round carried on through her and into the stomach of Teuton as she charged furiously at Freya.

She dropped abruptly, and Freya rolled and came back up on the other side of the large monitor on Kaiser's desk. By then he had already fired a second round, not realising he had shot his daughter, blowing a huge hole in the floor next to Freya.

"No," Kaiser exclaimed as he saw Teuton fall. She looked equally surprised, clutching at her gut, the colour draining from her face.

Freya shoved the monitor at Kaiser, forcing him back, its screen shattering and cables whipping free. Kaiser attempted to sidestep it, but it clipped his side and knocked him against the desk.

Freya scrambled directly over it, flinging a paperweight at him, knowing she had to close the distance before he got another shot off. The paperweight hit his hand as he raised the Protocol again, making him yelp and giving Freya time to get a punch in, flinging herself on top of him.

They went down together, Freya trying and failing to get a grip on Kaiser's wrist. She didn't know exactly where the pistol was, and when it went off again she expected to feel a fatal pain, but Kaiser's shot blew a chunk out of the old desk instead.

He bellowed and shoved back against her with a strength born of fury, belying his short stature. Freya was forced up against the table, but managed to get a grip on his wrist, twisting until he let go of the pistol. It clattered to the floor on the other side.

"You… shot my daughter," he snarled, spitting in Freya's face.

"You shot your daughter, you fool." Freya twisted out from against the desk and threw him against it in turn. "And I didn't kill your wife!"

Kaiser wasn't listening. Instead of remaining locked with Freya, he let go and scrambled across the desk. Freya thought he was going to Teuton, who had now slumped back and coughing up blood, but instead he snatched at the fallen pistol.

Freya charged after him, knowing this would end one of two ways – she, or they, wouldn't be leaving the Jägerhalle.

She kicked Kaiser in the back of the knee as he stooped for the Protocol, bringing him down. She grabbed his short, white hair, dragging him around so she could punch him.

"This is for my dad." She followed up with a second blow.

"Your dad… was a traitor," Kaiser snarled through bloodied lips before he wrapped both arms around Freya's left leg and heaved.

She cried out while falling back, knocking her head painfully off the tiled floor. She lashed out with her other foot and sent the Protocol skittering away again, but Kaiser wasn't after that anymore. He straddled her, grabbed her throat with both hands, bloody spit drooling from the snarling rictus his face had become as he leaned over Freya and choked the life from her.

"Now… die," he snarled.

Freya fought back, but his grip was good. Her lungs burned. Panic set in. She tried to turn it around, lessening her struggles even as her vision began to grey, every biological imperative screaming at her. Face flushed and eyes rolling back, she lay still, even as Kaiser's fingers dug into her windpipe with manic force.

It was too late. Breathless, she slipped away.

Will charged in through the office door, seeing Teuton lying in a pool of blood and a white-suited, feral-looking man he took to be Kaiser with both hands on Freya's throat. She was prone, motionless.

He instinctively shouted her name again and raised his pistol, firing.

The weapon clicked, empty.

Kaiser turned, locking his manic eyes on Will. He saw him with a gun, and likely assuming he was either about to shoot him or reload while Freya lay lifeless beneath him, he rose and charged him with a roar.

Will stood frozen until the crime lord slammed into him, tackling him back towards the office door and sending them both sprawling through it. Will yelped, finding himself under Kaiser much as Freya had been, but instead of strangling him Kaiser began to punch him, sending sharp pain through his cheek, his jaw, then bursting blood from his lip. His hands flapped desperately, first grabbing the front of Kaiser's white suit, then his waist in an effort to twist and throw him off.

In doing so, he brushed up against the one flare he'd been given, still stuck in his belt.

With wild strength he heaved, throwing Kaiser back against the door. He staggered as he attempted to rise, spitting blood, his vision swimming from the ferocious assault. The flare was in his hands, though.

Despite his apparent age, Kaiser was fast. He was back up and on him again, grappling with him as he forced them both out onto the bullet-riddled landing. He got in another punch, snatching his throat and forcing him onto his knees.

"Welcome to Berlin, little Englander," Kaiser hissed, slowly beginning to press Will's face against the remains of the banister railing while squeezing the breath from him.

Will was panicking, unable to get any air, unable to find the strength to throw Kaiser off, but he had unscrewed the flare's cap. With one last, desperate effort, he struck it, heard it spark up, felt the sudden, fierce heat.

He shoved it upwards. The burning tip hit Kaiser's jaw, making him scream and fling himself away from Will, clutching his face. Will gasped down air into his aching lungs, then choked and coughed as smoke began to broil from the flare, its crimson glare blinding.

"You little rat," Kaiser shrieked, lunging back at him. The flesh of his lower left face was already starting to twist and blister. He snatched at Will's arm, banging it off a banister railing until the wood split, and he released the flare with a cry. It dropped down into the lobby below, its smoke churning up to engulf them.

"I'm going to kill you, you pathetic little man," Kaiser hissed as he resumed strangling Will. "Just the way I killed Freya, your brute of an ex-wife!"

Freya's name brought her back.

For a while she had been with her mother and father, a child again, laughing and happy. Then she had heard her name, spoken by a voice at once familiar and strange.

That had done it. She had felt the burning in her lungs, the aching beat of her heart, and the brief, joyful illusion of an innocent past had evaporated.

She sat up, gasping and coughing. In an instant, it all came back. She stumbled to her feet, dizzy, chest still sore. Only then did she recognise the voice that had shouted to her.

Will had found her. He was now grappling furiously with Kaiser. Forcing herself through the pain and disorientation, Freya made towards them.

She had barely gone a few steps after them before something snagged her ankle and she went down once more, cursing.

It was Teuton. The wound in her stomach looked grim, but it seemed as though raw hatred had overcome the pain and shock. She had managed to snatch at Freya, and now she got in a weak punch while trying to headlock her.

Freya managed to prise her head free, but even dying, Teuton's strength was fearsome. Freya had a horrible sense that, in another life, they would have been friends. Instead, Teuton scrambled on top of her, clawing at her face as Freya grabbed her wrists.

"I'm sorry… about your mother…" Freya hissed. She realised there were tears in the other woman's eyes, even as she swallowed back blood.

"I loved her," Teuton managed.

"I loved my father," Freya replied. "No child… should lose a parent."

Abruptly, the tension vanished. She thought at first that the last of Teuton's strength had deserted her, but making eye contact she saw no more rage there, no more hatred, just a cold acceptance.

Teuton slumped off Freya, dead.

Freya stared at her, until a scream caused her to scramble back to her feet, hands and chest wet with Teuton's blood.

Will and Kaiser were still fighting desperately. Will must have popped his flare, then dropped it, because red-tinged smoke was billowing up from the lobby, framing and partially engulfing the two as they fought.

Freya thought of Teuton, of how in her last seconds she had let go, in every sense. Then she thought of her mother and her tears, of her son, who had never known his grandfather. She thought of Thomas Bauer, who had hugged her tight before he had left, never to return.

She ran at Kaiser. He had Will pinned against the broken banisters and was punching him again and again. He heard Freya coming at the last second. He looked up. The left side of his face was hideously burned. There was no calmness in his eyes, no acceptance, no dignity. Only the frenzied rage of an animal driven beyond reason.

Freya threw herself against him. He tried to dodge, but Will, his face a bloody mess, managed to snatch the front of his suit and hold him in place.

Freya's impact sent Kaiser crashing through what little remained of the banisters and out into the lobby, through the smoke of the flare. He barely had time to scream before there was a gristly thump, and silence.

Freya would have gone with him, locked in a final, deadly embrace, had Will not managed to absorb her impact and hold her back from the edge. They stayed there for a few seconds, panting, looking into each other's eyes.

"What took so long?" Will slurred through burst lips.

"Teuton," Freya said, standing up. She shook badly. She

leaned forward, looking over the edge of the landing, fearing that it wasn't high enough up to ensure Kaiser's death from the fall alone.

In the end, she needn't have worried. Kaiser hadn't even made it to the floor. He had been impaled through the back on one of the great, curving ivory tusks of the taxidermied elephant, facing up towards his office door. The tusk's crimson tip was protruding from his stomach, turning his white suit a shockingly bright red as smoke from the flare that had fallen beneath broiled up around him. He was dead, as glassy eyed as the hundreds of other slain animals in the villa.

"Nice catch, Dumbo," Will called out to the elephant that remained, standing tall and battle-scarred.

Freya fell to her knees and, before she had even thought about it, burst into tears. Will threw an arm around her shoulder, murmuring to her as they sat down on the edge of the landing, legs over the side.

"It's over Freya. It's over."

The emotion that had overwhelmed Freya receded as quickly as it had risen up. Will was right. It was over. She could take time to come to terms with exactly what that meant later on.

She coughed, turning her head away from the smoke before grabbing one of the snapped banisters and using it to support herself while she helped Will to his feet. They had been in a lot of scrapes down the years, but right now he really did look like hell.

"You're hurt," he said to her, somewhat ironically. Freya glanced at her shoulder, where the shot that had killed Teuton had grazed her.

"Just stings a bit," she said. "Can you walk?"

"Yeah, but my face feels like it's in bits and pieces."

"It is. What happened to VERT?"

"I think they pulled out. No idea why. We should probably get going though, before any of Kaiser's remaining minions show up."

Arm in arm, they helped each other down to the base of the lobby. Freya cast one last glance up at Kaiser's corpse, impaled above now like some sort of ghastly Halloween decoration. Well, it was almost that time of year. As they passed she looked towards the door to the trophy room.

Leona was standing there, supported by another of the Reboot crew, A-Grade. Leona looked wan, and Freya realised she had a nasty-looking leg wound.

"You got him then," the Reboot leader said, holding A-Grade tight as she looked up past Freya at Kaiser's body.

"Think so," Freya said. "Are you two all that's left?"

"No, I've seen at least Hangover and Lago," A-Grade said.

Freya heard the unmistakable sounds of police sirens, their wailing echoing from outside.

"I've already pinged the Optiks of the others to head for the back," Leona said. "We came to check if you two were still alive."

"Looks like it, but we might as well not be if the police cordon this place off," Freya said. "VERT must have been told to drop back. We need to get out of here."

She helped A-Grade support Leona while Will went ahead, passing back through the trophy room and on to the rear of the Jägerhalle. The remnants of M-Bahn and Kaiser's other followers had presumably taken the withdrawal of VERT as one last opportunity to make themselves scarce – the place was deserted, bar the dead bodies. No honour among thieves, it seemed.

"We might need to get you to a hospital," Freya told Leona as they went, knowing it meant certain imprisonment.

"I'll be all right once I get a proper bandage on it," she grunted. "It's just blood loss and a bit of pain."

"You're a tough one, Miss Lion," Will said as they helped her out through one of the shattered windows along the rear of the villa.

The deaths were on her, and that was something she was going to have to come to terms with. Perhaps she had just swapped one pain for another. But at least, tonight, there was a sense of closure, and the hope that, after the killing and bloodshed, some good had been won, something that would show its worth in the weeks and months to come.

They headed through the battle-scarred back gardens, hoping the van was still parked beyond. The sun was up now, but the world remained grey, and as they went snow began to fall. It seemed as though the skies themselves wanted to place a shroud over what had happened.

The sirens were getting louder. They got over the back gate with some difficulty, and help from Max. He was still there, as was Reboot's shot-up van.

"We're going to have to head out of town," Max said urgently as they helped Leona into the back. "There's police everywhere. I had VERT drones overhead too, but they pulled away."

"You know where Marko's safehouse is, in Brandenburg?" Leona asked Max. "We'll head there."

The rear of the van door, peppered with bullet holes, was slammed shut. Freya leaned back and let out a long, slow, shuddering breath, misting in the encroaching cold.

It was over.

39
Rebooting

Rammstein cut off abruptly. Freya pushed her way through to her fiftieth rep before setting the weights down and sitting up.

"Hey Chalmers," she said.

"Evening Freya," the gym owner replied. Freya frowned. He seemed almost hesitant, and that wasn't like him.

"You wanted me to turn the music down, all you had to do was ask," she said. He scoffed, trying to hide his moment's awkwardness.

"I mean that'd be nice, but that's not why I'm interrupting you. I just wanted to say thanks."

"Thanks? What for?"

"Well, thanks for getting your head on straight. You're a good PT. It would have been a shame to lose you. But the past month you've been more like your old self again. That's the sort of Freya I want around. That's the sort of Freya I'm finally giving a raise."

Had it really been a month? A month since the chaos in Berlin. A month, almost, since Reboot had smuggled her and Will all the way into Switzerland, where they'd been able to meet up with another fledgling DedSec branch that got them back to London.

It felt like a dream now, another life. The intervening weeks had been the most peaceful Freya had ever known.

"I had a few problems," she admitted to Chalmers, standing up and towelling the sweat from her neck. "One or two long-term issues that had been… keeping me up at night."

"What happened to them?" Chalmers asked, clearly intrigued. Freya shrugged.

"I confronted them, head on."

She walked past him, beginning to stretch.

"Finishing early tonight?" Chalmers asked.

"Yeah," Freya said without turning. "I've got a dinner planned."

Freya arrived at her mother's flat just as she was serving up her sauerbraten. Helen and Harriet were already seated at the table, and exclaimed happily when Freya walked in. It was the first time they had all been together since Freya had made it back to London and been reunited with her family.

"You've been at the gym all this time?" Harriet asked. "You make me feel very out of shape."

"You're young, enjoy being out of shape while you can still afford to be," Helen teased, rising to hug Freya. One of Helen's cats had made the short migration across the flat block's landing with them, and was now curled up next to the oven.

"Almost late," Belinda scolded as she plated up the last cut of beef. "I was going to give this to the cat. He's been eyeing it!"

"I'll fight him for it," Freya said. "Did you hear the news about that ghost you banished?"

The words were directed at Helen and Harriet. The latter smirked.

"You mean Damian Gruber? No wonder he went by a pseudonym all his life. Took the Met long enough to crack it. I was worried DedSec were going to have to pitch in and lend a helping hand, yet again."

"Mister Gruber will have a ghost or two of his own to confront in prison, I imagine," Helen said. "Once the authorities work out how many murders to charge him with."

"Funny how his last one actually deserved it," Harriet said. She had explained how herself and Helen had worked together to turn Wellend into the Ghost's last victim, using Andrew's Optik and the face-altering software Helen had been developing. The rat had been neutralised and the killer caught, a cautionary tale that was already doing the rounds among DedSec activists.

"Before I forget, I've got something for you, Mum," she said, changing topic before Belinda could sit with the others at the table. Freya reached into her backpack and pulled out a copy of her school Polaroid.

"I had it enlarged and framed," she said with a hesitant smile, wondering how her mother would take it. "Don't worry though, I still have the original."

Belinda held the photo of the young, smiling Freya, emotions visibly rising. She set it down on the counter and embraced Freya fiercely. Freya hugged her back, hearing her mother speak softly in her ear, in German.

"I'm so proud of you, Freya. Your father would be too."

Freya ate well, enjoying the company and the food, but didn't stay late. She needed to be at Paddington station early the next morning.

Andrew was coming home for Christmas. She met him off the train, grinning as she hugged him, then bombarding him with worrisome questions about his course and Bristol, all the way to Snax. They found a table and ordered breakfast.

"You don't see anyone funny hanging around your flat, or in lectures, do you?" Freya asked him for the umpteenth time.

"No, Mum," he said with more than a fair share of patience. "You told me what to look out for. Besides, Dad's around half the time, or it feels like he is anyway!"

"Well, he's not around today. I'm not waiting for him."

Sure enough, Will arrived after their food.

"Sorry I'm late," he said hastily, brushing fresh snow from the shoulders of his jacket. "Pretty sure I picked up a tail just past Camden. Had to take a detour to shake it."

"You were speaking to Leona, weren't you?" Freya said pointedly. Will had the decency to look shame-faced, taking a seat and pretending to scan the menu, as though he didn't know everything on it by heart.

"How's her leg?" Freya pressed.

"Hmm? Oh, seems fine. She's up and running, and so's Reboot. In fact, from what she tells me, they're rather keen on adopting the DedSec mantle after all."

"Is that so?" Freya asked drily, glancing at Andrew, who tried not to laugh as he watched his mother make his father squirm.

"Yes," Will said, finally finding the courage to set the menu down and look at Freya directly. "I'm actually thinking of heading back over. Giving them the help I couldn't provide before. Holloway might even be coming over."

"Leona will be delighted," Freya said. Will had told her that his former partner, Samantha, had broken up with him not long after getting back from Berlin. Things hadn't been right for a while, and Will's swollen and bruised face – and, presumably, his inability to adequately explain why he was in such a mess – had been the last straw for her.

"So much for getting out of DedSec," Freya pointed out.

Will shrugged. “You never really leave, right?”

“Speak for yourself.”

“I’m happy for you, Freya. But I’ve still got the bug. It still matters to me. Since being over there, seeing what we can do, seeing how important change is… just because VERT and their allies are out of power right now, doesn’t mean they won’t be back. There are always more like them. So yeah, some of the good guys need to stick around too.”

Freya realised Andrew had been quiet during the exchange.

“You OK?” she asked, her concern evaporating when he smiled.

“Yeah,” he said. “It’s strange, all of us being here. It feels like a long time since that happened.”

“Guilty as charged,” Will said. “I took being late to new extremes.”

“It’s all right, I think,” Andrew said thoughtfully. “That’s all in the past. It’s the future that counts. Speaking of, I’ve thought of a way you can make it up to me. Take me to Berlin before next semester starts.”

“No,” Freya and Will both said together, loudly.

“It’s the Bauer in him, I swear,” Will said. “One whiff of adventure, and he wants his own DedSec mask and hacker name.”

“You’re the one who reiterated undying loyalty to the movement,” Freya said.

“Fine, but I’m halfway through uni now,” Andrew pressed. “If I graduate with a first, will you, y’ know, show me the ropes? Get me in on an operation or two?”

He was deliberately baiting them. Freya shot her son a look only a mother could.

“You and I are going to have a serious talk about your future over Christmas, young man,” she said.

"In the meantime, maybe we could eat, like a normal family, and forget all the trouble in the world?" Will asked.

Freya nodded. And so, for a short, precious time, they did just that.

ACKNOWLEDGMENTS

I would like to thank the Aconyte team, including Marc, Lottie, Jack, Joe, Ashley, and Nick, but most especially my editor, Gwendolyn Nix, who stuck with me throughout the thick and the thin of this novel. I may not be any better at hacking than when I started, but hopefully I'm a bit better at writing!

ABOUT THE AUTHOR

ROBBIE MacNIVEN is a Scottish highlander with a PhD in Military History from the University of Edinburgh. As a freelance author his work features, among others, novels in the *Warhammer 40,000* and X-Men settings, as well as digital game narratives, comic book scripts, and military non-fiction. Outside of writing his hobbies include historical re-enacting and making eight-hour round trips every second week to watch Rangers FC.

robbiemacniven.wordpress.com
twitter.com/RobbieMacNiven